# DANGER AT PEMBERLEY

FENELLA J MILLER

Boldwood

First published in 2016 as *A Spy at Pemberley*. This edition published in Great Britain in 2024 by Boldwood Books Ltd.



Cover Design by Colin Thomas

Cover Images: Colin Thomas and Alamy



A CIP catalogue record for this book is available from the British Library.

Paperback ISBN 978-1-83518-742-5

Large Print ISBN 978-1-83518-743-2

Hardback ISBN 978-1-83518-741-8

Ebook ISBN 978-1-83518-744-9

Kindle ISBN 978-1-83518-745-6

Audio CD ISBN 978-1-83518-736-4

MP3 CD ISBN 978-1-83518-737-1

Digital audio download ISBN 978-1-83518-740-1

This book is printed on certified sustainable paper. Boldwood Books is dedicated to putting sustainability at the heart of our business. For more information please visit https://www.boldwoodbooks.com/about-us/sustainability/

Boldwood Books Ltd, 23 Bowerdean Street, London, SW6 3TN

www.boldwoodbooks.com

## AUTHOR'S NOTE

The characters in this story are an accurate reflection of the time they are living in. As such, their thoughts, speech and actions are normal for this era. Thankfully we now live in a more enlightened time.

# 1

## PEMBERLEY, MARCH 1812

Fitzwilliam Darcy put down the letter he had been perusing in order to talk to his wife, Lizzy. 'My love, my cousin Colonel Hugo Fitzwilliam has written informing me he intends to call in here. We haven't seen him since the christening of the twins last year and it will be pleasant to catch up with him again.'

Lizzy nodded. 'Indeed, it will. Is this a social call or will he have another task for you?' She pursed her lips. 'You have been away on business for him twice in the past six months. Surely he can find someone else to run about the country for him?'

This had become a bone of contention between them. His wife believed he should spend more time with her and the children. However, he disliked being confined for weeks on end at Pemberley surrounded by endless domesticity and babies, and he welcomed the opportunity to get away on business for the government.

'I cannot refuse to serve the king, my dear, as you very well know. Poor Bingley is being worn ragged by your sister's demands. I think...'

She tossed aside her periodical and stood up, her magnificent eyes flashing with annoyance. 'Jane's marriage is no concern of yours, Fitzwilliam. Their daughter, Charlotte, is a constant worry to both of them as she's not as robust as our babies. Think yourself fortunate that Fabian and Amanda are thriving and so very advanced for their age.'

He stood up and walked across the drawing room to her side. 'I apologise unreservedly, Lizzy. You are right to chide me. You and my children are the most important thing to me but, like all gentlemen in my position, I am also obliged to complete tasks occasionally for Mr Spencer Perceval, our esteemed prime minister.'

'I suppose with the king indisposed and the prince regent in charge they need all the help they can get from gentlemen such as yourself. I cannot like it, however; you were almost caught up in the last Luddite riot and could have been injured.'

When he cupped her face and tilted it to receive his kiss she didn't shy away. Things had changed between them since the birth of the babies last July and they were no longer quite as close as they used to be. Her attention was given mainly to their son and daughter, then to her sister's sickly baby, and he believed that he came a poor third.

Perhaps he should be more insistent that she leave the care of the children to the team of nursemaids employed upstairs and concentrate more on his needs. His father had been a dictatorial man and his mother had not been allowed to spend time with her children unless her husband was away. When he had married Lizzy, he had been determined not to behave in such a way. He wanted to be involved in the care and upbringing of his children, not be a distant figure of fear as his father had been to him and Georgiana.

'Would you like to have a house party in the summer? You

could invite your parents and sister – I believe it's time to forgive Mary for her involvement in Georgiana's abduction last year.'

'I should like that above anything, my love. Although Georgiana and Kitty are in an interesting condition, there could be no objection to them attending a house party here.' She clapped her hand to her mouth. 'Oh dear! I was not supposed to reveal this news as they are both in the early stages.'

'When am I to be an uncle again? Presumably at the end of the year.'

'Kitty is expecting her baby in November and Georgiana in December. Neither of them is feeling quite the thing at present so they won't be visiting.'

He well remembered the nausea Lizzy had suffered in the early months of her pregnancy but if he recalled correctly this passed and was perfectly normal.

'They will be well soon enough and able to enjoy the summer's events. I did wonder why I'd not seen either of them recently.' He gently squeezed her shoulder. 'I have letters to write, my love, and then the colonel should be here. I shall see you, no doubt, at dinner.'

He strolled from the room as if he had not a care in the world, but as soon as he was out of her sight he lengthened his stride and hurried to his study. He thought he'd dissembled well – Lizzy couldn't have guessed that the news he'd received was so disastrous.

He wished to have no interruptions for the next hour or so. The butler, Peterson, had instructions to conduct his visitor directly to him. He opened the letter and read it a second time.

*Darcy,*

*I write to you in haste with the most serious news. We are certain that information is being sent to France about the dispositions of our troops and the plans of our generals.*

*The prime minister is already under pressure and the prince regent appears more interested in his mistress than the war.*

*It is my surmise that two English families are involved in this traitorous activity and they are passing the information to Bonaparte via Count Duvall, a so-called émigré.*

*This needs to be stopped and we need your help to do so. Frederick Hall is a close friend of Sir Robert Sinclair and we think he too is up to his neck in the business.*

*You need to invite them to your house so I can investigate them further. I'll explain when I arrive later today.*

The signature was scrawled underneath this missive. He had only made the suggestion that Lizzy organise a summer house party because of this letter. He disliked having strangers in the house – family and close friends were another matter – but this event must include the Sinclairs and Halls, as well as other families from the *ton*.

God knows how he was to manage this, as he'd never met the people in question. He was notorious for being over-particular in his acquaintances and to invite complete strangers to stay with him for the summer would cause unnecessary speculation.

No doubt his cousin would have a scheme in hand to overcome this problem. Whilst he waited he would take care of some other estate business that needed his urgent attention. He would be damned glad when Ingram, his steward, returned from visiting his ailing mother and could take back these time-consuming tasks.

When the colonel was announced, Darcy was more than ready to put aside his tedious duties. He went to greet his friend and cousin. 'Welcome. I was shocked to read your letter and will do everything I can to assist in this difficulty.'

'I knew you'd not let us down, old fellow. Forgive my disarray – I didn't stop to tidy myself as this matter is of the utmost importance. I've not eaten since before dawn – would you be so kind as to send for refreshments?'

'Of course – the matter is already in hand. Sit down. Would you like a brandy to revive you after your long ride?'

'I would indeed. I'm not in favour of strong liquor so early in the day, but today is different.' He collapsed onto a leather seat to the left of the fire and Darcy took his drink over to him.

'Here you are – forgive me if I don't join you but my wife would not be impressed if she smelt alcohol on my breath before dinner.'

One footman arrived with a tray laden with cold cuts, fresh bread, cheese and a selection of pastries. A second followed behind carrying the necessary crockery and cutlery plus a silver jug of coffee. They set it out on two tables at the far end of the room.

He waved the servants away and they vanished. 'Help yourself, Cousin. I'll join you at the table. I don't usually take luncheon, but today I'll make an exception in your honour.'

The colonel was too hungry for conversation and munched his way through a substantial amount of food and consumed three cups of coffee before he was ready to talk. Finally he wiped his mouth on his napkin and resumed his seat by the fire. Darcy followed his lead.

'Both families we are interested in are going to be in Town for the Season. I need you to open your house in Grosvenor Square and make sure that you attend the events that they do. Sinclair moves in the same circles as you. He has deep pockets and his estates are substantial.'

'In which case there should be no difficulty making his acquaintance. If he is a member of the *ton* how is it that I've not met him before?' Darcy frowned. 'Why has he become embroiled in this matter if he's a wealthy man?'

'He's a hardened gambler – need I say more. He has been living abroad for the past few years and only returned last summer. As you've not been to London to socialise in the past few months, there's no reason you should have met.'

'What about the other family?'

His cousin frowned. 'Wealthy cits – he made his money with the East India Company and he too has only recently got back to England. Hall, unlike Sinclair, had no properties of any importance until he purchased a large estate in Hertfordshire and a house in Grosvenor Square. This makes things easier as he will now be a neighbour of yours and I'm certain your wife can make a morning call and thus establish the connection.'

Darcy's eyes narrowed. 'I've no intention of involving Lizzy in this. As you know, I keep my work for the government separate from my life here.'

'This won't work unless you have her with you. A gentleman doesn't go willingly to Town to attend routs, balls and soirées – he's always dragged there by his spouse.'

'Dammit to hell! She will bring the babies and I won't have them there. This will cause dissent between us, as Lizzy hasn't been separated from the twins since they were born last July.'

Hugo shrugged. 'You have no choice. King and Country must come before family. Good God, man, why do you think I've not yet married? Being an intelligence officer and a husband do not sit comfortably together.'

His cousin was right. He would have to persuade Lizzy to accompany him and leave the children with their nanny and nursemaids for as long as it took to accomplish his mission. She wouldn't agree willingly and he would have to insist she did as he bid. That didn't bode well for his marital happiness in the future.

Hopefully she would understand when he was in a position to tell her the real reason for dragging her to Grosvenor Square. Neither of them enjoyed attending fashionable parties where it was impossible to hold a sensible conversation and one was obliged to do the pretty with people one would prefer to ignore.

'I'll not mention it whilst you're still here, my friend; better to wait until you've departed so you're not involved with the inevitable row that will follow.' Darcy glanced at his gold pocket watch. 'We've barely time enough to change for dinner. You are staying in your usual apartment. You will have to come up with something feasible to explain why you arrived here in such a rush.'

* * *

Lizzy completed her toilette and was ready to go down and still Fitzwilliam had not appeared to change. What could be keeping him so long? She would go to the nursery and check that Amanda and Fabian were sleeping peacefully.

Even Dawson, her husband's efficient valet, could not change his master and prepare him for the evening in less than a half an hour. This gave her ample time to slip upstairs and return without keeping him waiting.

As always the sconces were lit everywhere. The staircase leading to the nursery floor was carpeted and her children were as comfortable up here as she and Fitzwilliam were in their own apartment. She had wished to have the children moved downstairs so she could visit them more easily, hear if they cried in the night, but Fitzwilliam wouldn't hear of it. So they remained where he, and all the Darcy children, had been raised – on the nursery floor looked after by a positive regiment of nursemaids. The nanny had been appointed by Lizzy, as had the nursemaids, so she had no complaint on that score.

In some households it might have been considered unusual for the mother of the children to be seen up here – but she had no intention of allowing her children to be brought up by servants. She would have fed them herself if she hadn't been so unwell after the delivery.

Nanny was sitting by the fire reading a book. She looked up, jumped to her feet and dipped in a curtsy. 'Good evening, madam. I'm afraid Miss Amanda and Master Fabian are already asleep. They quite exhausted themselves crawling about the drawing room all afternoon.'

'I'm not surprised. I think that Amanda will be walking soon as she's already attempting to stand up. I'll just look in and then leave them in peace.'

The nursery door was open so Nanny could hear if they stirred. Although there were no candles burning, the light from the fire was more than sufficient to make her way to the children. Her son was spreadeagled like a starfish and she pulled the comforter back over him. His sister was scrunched up into a corner of her crib, her thumb tucked firmly in her mouth and her bottom in the air. She too needed recovering.

How she loved these babies – if she was honest they came first with her now; Fitzwilliam was no longer the centre of the universe. She loved him as much as ever, but what a mother felt for her children was stronger than that between a man and a woman. She supposed this was nature's way of making sure the babies survived.

Her eyes prickled as she thought of the anguish Jane and Charles had gone through so often since their daughter, Charlotte, had been born last summer. Thank God the infant was thriving at the present, but she was still not as robust as her two – even though they had been far smaller when they were born.

She bid Nanny goodnight and hurried back to her apartment. She was greeted by her husband. His smile still made her toes curl in their slippers.

'Good evening, my darling, might I be permitted to say you look enchanting tonight? Is that in my honour or for our guest?'

She stepped into his open arms and his kiss was hard, demanding; she wished they didn't have to go downstairs but could tumble into bed immediately. This thought made her speak of something that had been bothering her.

'Fitzwilliam, I'm concerned that I'm not yet with child. Initially I was glad not to be increasing so soon, but now I would like another infant and there's no sign of one.'

'I'm sure there's nothing to worry about. To tell you the truth, I'm relieved that we've had a few months' respite. You had a difficult pregnancy and there's always the danger you could have twins again and we might not be so lucky next time.'

'I know, and I thank God every day that we have two such healthy children. I would like a large family, but if the good Lord chooses to only give us Amanda and Fabian then I shall be satisfied with that.'

'As shall I, my love. We had better go down or the colonel will think we have deserted him.'

She knew better than to ask him why his cousin had arrived so precipitously. Being married to a man of his position it was only to be expected that he would be asked to take an interest in politics.

His cousin was not attached to a particular regiment and appeared to spend his time gallivanting about the country and the peninsula involved in secret missions of some sort. No doubt he was what was known as an *intelligence officer* – a polite word for *a spy*. Hardly a gentlemanly occupation, but someone had to do it.

After a pleasant evening spent with two Fitzwilliams Lizzy retired and left the men to their conversation. They would have plenty to talk about; she climbed into bed in the expectation her husband wouldn't join her until long after she was asleep.

Less than a quarter of an hour after she settled, he slid in beside her. His naked thigh touched hers and his intentions were obvious. As he deftly removed her nightgown he whispered in her ear. 'My darling, if we are to produce another offspring then we must be more diligent in our efforts.'

'I think that an excellent notion, my love. Are we not told at every turn that the more effort we put into something the greater the reward?'

His hands began to work their usual magic and soon she was incapable of speech. It was a considerable time before she was allowed to sleep.

# 2

Darcy thought it might be beneficial for him to spend the day with his beloved Lizzy before he broached the subject of removing to London in April. Although she had no option in the matter, he wished to use his considerable powers of persuasion to convince her she should like to come and leave the children behind.

He rolled out of bed at his usual time of seven o'clock, making sure he didn't disturb her slumber. His cousin would be departing early and he wished to speak to him again before he left. As expected Hugo was attacking a full plate of breakfast before he left Pemberley.

'Good morning, Darcy, I didn't expect you to join me so early.'

'I've come up with what I think might be a suitable reason for wishing to spend part of the Season in Town.' He piled his plate and joined his cousin at the table before continuing. 'I think we should tell Lizzy, and anyone else who might be interested, that you've decided to become leg-shackled. Therefore, you enlisted our assistance to find you a suitable wife.'

His cousin choked on his coffee and was incapable of speech

for several minutes whilst he spluttered into his napkin. 'Good God! Have you run mad? The last thing I require is a wife.'

Darcy laughed at his friend's horror. 'Come now, you are five-and-thirty – high time that you set up your nursery. After your recent inheritance you have a substantial income and a handsome estate. What could be more natural than your wishing to get married?' He waved his fork in the air. 'You don't have to make any hopeful young debutante an offer – just appear to be looking.'

'For a nasty moment I thought you were in earnest. If the whole thing is to be a pretence then that's a different matter altogether. Just make sure the Sinclair and Hall families are included on the list.'

'I've already suggested to Lizzy that we have a house party in the summer. If she believes she is to invite suitable young ladies, as well as friends and family, this will make the whole thing more credible. I hate to deceive her, but it's better this way. If she was to know the truth she might reveal something and put her life in danger.'

'I agree, my friend. The Season has hardly begun – no one of any importance will be in London until April. You must hold a ball or some such nonsense. I'll leave it to your wife to decide which is the best option.' He tossed his napkin aside and stood up. 'Forgive me, but I must get on my way. I have to report at Horse Guards as soon as possible and, even travelling post, it will take me two days.'

Darcy nodded and his cousin marched out. Lizzy had taken to having her breakfast in the nursery with the children so he would seek her out up there. He enjoyed playing with the twins but was looking forward to the time when they could communicate with words rather than screeches.

Whilst he finished his meal, he rehearsed what he would say

to Lizzy to convince her that Hugo was genuinely in search of a wife. Although his cousin wasn't exactly a misogynist, he wasn't famous for his success with the fairer sex. As far as he knew the colonel didn't even keep a ladybird tucked away somewhere.

However, he was a handsome man, in his prime and had good teeth and a full head of dark hair. The fact that he was wealthy, and his pedigree was second to none, would be of more interest to the matrons seeking husbands for their daughters. Darcy smiled to himself. He rather thought the fact that his cousin was personable would be what attracted the young ladies.

He slammed his palm down on the table, making the cutlery and plates jump into the air. Tarnation! He was thinking as if the search was genuine and not a fabrication to aid the government mission. He frowned. He sincerely hoped that no hearts would be broken by this duplicity.

His appetite had deserted him. He was a straightforward man and disliked dissembling of any kind. Now he was obliged to not only lie to his dearest Lizzy, but also to risk the happiness of an innocent girl. He pushed himself upright, hating what he had to do. It would be better to hurt two people than have thousands of British soldiers put at risk by the traitors sending information to France.

The nursery was empty. He scowled and a flustered nursemaid curtsied and explained. 'Madam has gone with Nanny and the twins for a walk.'

Darcy glanced out of the window. It was hardly the weather for perambulating around the garden, but his wife believed fresh air was essential for their offspring – whatever anyone might think to the contrary. He nodded to the girl and strode off in search of them.

* * *

'Madam, the master is coming this way,' Nanny said nervously.

Lizzy turned and saw that Fitzwilliam looked far from pleased. Why had he come out here to find her? Was there something of importance he had to tell her?

She handed Fabian to the nursemaid who had accompanied them to the parterre. 'Continue with the walk. I must see what Mr Darcy requires of me.'

When he saw she was heading his way, he stopped and his expression changed. His eyes lit up and his smile warmed her, sending heatwaves to a most intimate place.

'Sweetheart, I'm glad you returned. I've something quite extraordinary to discuss with you and I think it best done inside.'

He offered his arm and she placed her hand on it. If she was honest she was quite glad to return as the March wind in their part of Derbyshire was decidedly cold. But her children were well wrapped up and would come to no harm in the bracing weather.

'Do you think we would scandalise Peterson and Reynolds if we were to run the remaining distance?' His grin made him look almost boyish.

'It's not their place to have opinions on such matters. If we are inclined to run and behave like children then surely in our own home we can do it?'

He needed no further urging and snatched her hand into his, held it hard, and then took off like a rabbit from a fox. By the time they reached the terrace she was breathless, her bonnet was askew and her hair tumbling from its pins.

He, as always, looked immaculate. Instead of being shocked at her appearance, he put a hand on either side of her waist and lifted her from her feet. 'You look enchanting, my darling. I almost wish we could continue this conversation in our bedchamber.'

She threw her arms around his neck and pulled his head down so she could kiss him. His lips were cold, but still sent heat-waves racing around her body.

She pressed her scarlet cheeks into his shoulder. 'If we haven't scandalised the staff by running, we will certainly have done so by embracing so publicly.'

Gently he removed her hands from behind his head and smoothed away two strands of hair that had escaped from beneath the rim of her bonnet. 'I love you, Elizabeth Darcy, and I don't care who knows it.'

Hand in hand they entered the house and made themselves comfortable in front of the substantial fire in the drawing room. Refreshments were brought without being asked for. Whilst she busied herself pouring out the coffee and cutting them each a generous slice of cake, he watched her through half-closed eyes. She didn't trust him one jot. He was quite capable of snatching her up and carrying her to bed, whatever she might say about the matter.

'Don't look at me like a wolf about to seize a lamb, my love. Take your coffee and cake and behave yourself.'

He lounged back against the chair, stretching his long legs out towards the flames. 'Cousin Hugo wishes to get married and has asked for our help to find him a suitable bride.'

Her cake slid from the plate and she stared at him open-mouthed. 'Good heavens! If you told me he was about to sprout wings and fly I couldn't be more surprised. I thought him wed to his job – a lifelong bachelor. Whatever has made him change his mind?'

She scooped the cake back onto the plate and took a large bite. It was far too good to be wasted just because it had spent a brief moment on the floor.

'I am as shocked as you are, my love. I think the fact that he's just passed his birthday, and is now nearer to two score years, might have been the impetus for this decision. I suppose he's thinking that his active service days will soon be over and then he will need someone to run his house in his retirement.'

She snorted inelegantly. 'A housekeeper would be adequate for that. He's never shown the slightest interest in our children – although he's always been kind to your sister.' She munched on the delicious cake as she thought about this extraordinary development. 'I suppose if he's serious in his intention we are the best people to assist him in this endeavour. Unfortunately, as I've not spent any time at all in Town, I've no idea where to look for suitable candidates.'

'I've already decided how best we can help him. We shall go to Grosvenor Square next month and accept as many invitations as we can. I'll go to the clubs and listen to the gossip and you can pay morning calls and make discreet enquiries about the eligible girls this Season.'

'That sounds like an excellent notion, my love. I believe we could accomplish that in a week or two and then be able to return here with a list of names to invite to the house party. Of course, some of the most likely debutantes will already be spoken for by the time summer comes – but I'm sure we can find a dozen from which the colonel can make his choice.'

'In which case there's no need to take the children with us. They will be perfectly well here in our absence.'

She was about to protest that she had no intention of leaving her babies for even so short a time, when she realised his unwelcome idea made sense. 'As long as you promise we shall be there for no more than three weeks, and that we travel as speedily in both directions as we may, then I agree your suggestion has merit. I shall find it very difficult being parted from the children, but transporting them so great a distance doesn't make sense when we are only remaining for a week or so.'

'Do you think we should hold a rout or some such thing?'

'Absolutely not. It's only necessary to make our list – we won't be there long enough to arrange a social event of any significance. I'm not averse to inviting a dozen or so to dine with us as that doesn't require a lot of planning, or sending out invitations weeks in advance.'

'I hope you have an inkling as to what sort of girl he might be looking for, as I certainly don't. You must speak to him in more depth before we begin our search, for there's no point inviting anyone who doesn't fit his criteria.'

'I should have asked him whilst he was here, but it didn't occur to me to do so. One would imagine he would like a robust young lady, who prefers to be outside rather than indoors eating sweetmeats and reading periodicals.'

'I'm sure you're right, my dear. She must have a lively wit, be from a good family and not be an antidote or at her last prayers. The girl I think would suit him best wouldn't be straight from the schoolroom, but perhaps in her second or third season. As long as she is young enough to provide him with children, I don't think even someone in her mid-twenties could be considered too old. Your cousin is a serious man and would not deal well with someone fifteen years his junior, with her head stuffed full of romance and other such nonsense.'

'Then let us hope we can find someone speedily, because I'd rather have my teeth pulled than spend time mingling with the *ton*.'

Although Fitzwilliam had changed in the time they'd been together, he was still a gentleman who preferred to be with close friends or family. He was thought of as proud and arrogant – but she knew him to be neither of those things. He found it difficult to engage in trivial conversation, became uncomfortable and silent, and this was often misinterpreted as him being toplofty.

'I shall set things in motion, my love. We should be ready to travel by the end of the month. Before we leave we must spend time with Kitty and Georgiana. I could not possibly leave Derbyshire without knowing that my sisters are well.'

Darcy nodded. 'I'll leave things in your capable hands, Lizzy. I'll send two teams ahead of us so we can change horses when we stop for the night. If the weather remains clement, we should complete the journey in less than three days if we take things at speed.'

'We shall still be obliged to use post-horses when we stop for refreshments. I assume that the horses must set off several days before us so they can have time to rest. Surely even your extensive stables cannot do without so many horses? You will have to send four grooms, two with each team, and they will need to be mounted as well.'

'We can use the gig, or ride if we need to visit anywhere in the neighbourhood.' He stood up. 'I'm going next door to speak to Bingley. Are you coming with me?'

'No, Jane has gone to visit Kitty today. Are you sure that Charles hasn't gone with her?'

'I'll take the chance. I'll not be above an hour – shall we spend time with the children after they've had their afternoon nap?'

* * *

Her delighted smile told him he'd said the right thing. She rang the bell to summon the housekeeper and he left the premises through the side door. The Great Hall was rarely used nowadays and neither was the main staircase.

Pemberley was too large and although he'd spent most of his adult life living here he wished they could move somewhere more manageable. Even Bingley and Jane were more comfortable living in the east wing, which had been converted for them.

He could reach their home by walking along the terrace and through the orangery. His friend must have seen him and was waiting for him by the door. Bingley's usual cheerful smile was absent. He looked distressed.

'Darcy, old fellow, I was coming to see you but it's better that we talk here as neither Jane nor Lizzy will be present.'

What now? He hoped it wasn't bad news about their baby – the thought of them losing their precious daughter made a cold lump form in his stomach.

His friend didn't elaborate but led him through the house to his study. He closed the door firmly behind him. 'It's my sister, Caroline. She's eloped with a damned fortune hunter. I had word by express just now. I should go after her but I cannot leave Jane as she's increasing again and baby Charlotte has only just recovered from a fever.'

'Did you know that both Kitty and Georgiana are also in an interesting condition?' He spoke without thought – and he'd given his word not to mention this to anyone.

'I did know and that's why Jane has gone to see Kitty. You have been involved in this sort of thing twice before, Darcy. I'd not know where to start.' He delved into his pocket and passed over the letter that had given him this disastrous news.

Caroline Bingley had run off with one David Forsyth – the youngest son of a baron. They were travelling in a hired carriage and, thank God, she'd had the sense to take her maid with her. Mrs Hurst, Bingley's sister, stated quite clearly the exact routes they would be taking. He looked up from perusing the letter.

'This has come at a most inopportune time. Lizzy and I are

going to London in two weeks. She believes it is to find a husband for my cousin, but in fact I have business to undertake for the prime minister. You must give me your word you'll not reveal this to Jane or Lizzy.'

Bingley looked even more worried, if that were possible. 'I'll say nothing. Caroline is headed for Gretna Green – she must travel north in order to reach the border. She departed from my townhouse late yesterday and will have had to stop overnight somewhere. You should be able to catch up with her easily.'

'And what do you expect me to do when I find her? Her reputation will be gone – she has no choice but to marry this blackguard or she will be a ruined woman.'

Bingley dropped his head in his hands and Darcy was sorry for his harsh response. He patted his friend on the shoulder. He had no choice. He would have to do what he could – but he didn't intend to do it alone.

'The fact that your wife is increasing and your daughter recently unwell is no reason for you to remain here and leave this matter entirely to me. Bingley, you will come with me. Together we will rescue your sister and do our best to keep the matter from the tabbies.'

'You're right. I'm her brother and protector and I must do my duty. Caroline can come here – even if she is a fallen woman there's nobody to point fingers. As long as there's no bastard born, then she might come out of it unscathed.'

Hearing his friend speak so bluntly was quite shocking. 'I'll explain to Lizzy; you must leave a note for Jane. We'll ride. But I warn you, it's still possible we won't catch up with them. I cannot gallivant all over the country. If we do not waylay them today then they must deal with the repercussions themselves.'

'There's no need to elaborate. As long as we try to find her then I must be content. At least if she is obliged to marry Forsyth, he comes from a decent family. My sister has always been particular in who she befriends so the man must be personable at the least – and move in the same social circles as her.'

Darcy frowned. There was something about this that bothered him. 'Good God! What makes Mrs Hurst think they are going to Scotland to marry? Your sister is able to marry without getting permission from anyone – all they need to do is obtain a special licence and they can be married anywhere.'

'I'd not thought of that. This could be a fool's errand, couldn't it? Caroline has always known her own mind. She will marry the man and then reappear as if nothing has happened.'

'In which case, Bingley, why have you been sent to in a panic, demanding that you do something?' Enlightenment dawned. 'There's only one reason why your sister is heading for Scotland – Forsyth must be underage.'

# 3

Lizzy was busy writing a list of tasks to be completed before they moved to London when her husband burst in.

'Caroline Bingley has eloped with a man several years her junior – so young that I believe him to be below the age of consent. They are heading for Gretna Green and Bingley and I are going to make an attempt to prevent them.'

She dropped her pen and jumped to her feet. 'Good gracious! How very unlike Miss Bingley to do something so wild. Of course you should go, my dear. You must do everything you can to prevent her making such a catastrophic error of judgement.'

'I think it to be a futile effort, Lizzy, as the chances of us coming across her are remote. She could be travelling by any one of a dozen routes – but we must make the effort and try to avoid an unpleasant scandal.'

'Shall you be gone for long? Are you taking the carriage and your valet?'

'We are riding and will travel light. It's a good fifty miles to the nearest direct route to Scotland. We know that she is travelling on this so have a chance of stopping her.'

He kissed her briefly and then strode off, his mind no doubt already on the search. This morning she had been bemoaning the fact that her life was lacking excitement and now, not only were they to go to London, but Fitzwilliam was off to rescue Caroline.

In her opinion he was chasing a lost cause, for if a lady spent the night with a gentleman without the benefit of clergy her reputation was already gone. Marriage was the only way to rectify the situation. After all, had not her husband persuaded the dreadful Wickham to marry her youngest sister, Lydia, after they had been living as man and wife for more than a week.

She shuddered as she recalled how that marriage had ended. He had been killed whilst holding Georgiana prisoner in the hope that he could force her to marry his friend. Lydia had been packed off to India with a relative of Georgiana's husband. The last she'd heard was that her sister had already found herself another husband. She hoped this second marriage would be more successful than the first for all their sakes.

Jane was visiting Kitty and would be unaware of the drama unfolding at her home. Charles would have to leave her a note and this would be most unsatisfactory. Her sister must be told in person so Lizzy must go herself to the Old Rectory.

In less than half an hour she was bowling along the lane that led to the village of Bakewell where Kitty lived. This was no more than a short drive and the lane was free of ruts and potholes since her husband and Adam King, Kitty's husband, had set the villagers to repairing it.

She would spend an hour with her sisters and then travel the extra three miles and call in on Georgiana and Jonathan Brownstone. The major had resigned his commission and appeared to be enjoying life as a civilian.

When the carriage rattled to a stop she didn't wait for a

servant to open the door but kicked down the steps. Picking up her skirts she dashed to the front door and was unsurprised that it opened as she arrived. Vernon, the butler here, was ever vigilant and would have seen the chaise approaching.

He bowed. 'Welcome, Mrs Darcy. Mrs Bingley and Mrs King are in the drawing room. Shall I announce you?'

'There's no need – I can see myself in.' She was familiar with this house as they had all been obliged to live here whilst Pemberley was being repaired two years ago.

The door was open and she walked straight in. Jane and Kitty were already on their feet. They must have heard her arriving.

'Lizzy, we didn't expect you to come today. Is something amiss?' Kitty ran across and embraced her.

'You look well, my love. Pregnancy obviously agrees with you.'

'It's only if I step into a carriage that I feel so ill – as long as I remain on my own two feet I'm absolutely fine.'

Lizzy turned to Jane. 'How is the nausea? You look less wan today.'

'I'm feeling more the thing, Lizzy dearest. Like last time, the sickness only afflicts me on waking.'

Kitty gestured to the seat opposite the daybed upon which they had been sitting and reading the latest *Ackermann's Repository*. 'I've already sent for refreshments and they should arrive at any moment. Sit down and tell us why you arrived here so unexpectedly.'

Lizzy explained the circumstances. When she'd finished her tale, her sisters were as mystified as she that Caroline Bingley – such a stickler for protocol – had abandoned her principles in this way.

The tray arrived and they were obliged to talk of something else until they were private. It wouldn't do for the servants to hear this piece of gossip – it would be all over the county by suppertime if they did.

'Poor Charles, he will be so shocked by his sister's behaviour,' Jane said as she sipped her coffee. 'Like you, Lizzy, I think it unlikely they'll manage to find them. What I find quite astonishing is that Caroline should fall in love with a man she is obliged to elope with. She is no longer in her first youth and is certainly what one might refer to as a mature young lady.'

'No doubt we will hear all about it when the gentlemen return. Now, girls, I have some other news to impart.' Lizzy told them about Fitzwilliam wishing her to go to London to find his cousin a wife and they were as astonished by this piece of information as by the previous one.

'The colonel married? I can scarcely believe my ears. I thought him a confirmed bachelor. I cannot think he will make a comfortable husband.' Kitty giggled. 'Mind you, both Georgiana and I married ex-soldiers and couldn't be happier with our choices.'

They talked of this for a further hour and then both Lizzy and Jane took their leave, promising to return very soon.

'I must get back, Lizzy, as you know. I don't like to leave Charlotte for more than an hour or two. Give my love to dearest Georgiana.' They embraced and got into their respective carriages – Jane to return to Pemberley and she to continue to Brook Manor, the estate that Fitzwilliam had given to his sister as a wedding gift.

* * *

Darcy thundered through the countryside, travelling across the fields and jumping hedges and ditches with no thought to his own safety. Bingley, a bruising rider, had no difficulty keeping up the punishing pace.

Their horses were exhausted after three hours of travelling at breakneck speed. They stopped to change to fresh mounts and grab a quick drink and meat pasty.

'We should reach our destination in a couple of hours. With luck your sister and her paramour will not have risen at dawn and should still be en route.' Darcy checked the girth of his rented mount and vaulted into the saddle.

'I'll be dashed glad if we do find them soon. All this galloping about isn't good for a fellow's constitution.'

There was no opportunity for further conversation as they resumed their chase. Neither Bingley nor himself were in their prime and he agreed with his friend's comment.

The coaching inn they intended to wait at was famous for its hospitality and excellent stabling. Darcy tossed the reins of his horse to a waiting ostler. 'Take care of these. We shall need fresh mounts in a while. Make sure they are as good as these two.' He tossed the man a silver sixpence. 'Have any carriages pulled in this morning containing a young lady and even younger gentleman?'

Immediately the man understood why he and Bingley had arrived so precipitously. 'No, sir, nothing so far today. And there ain't been no one matching that description staying overnight. I reckon you're in good time.'

'My friend and I will be waiting inside – be so good as to send us word if a post-chaise or carriage arrives containing passengers of that ilk.' Darcy tossed him a further coin and the man touched his cap.

The interior of the hostelry was dim, but everywhere looked well cared for. He had no need to ring the bell on the counter as a tall, elderly gentleman hurried forward to greet them.

'Welcome, sirs, how may I be of assistance?'

'We require a chamber in which to restore ourselves and then a substantial meal. Serve this in a private parlour, if you can.'

The landlord snapped his fingers and a serving maid appeared. 'Betty, show these gentlemen to the empty chamber above the snug. Take hot water and towels to them immediately.'

The girl, little more than a child, curtsied and headed for the staircase in the far corner of the vestibule. Both he and Bingley were obliged to duck their heads as they went in – but apart from that small inconvenience he was well satisfied with the room he'd been shown to.

The girl scurried off to fetch the water, leaving him alone with his friend. 'I think we probably have an hour or two to wait. That's if we've chosen correctly. Your sister, if she is travelling this way, will stop here – if not to take refreshments, then to change the horses.'

'To tell you the truth, Darcy, I'm not sure I actually need to find her. Fond as I am of my sisters, I get on better with them in their absence than I do when we're together. I'll have no option but to take her back to Pemberley and she'll be in high dudgeon and make my life a misery for interfering in hers.'

This was the longest speech Bingley had made in some time and he had yet more to say.

'Jane and I will be obliged to have her stay until the fuss dies down – God knows what we will do if she's with child. I'll have to fetch the erstwhile bridegroom and insist that he does the right thing.' He sank onto a chair and closed his eyes, as if wishing to shut out his problems.

Darcy thought for a moment, allowing Bingley to recover his composure. 'Your sister is quite capable of making up her own mind. If she's decided this gentleman is for her, then perhaps instead of blocking her, we should support her in her endeavour to get married?'

Bingley sat up. 'What are you thinking?'

'If we escort the pair of them back to Pemberley then we can have the banns called and arrange for them to be married in the chapel. The marriage would be viewed as more acceptable when people hear that it has taken place with friends and family present.'

'I think it might work. It's unlikely anyone would think to look for them in Derbyshire.'

'They will have to reside at Pemberley long enough to claim it as their residence, otherwise the banns will have to be called in Forsyth's local church.'

'If Caroline's intended husband is underage then they will have to lie, and that would make the marriage invalid.'

A knock on the door prevented further conversation and two maids staggered in carrying the requisite water. In less than half an hour, Darcy was satisfied with his appearance and ready to go down and eat.

* * *

Georgiana was delighted to see Lizzy as her husband, Jonathan, was away on business until the next day. 'I would much prefer to return to Pemberley when he's away – but I cannot be forever running back home just because I'm lonely.'

'My love, I'm sure that he wouldn't object in the slightest if you were to stay with either Kitty or myself in his absence. Come back with me now. Fitzwilliam and Charles are also away until tomorrow.'

Lizzy quickly explained the drama that had been enacted

earlier that day and her sister-in-law was as surprised as Kitty had been at Caroline Bingley's extraordinary behaviour.

'I shall come with you – I wouldn't miss the excitement for all the world. Although I prefer a quiet life, I must own I find domesticity a trifle flat at times.'

'It's a shame that Kitty is unable to travel at the moment or she could come too.'

Georgiana hurried off to ask her maid, Ellie, to pack an overnight bag for them both and to change from her morning gown into something more elaborate.

Soon Lizzy was in the carriage with Georgiana and her maid and returning to Pemberley. 'I'm sure that the gentlemen won't be back before morning. I wonder if they will bring Caroline with them.'

'There must be more to this than we understand, Lizzy, for I cannot believe any family would refuse permission for their son to marry a modest heiress even with the supposed disparity of age.'

'Well, my love, we will have to contain our curiosity until tomorrow when all will be revealed. Jane will be delighted to see you, as will the twins and little Charlotte.'

The remainder of the journey passed in such pleasant conversation that when the vehicle arrived they were both surprised.

'Georgiana, why don't you go directly to see Jane? Ellie can see to your belongings whilst I speak to Reynolds and have two guest chambers made ready in case Fitzwilliam brings the runaways back with him.'

After speaking briefly to the housekeeper, Lizzy ran upstairs to check on the well-being of her children. They were, of course, content to be with Nanny and she left them playing with their bricks. She paused at the window at the end of the nursery corridor and stared out at the grounds.

Although Jane hadn't mentioned it, she was almost sure her older sister was increasing too. This meant that she was the only one of the four not be expecting a happy event later in the year. She blinked away tears. There were already two children in the Darcy family – so she must view these new arrivals as her sisters catching up with her.

Why wasn't she having another baby? Had her difficult pregnancy and delivery damaged her internal workings so that she was now unable to conceive? This would be preferable to the conclusion she was coming to: that the lack of another baby was due to the fact that she and Fitzwilliam were no longer as close as they had been.

When they had first been married they had spent every minute together, and he had been vigorous in his attentions in the marriage bed. However, since the arrival of the twins things had changed. He no longer spent every night beside her. Sometimes he didn't come to her but remained next door in what had once been her domain.

This wouldn't do. She loved him as much as she had always done and he returned her affection in full measure. No doubt things changed between a married couple once there were children. It was impossible to pay one's husband the same amount of attention as before. In her opinion a mother must always put her offspring first – at least until they were old enough to take care of themselves.

She sniffed and wiped her eyes on her cuff. Fitzwilliam would be horrified at such behaviour, but she cared not for such things. At least she wasn't blowing her nose on her sleeve, which would be far worse. On the way downstairs she called into her rooms and collected her reticule so she would have her handkerchief to hand if it was needed again.

Jane had her baby on her lap and Lizzy was delighted to see the little girl was looking well. She had roses in her cheeks and was more animated than she'd been for weeks. Georgiana was playing peekaboo with Charlotte and the baby was screeching with joy and clapping her hands.

'I should have brought Fabian and Amanda with me. I love to see the three of them playing together.' She smiled sadly at Jane. 'I wish I was having a child this year like the rest of you.'

'I didn't like to tell you my news, dearest Lizzy, because I know how much you desire to add to your family. I'm sure in God's good time there will be more babies in your nursery as well.'

Georgiana laughed. 'You already have a boy and a girl – it's only fair that we catch up with you before you produce another set of twins.'

'I sincerely hope I don't – I'd much rather have them one at a time. Anyway, I was at a loss at what to tell Peterson and Reynolds about the possible arrival of uninvited guests. They must be aware that Fitzwilliam and Charles have rushed off and must be wondering why they did so.'

'I think it highly unlikely that my brother will actually locate the runaways. Therefore it must be better not to mention any names and possibly start rumours spreading throughout the county. Servants are always the first to hear and the first to spread a juicy titbit of gossip.' Jane handed her baby to Georgiana.

'I've been thinking about your task, Lizzy, and I think the names of this year's eligible young ladies are written somewhere in one of the periodicals.'

'Unfortunately, Jane, this list will only tell us the status and wealth of the family. In order to provide a selection of young ladies for Cousin Hugo, I must see for myself that they are suitable.'

# 4

After a substantial luncheon Darcy was feeling more optimistic about this adventure. 'I think it might be wise to take a turn outside, Bingley. It's possible your sister might only stop here to change the team and not come into the inn.'

'I suspect that you're correct. She'll not wish to be seen.' He tossed his napkin onto the table. 'I'm replete – I've no intention of getting on a horse again until my food has settled.'

Black clouds had rolled in whilst they'd been inside. 'Let's hope the rain holds off for a while. I've no inclination to get drenched on our return journey.' Darcy frowned. 'Perhaps it might be wise to reserve a room for the night just in case the weather turns nasty.'

'I've no intention of being away overnight, my friend. I've not been apart from Jane since we were wed and don't want to set a precedent today.'

There was no point in arguing with Bingley on this point – where his family was concerned he was obdurate and could never be persuaded to change his mind about the smallest thing. It had been far easier to alter his viewpoint in the past.

They strolled around to the stables and selected two mounts for their return journey. 'Our own horses will be sufficiently rested by the time we reach them. You do realise, Bingley, that it will take far longer to return than it did to arrive here. We shall also have covered more than sixty miles.'

His friend nodded. 'No need to risk our necks – we can stick to the lanes, even if it takes more time. I expect it will be dark before we even set off at this rate.' He gestured towards the gloomy sky.

'I'm going to book a room for us. Do you honestly believe that Jane would like you to ride through the night in pouring rain just to be with her? Think about it, man, she'll have retired before we could be halfway home.'

As he was about to go inside, a travelling chaise turned in through the archway. The blinds were drawn and the horses flecked with sweat. The coachmen shouted for attention and two ostlers hurried across to unharness the exhausted team and replace them with fresh nags.

He exchanged a glance with Bingley and together they strode over. Darcy stepped aside and allowed Bingley to fling open the door of the vehicle.

'Bingley, Darcy, whatever are you doing here? This is none of your concern.' Caroline looked and sounded as she had always done. Sharp-tongued and completely in command.

The gentleman sitting opposite her must be Forsyth. His exact appearance was hard to discern in the dimness of the interior. Was he eloping because he was less than one-and-twenty years of age?

The shadowy figure at the far side of the carriage scrambled forward and tumbled out. 'Thank God! I'm Forsyth – you must be Caroline's brother.' He looked so pleased to see them Darcy was at a loss to know what was going on.

'I'm Darcy. A word with you, sir.' He indicated that they step away from the carriage where they could converse without being overheard. Bingley jumped into the carriage to talk to his sister.

The young man was tall with a shock of corn-coloured hair. He was certainly an attractive gentleman and he could see why Caroline might have been infatuated with him. 'Forsyth, what madness is this? Nobody in their right mind elopes to Gretna Green.'

'I told Caroline it was a ramshackle thing to do, but we could think of no other way. Only after we set out did I consider the repercussions of doing something so foolhardy, but by then it was too late. I was praying that somehow her brother would hear of this venture and come to intervene.'

'Why would your parents feel the need to stop you marrying Miss Bingley? She is a personable young lady and from an excellent family. The fact that she is also an heiress must be in her favour too. Is her age the problem?'

'Not at all – I will reach my majority next month. They object because I've been promised to the daughter of my father's closest friend since I was in leading strings. Eleanor has no more desire to marry me than I do her, but neither her parents nor mine will listen.' He stretched out a hand and was about to grasp Darcy's arm but then thought better of it. 'I love Caroline. We might be considered chalk and cheese, but I knew the moment I set eyes on her she was the one for me.'

'Might I enquire, sir, if you would be prepared to accompany Bingley and myself to my home, Pemberley, and get married in the family chapel once the legal requirements have been settled?'

'That would be ideal. I didn't see the need for such a havey-cavey business, but Caroline decided we must take matters into our own hands, as my parents were about to announce my forthcoming nuptials to Eleanor. I would be in breach of promise if they did so.'

'If we set out immediately your team is changed, and the weather holds off, it's possible we will complete the journey today.' Darcy saw his friend emerge from the carriage looking far happier than he had when he'd got in.

'My word, Darcy, I never thought to live to see the day when my sister should risk everything for love. She is overwhelmed by your kind offer and would much prefer to marry with her friends and family present than do it over the anvil.'

'Excellent. I'll pay the shot whilst you send for our fresh mounts. You never know, we might get home this evening.' Before he went inside he thought he'd better pay his respects to Caroline. As he reached the chaise she appeared in the doorway and beckoned him over. He'd never seen her look so pretty – her smile was radiant.

'Darcy, I cannot thank you enough for your generous offer to allow David and me to stay with you and marry at Pemberley. To have dearest Georgiana and her new husband present will make my day even more special.'

He took her hand and held it for a moment, remembering the many years that he'd known her. At one time he'd thought he might even make her an offer – but then he'd met Lizzy and everything had changed.

'I'm delighted to be able to help. I like young Forsyth and believe that you might be happy with him. I'm not sure if we will reach our destination today – but if not, we'll overnight and arrive first thing tomorrow. Lizzy is expecting you both. Once you have fulfilled the residency requirements you can arrange for the vicar to call the banns.'

Forsyth bounded up behind him and he stepped aside to allow the young man to rejoin his future wife. By the time he'd settled with the landlord, Bingley was mounted and his new horse, a rangy chestnut gelding, was waiting for him.

He would have to delay the departure to London until after the wedding – but leaving a few weeks later would hopefully make no difference to his plans.

* * *

When Lizzy awoke, the rain was rattling against the windowpanes. She hoped Fitzwilliam and Charles had had the good sense to stay overnight and had not attempted to return in such foul weather. Her maid had yet to come in with her morning chocolate and sweet rolls so the hour must be early.

As she was now fully awake, she might as well rise and begin her morning ablutions. She was quite happy to use the cold water from last night. After stripping off her nightgown she rubbed a little of the rose-scented soap onto her washcloth.

'Good morning, my darling, I thought I heard you stirring.'

Lizzy dropped both items and spun round to see her husband approaching with a wicked glint in his eye. He too was unclothed.

'I'd no idea you had returned last night. I'm so glad to see you. Is Caroline with you?'

His arms encircled her waist and he lifted her from her feet. 'I'll tell you later – I've more interesting things to do at this moment.'

He carried her into the bedchamber she'd just left and tumbled her between the sheets. After a delightful interlude, she finally caught her breath and eased herself away from him so she could see his dear face.

'Is she with you? Have you brought Mr Forsyth as well?'

His smile was tender and he smoothed a damp tendril of hair

from her cheek before speaking. 'I can answer in the affirmative to both questions. They are to be married in our chapel as soon as we can legally have the banns read. This means we cannot depart for Town before their nuptials have taken place.'

She relaxed into his arms, delighted with his reply, then sat up abruptly jabbing her elbow into his chest. 'How did our guests find their rooms? What time did you return? Peterson was already locking up when I retired at ten o'clock last night.'

'There's no need to panic, my love – we were able to rouse him, and Reynolds conducted Caroline and Forsyth to their apartments. Fortunately we got here before the heavens opened and so avoided a soaking.'

'I can hardly comprehend that you were able to waylay them and also persuade them to come here. Why did you travel in the dark? Surely it would have been better to stay overnight than risk an accident?'

'That was my intention, sweetheart, but Caroline refused. She insisted that they would be recognised and word would be sent back to Mr Forsyth's family. If Bingley and I hadn't continued as well, she would have arrived here unannounced and I couldn't allow that.'

Lizzy stretched up and kissed him, intending this to be no more than a thank you gesture but he took it as licence to begin another enjoyable episode of bedroom sport. When they eventually emerged it was after eight o'clock.

'The babies will be awake now and I always go up to spend time with them.'

He nodded and smiled. 'I didn't know that, but I intend to make it my business to accompany you every morning in future, my love.'

She couldn't help her tart reply. 'You would have known if you remained at my side all night as you used to and hadn't started sleeping next door on numerous occasions.' She wished her words unspoken when she saw his eyes narrow.

'Where I choose to sleep is my business, my dear, and I believe that I spend far more time in your bed than most husbands.' He stopped. 'Forgive me, I must send a note to the curate asking him to attend me here. I shall see you downstairs in due course.'

He was gone before she could apologise. How could she have been so foolish as to ruin what had started out as such a wonderful day? She couldn't remember the last time they had made love so passionately and now she had offended him.

Spending time with her babies was as pleasurable as always and, when she headed for the breakfast parlour, her good humour was restored. She was eager to speak to Caroline and be introduced to her future husband.

The sound of laughter and voices echoed from the room – she was tardy and everyone was there before her. She paused at the door and watched unobserved for a few moments. Caroline was a woman transformed. The habitual sneer and supercilious look had gone to be replaced by a smiling, happy countenance.

The young man who had brought about this change was a veritable Adonis – small wonder she had fallen in love with him. To Lizzy's surprise he appeared as besotted with Caroline as she was with him. The fact that he was somewhat younger than her made not a jot of difference to either of them.

Fitzwilliam became aware of her presence and looked over. She stiffened, expecting him to have remained cross with her. Instead he dropped his cutlery with a clatter and bounded to his feet. In two strides he was next to her and pulled her almost roughly into his arms.

'Darling, I apologise most humbly for my bad temper. Put it down to lack of sleep and overexertion...'

'Fitzwilliam – you must not say such things.' Her cheeks were scarlet thinking they might have been overheard.

His laughter did draw the attention of their guests. 'I was referring to having spent almost a day in the saddle. Come and meet Forsyth.'

He kept his arm around her and guided her forward. Both Caroline and her betrothed were also on their feet. After cordial introductions they all resumed their seats. Her husband collected her breakfast for her as he always did and the remainder of the meal was spent in convivial conversation.

'I hope I may come up to the nursery and meet your children, ma'am?' Caroline said.

'Please call me Lizzy – we stand on no ceremony here.'

Fitzwilliam choked into his napkin and his eyebrows disappeared under his hairline. Pemberley was renowned for its formality and he for being the most formidable of hosts.

Caroline smiled. 'Thank you, that is most kind of you. Do you spend much time with your little ones or leave their upbringing to their nanny?'

For some reason her husband chose to answer this question for her. He was no longer smiling. 'My wife spends an inordinate amount of time with our offspring – if I had not refused they would have their cribs in our bedchamber.'

Their guest chose to ignore the implied criticism. 'How splendid! If David and I are fortunate enough to have children of our own I intend to be the most devoted of mamas.'

'I know it's unfashionable to be so involved, but I believe that the more time spent with one's babies the more they thrive.'

She pushed back her chair and nodded to the gentlemen. 'Pray excuse us. Caroline and I are going to the nursery.'

* * *

Darcy watched them leave and wished he'd kept his opinion to himself. When Lizzy had eventually agreed to marry him, he had been determined not to be a proud and dictatorial husband. Why was he now behaving like his father?

He had no time to dwell on this thought as Forsyth spoke up from the other end of the table. 'I expect you're wondering how I met Caroline.'

He had absolutely no interest in the subject but could hardly tell the earnest young man this fact. He forced a look of curiosity on his face. 'I am indeed, sir, but there's no need to tell me if you would prefer to keep this matter private.'

Forsyth beamed. 'It's no secret, Darcy. I met her at a musical evening I was attending with my family. The performances were appalling – no professional singer or player had been retained – and halfway through I slipped away. Caroline had done the same and for both of us it was a *coup de foudre.* Love at first sight and from that moment we were both determined we would be together somehow.'

'I'd not thought of her as having a romantic nature – but love can do strange things to a person. You must remain here for several weeks until your residency can be established.'

'I shall have reached my majority by then. I cannot imagine that my father will think to look here for us. I've no idea where we shall be living once the knot's tied. I have a very small estate in Essex but I hardly think Caroline will desire to live there.'

'I'm sure that you can remain at Bingley's place in Town. He rarely goes to London nowadays.' Surely Forsyth was aware that once he was married to Caroline, her fortune would be his own?

'You will be able to buy something more substantial anywhere in the country. Does Caroline intend to live near Mrs Hurst?'

'Absolutely not. She has little time for her older sister or her husband. Derbyshire seems a pleasant place to live and I'm sure she would love to be close to her brother and his wife.'

Caroline might be Bingley's sister, but she could be considered almost as a member of his family, so why did his spirits fall at this news? 'I'm sure that my steward could find you something suitable when he returns if that's what you require. Please excuse me; I have estate business to attend to.' He nodded and strode off, belatedly realising his unfortunate guest would have no notion where to find his future wife or indeed anywhere else in the vast establishment that was Pemberley.

The study was his retreat. He was rarely disturbed when working there, although Lizzy had often come to sit with him when they were first married. He missed the closeness they'd once had. He'd only become involved with his cousin's intelligence work because Lizzy had less time for him since the twins were born. He now understood that his being away so much had just compounded the problem.

They would be alone in London. She wouldn't have the distraction of the children, and he was determined to court his beloved Lizzy and persuade her to fall in love with him again.

# 5

Caroline had never been a particular friend of Lizzy's – if she was honest she had never taken to her from the first moment they'd become acquainted at a ball at Meryton so many years ago. Neither of Charles's sisters had been invited to the recent weddings, as they were not included in the close family circle.

Therefore Lizzy wasn't sure she wanted Caroline to accompany her to the nursery. No doubt she would sneer and make supercilious comments as was her wont. Miss Bingley had expected to be mistress at Pemberley and had made her displeasure clear when she and Fitzwilliam had married.

'How old are the twins? I misremember exactly when they were born last year.'

'They are not quite nine months old. You will see how advanced they are, which is unusual for twins. They are both crawling and have been sitting up unaided since November.'

They had reached the nursery floor and Fabian and Amanda could be clearly heard banging about and laughing as they did so. Lizzy rushed in and immediately the babies stopped what they were doing and crawled towards her.

She dropped to her knees so she could embrace them, forgetting she was accompanied this morning by an unwanted visitor.

'May I hold one of your babies, please? They are quite delightful – Amanda looks just like you and Fabian like Darcy.'

Lizzy was cradling her babies on her lap. 'I'm not sure if either of them will go to you without protest, but we can see.'

Caroline stretched out her arms towards the nearest child, which happened to be Amanda. 'Come to your Aunt Caroline, little one. How pretty you are – just like your mama.'

The baby didn't hesitate. She launched herself across the gap and was soon babbling and gurgling happily, as if she'd known her new Aunt Caroline forever.

They stayed for an hour or more and by the end of it Lizzy was a fair way to having changed her mind about their guest. Gone was the unpleasant, manipulative young lady and in her place was a charming, happy person who could now be recognised as being a member of the family.

Lizzy had been expecting her husband to join them as he'd promised and was disappointed that he'd changed his mind. Perhaps he thought he would be intruding – but she was beginning to wonder if he found his son and daughter tiresome and that was the reason he didn't visit.

As they were making their way to the ground floor, Caroline touched her arm. 'You must be wondering how someone as... as proud as myself has behaved with such a lack of decorum.'

'We were certainly surprised to hear that you had eloped – but love will make the most sensible of people behave out of character.'

'How right you are, my dear Lizzy. I thought I was immune to this emotion but the moment I set eyes on dearest David everything changed. I hope you can forgive me for my previous behaviour.'

'It is forgotten. From now on things shall be different between us. Charles will be happy that you're to be back in his life again. Shall we find the gentlemen, or are you going to go next door and become reacquainted with your sister-in-law?'

'I must speak to David first, but then I should dearly love to see Jane and my niece. I barely had time to talk to Charles either yesterday. I've so much to tell him.'

There was no need for Caroline to go elsewhere as Charles, Jane and Charlotte were in the drawing room with Mr Forsyth. There was no sign of Fitzwilliam.

It was a merry party indeed and Lizzy immediately sent up for the twins to join them. Rugs had been spread on the priceless carpet so the children could play with their toys. She had arranged for a cold collation to be served on tables halfway down the room as midday approached.

The nursemaids, who had been chatting together on the periphery of the family group, were beckoned forward and took their charges to the nursery where they could eat their own lunch.

'Forgive me, everyone, but I must go and find Fitzwilliam. I cannot think what has been keeping him busy all morning.' Lizzy nodded and headed for the study. He had better have an excellent excuse for his bad manners.

Was he regretting his decision to invite Caroline and David to live with them until they were married? She could think of no other explanation that made sense. Then she understood. The couple should be staying with Charles and Jane, not with them. There was ample room in the east wing for a dozen guests and this didn't prevent the marriage eventually taking place in the chapel.

This she could arrange before searching out her husband. She walked briskly back to the drawing room and beckoned to

Jane. Immediately her sister left the group and came to join her. 'What is it, Lizzy? You look most perturbed.'

'Could you take Caroline and Mr Forsyth back with you? They should be staying in your home – after all they are your family not ours.' She regretted the bluntness of her words when she saw the shock on Jane's face.

'Of course, I cannot think why Charles allowed them to move in here. I know how much Darcy dislikes having strangers around him. I shall send word next door and have rooms prepared immediately. Is that why your husband has been absent all morning?'

'I think it might be – but there is no excuse for his incivility and I intend to have stern words with him. Please don't wait for us to join you but enjoy your luncheon.'

'We shall be gone as soon as we've eaten and leave you to yourselves. Between us we have made a sad mull of things.'

Lizzy took her sister's hands. 'I believe that Charles was protecting you. Caroline treated you disgracefully…'

'Good heavens! That was so long ago I'd quite forgotten. Go and find your errant husband, my love, and tell him the good news.'

* * *

Darcy looked at his pocket watch and swore under his breath. Lizzy must think him deliberately avoiding their guests. First he'd become caught up in an estate matter that had required him to write to his lawyers and then a missive from his cousin had arrived by express. The information contained therein also required an immediate response. Then the curate had arrived and it had taken an interminable time to arrange things for the wedding.

The colonel wanted them in London immediately but this was now impossible. By the time he'd written this second letter explaining the reasons he couldn't come, two hours had passed. He'd given his wife his word he would spend time with her and the children and he'd broken it.

He hoped he could smooth things over by being at his most charming when he joined them. He was about to head for the drawing room when the door flew open.

'Fitzwilliam, have you been hiding from us?' Lizzy looked less than delighted to see him.

'I beg your pardon, sweetheart, I had letters to write that couldn't wait. I'm coming now.'

'I know why you remained here so long – you don't enjoy having Caroline and Forsyth staying with us. I cannot think why you invited them to come here in the first place. I've arranged for them to move next door. They are not really our family – but my sister's.'

He was about to protest but decided against it. 'You're right, my love. Bingley should have spoken up. This place is big enough to avoid a person one doesn't feel inclined to speak to, so they could have remained here. However, they will do better next door.'

'A buffet has been set out in the drawing room. I am sharp-set as it seems an age since breakfast. I have sent a note to your sister to invite them to dine on Tuesday. Jonathan should be back from his business trip by then.'

'It's a great pity that Kitty is unable to travel at the moment – how much longer will she be so discommoded?'

She shrugged. 'One would hope that she will recover when she reaches her fourth month – but unfortunately not every pregnancy follows the expected pattern.'

He could hear voices from the drawing room and was

relieved everyone was still there. 'I apologise for not being able to spend time with our children as I promised, my dear.'

'You refine on it too much, Fitzwilliam. I do not expect you to be as involved with the twins as I am. I'm sure you will find them more interesting when they are able to communicate.'

This wasn't what he'd meant at all but they had arrived at the door and he had no opportunity to tell her she was quite wrong on that account.

After a pleasant hour Bingley and his family rose to leave. 'We shall see you at matins on Sunday, Darcy. I believe we are all coming here to dine on Tuesday night with your sister and her husband. We shall not importune you further.'

He and Lizzy walked to the door and then a footman conducted their guests through the Great Hall. For some reason Peterson had decided the group must exit through the front door, which was rarely used nowadays.

'We need to talk, my love. Are you free to do so or do you have a more pressing engagement?'

'What could I possibly have to do that is of more importance than conversing with my lord and master?' Her smile told him he was forgiven.

Once they were comfortably settled in front of the fire he explained to her why he had been so delayed.

'Did your cousin not explain to you why we should go to London so urgently?' she asked.

'He didn't. I've told him we cannot go until the end of the month as planned but I couldn't tell him why – that's not my secret to reveal.'

'Forsyth could send for a special licence and then they could be married immediately.'

'He could if he was not underage. I cannot think it matters if we arrive a few weeks later than planned.'

'I have already written to the butler and housekeeper at Grosvenor Square. I have been thinking, my dear, that nobody will know we are in residence until we arrive. How then can we go to the requisite number of events in order to meet sufficient suitable young ladies?'

'My cousin will mention it and word will soon spread. I can assure you there will be dozens of suitable invitations waiting for us when we eventually arrive.'

'In which case, I cannot think of anything else that needs to be done to make this a successful venture. I still find it incredible that such a confirmed bachelor has finally decided to seek out a wife.'

'As do I, but we shall do our best to help him in this endeavour. Did I tell you that Forsyth intends to settle in Derbyshire so they can be close to Bingley and Jane?'

'That will be quite delightful for them.' She pursed her lips and he laughed.

'There will be no necessity for us to see them any more than you wish to, Lizzy. Caroline might appear to have improved her character but...'

'But leopards do not change their spots.'

'Indeed they do not, my love. Now, if there isn't anything else you need to say on the subject I must visit one of my tenants this afternoon. Do you intend to come with me?'

She gestured towards the rain-filled clouds. 'Thank you, but I've no desire to be drenched.' She stretched up and kissed him but skipped away before he could reciprocate.

He watched her sadly. He hated having to lie to her and dreaded to think what she would say if she ever discovered his deception.

* * *

Caroline came round every morning – sometimes on her own and sometimes with Jane, Forsyth and Charles. On the day of the dinner party, Lizzy was playing with the babies in the nursery and Fitzwilliam was dealing with a letter that had come from London by express.

The door opened and Caroline drifted in. 'Good morning. On your own again, I see?'

Lizzy didn't see why she should explain her husband's actions so ignored the comment. Her unwanted visitor pulled over a footstool and joined her on the floor. 'I think it sad that Darcy has not taken to fatherhood. One cannot help but notice that Charles spends so much more time with his baby.'

'He is an excellent father but has more to do than Charles.'

'I'm sure he does, my dear Elizabeth, and like most gentlemen he prefers to leave the rearing of the children to his wife.'

There was something about Caroline this morning that made Lizzy wary. Was she getting up to her old tricks and doing what she could to cause dissent?

'Pray don't let me keep you, Caroline. I'm sure you have better things to do with your time than be up here with my children.'

'It must be a comfort being able to spend time with Amanda and Fabian. It will be hard for you to leave them behind when you go to London – but I shall come every day in your stead so they will not go without loving attention.'

This would not do at all. Lizzy couldn't get up, as she had her son on her lap, but she straightened and answered icily. 'That will not be necessary, but I thank you for your offer. Only immediate family will be welcome in Pemberley in my absence.'

Caroline stood up gracefully; her lips smiled but her eyes were hard. 'Dearest Darcy considers me a sister. We have been closely acquainted for many years – far longer than you and he have known each other. I can see that you are drifting apart. I'm certain he regrets his choice and...'

Lizzy deposited her son on the carpet, much to his annoyance. Ignoring his howls of protest she moved until she was an arm's length from her tormentor. 'How dare you come into my home as if you had a right to be here? Remove yourself immediately and do not come again. Your invitation to dine tonight is cancelled, as is the offer for you to be married in our chapel.'

'We shall see about that, madam. When I have spoken to Darcy, you will find that he takes my side – as will my brother and dearest Jane.'

Lizzy's fist clenched and the wretched woman saw the danger sign and fled. Nanny had come in unnoticed and scooped up the disgruntled baby.

How much had been overheard? This was an unmitigated disaster. She must get to Darcy before Caroline could burst in with a string of accusations. She didn't for a minute think her husband would believe a word of it – instead he would be enraged and goodness knows what the outcome might be.

'You run along, ma'am. Take the servants' stairs; you will reach the study quicker that way,' Nanny said quietly.

Without stopping to think about the consequences of being found running about in such a place, Lizzy did as suggested. She snatched up a candle, lit it from the fire and then ran into the maids' room and out through their exit.

She would have soon been lost in the rabbit warren of passageways and staircases if numbers, arrows and directions had not been written on the walls. She emerged breathless on the ground floor and crossed the central stone passageway and threw herself into the study.

Fitzwilliam dropped his pen and surged to his feet. 'Lizzy,

sweetheart, whatever's wrong?' He strode across and gathered her close to his chest.

Her heart was pounding so loudly she thought he must be able to hear it. She was trembling and unable to explain why she'd arrived so precipitously. He stroked her back and murmured reassurances until she'd recovered sufficiently to speak.

'Caroline Bingley is on her way to stir up trouble between us.' Quickly she explained what had taken place in the nursery and his expression was grim by the time she'd finished.

'The woman hasn't changed – she's still as pernicious as ever she was. I thought that love had changed her. Hide in one of those high-backed chairs at the far end of the room. When I've done you can reveal yourself.'

Gently he pushed her away. Lizzy ran to do as he suggested and was barely settled before there was a soft tap at the study door.

# 6

Darcy could barely contain his ire. This was the last time Bingley's sister caused an upset in his family. He tried to keep his voice even as he invited the woman in.

'My dear Darcy, I would not come to you if I did not think you would desire to hear…'

He allowed her to say no more. 'Silence. My wife asked you to leave these premises. You will do so forthwith and not return. Do I make myself clear?'

Her reaction could not have been more extreme if he had struck her. She recoiled, colour left her cheeks and her hands fluttered uselessly in front of her. For a second he regretted his harshness and was about to say something a little more conciliatory when she spoke again.

'I see that you have been poisoned against me. I've always considered you a dear friend; I have only your best interests at heart.'

He reached out and pulled the bell strap. Peterson must have been outside the door as he stepped in immediately. 'Please conduct this person from the house. She is not to be admitted again under any circumstances.'

The woman's shoulders slumped and she turned, defeated, and followed his butler from the study. He hoped Lizzy had not been too distressed by the unpleasant scene. He was about to go to her when she emerged – to his surprise she was smiling.

'Fitzwilliam, that was masterly. I almost felt sorry for her.' In three steps she was beside him.

His reply was to gather her close and demonstrate just how much he loved her. They were standing within arm's reach of the door and he leant backwards and firmly turned the key. They'd never made love in his study and now was the perfect time to do so.

A most enjoyable time later he sat up and helped Lizzy adjust her clothing. 'Your hair is sadly disarrayed, my darling – you might as well remove the final pins.'

Her cheeks were flushed and her eyes bright. She had never looked more lovely. 'You are incorrigible, Mr Darcy. This was hardly the time nor the place for such a pastime.'

He reached over and tugged gently at her hair so it tumbled about her shoulders. 'If I wish to make love to my wife in my study then I shall do so. As you are always telling me, I am the master of Pemberley.'

She gathered up her tresses and with a few deft strokes restored her appearance. Watching her do something so intimate made him feel the urge to tumble her to the floor again.

'Don't look at me like that, Fitzwilliam – once is more than enough. Now, kindly behave yourself whilst I make sure I am looking respectable.' She waved towards his untucked shirt and barely buttoned breeches. 'You would do well to restore your appearance, sir, before we send the entire staff into palpitations.'

'My stock is ruined – I shall have to return to our apartment for a new one.' He shrugged into his discarded topcoat and pulled his boots back on. 'We shall go there together...'

'We shall do no such thing. I shall go first and you will follow after a respectable time has passed.' Her smile was loving but he knew better than to disagree.

* * *

As she reached the door he swore and she turned in shock. 'My love, whatever's wrong?'

'I must send for Bingley at once. I can only imagine what that woman will have told him. I should have thought of that immediately.'

'As should I – Charles and Jane will feel obliged to take her side, but I doubt that they will do anything precipitous. However, I cannot say the same for her future husband. I do hope he doesn't arrive to call you out.'

Her attempt to lighten the mood had the opposite effect. His eyes widened. 'Devil take it! That's exactly the sort of thing he might do. Sweetheart, we must repair the damage our lovemaking has wrought on our appearance and then go next door and speak to your sister and Bingley.'

'If we return by the route through which I arrived we will be there more quickly.' He followed her into the servants' domain and thus up the narrow wooden staircase staff were obliged to use.

When she reached the floor where she was certain their apartment was situated she stopped, not sure in which direction to go as previously she'd made her way down from the nursery floor. 'I don't suppose you know the correct turning to take, Fitzwilliam?'

He was standing so close behind her, his breath tickled her

neck. He raised the candlestick so he could see the arrows and numbers. 'My father must be rotating in his grave at our behaviour today. Firstly, what took place in the study and now becoming lost on the servants' staircase. Although I've never used this route before, I think we must turn here.'

They moved forward and she prayed they were near their destination as she was no longer comfortable wandering around these narrow passageways.

'Yes – if we exit here we should be in our own apartment or fairly adjacent.'

He reached over her shoulder and pushed open the door and immediately she recognised her surroundings. 'We are in the dressing room attached to my bedchamber. I must change my gown as it is sadly creased and quite unfit to be seen.'

'I only need a new stock – I'll wait for you in the sitting room.'

Fortunately her maid had been doing some mending and was able to assist her. In a quarter of an hour she was in a fresh dress – a pretty russet chenille with long sleeves and high neck – ideal for the chilly weather.

Fitzwilliam smiled his appreciation at her speedy arrival. 'I've sent a servant next door to request that Bingley and Jane call here as soon as they may. I think it better than us going to visit them. I hope to avoid an unpleasant confrontation with Forsyth or Miss Bingley.'

'I'm so relieved we don't have to go in person. We had better hurry, for it would not do for us to keep them waiting.'

* * *

Bingley and Jane were ahead of them. She was in tears and he little better. 'I apologise for keeping you both waiting. Thank you for coming round so speedily.' Darcy indicated that they should go into the drawing room.

Lizzy rushed to embrace her sister but Jane seemed reluctant to be embraced. This was an ominous sign.

'Before you speak, let me tell you what took place here – I doubt that you got an accurate picture from Miss Bingley.' He gave them a brief explanation but his words appeared to make little difference to their distress.

'Jane, we both know what Miss Bingley is capable of. Please don't let her machinations come between us.' Lizzy was having difficulty holding back her tears and seeing her so distressed made him more resolute.

'Well, Bingley, can you now say that we were not justified in ejecting your sister from these premises?' His friend wouldn't look directly at him and his mumbled reply wasn't clear. 'Would you please repeat what you said, as I didn't hear you?'

'Caroline is beside herself with grief. She knows she should not have attempted to offer advice but it was well meant...'

Lizzy was about to disagree but Darcy shook his head and she remained quiet.

'She has changed, Darcy. She is no longer the person who behaved so poorly at Netherfield. You have both misjudged her and caused us all a deal of pain.'

Jane was still sniffing into her handkerchief but appeared to be in agreement.

This time he couldn't prevent his wife from speaking out. 'Jane, I cannot believe that you would side with that woman. That you are prepared to sever relations with your real family...'

Finally Jane spoke. 'You are my sister, but Charles is my family now. I beg you, dearest Lizzy, don't make me have to choose, as my loyalty must be with him.' She stood up, her cheeks pale and her expression sad. 'Do we have two find ourselves another home if we are no longer welcome at Pemberley?'

'Don't talk fustian. Bingley, explain to your wife that although you are my tenants you have as much right to live there as Lizzy and I do to live in this part of Pemberley.'

His erstwhile friend stood up and pulled his wife up beside him. 'I intend to return the lease to you, Darcy. We shall not remain if my dearest Jane wishes to leave.' He nodded to Lizzy and bowed to him. 'We have been friends for many years and I am saddened that things have ended in this way. I bid you goodbye and wish you good luck in your London venture.'

Lizzy made a move towards her sister but he restrained her. 'Not now, leave things until they have had time to reflect.'

She turned her face into his shoulder in despair. Caroline Bingley had caused this misery and he was determined she would get her comeuppance – but it would have to wait until he'd completed his mission for the government.

'Don't cry, my love. I promise Jane will be restored to you. This will be but a temporary separation.'

She raised a tear-stained face. 'This is different. She is right to say she must put Charles ahead of her feelings for me. We love each other dearly but I believe that I would do the same if I was in her situation. Caroline has poisoned them against us and I can't see how this can be resolved amicably.'

'I shall leave it a day or two and then speak to Bingley. Anyway, it will take them several weeks to find another estate to buy and by the time we return from Town...'

Her expression changed. 'Surely you do not intend to go to London as things are? Your cousin's marital needs are nothing in comparison to restoring my relationship with my sister.'

Although what she said was true, she didn't know the real reason they were going. He had given his word to the colonel. He would have to insist they leave as planned and this might irreparably damage his marriage.

He had to give her an answer and when he did things would change between them. His chest constricted and he swallowed a lump in his throat. 'I appreciate your sentiments, my love, but we shall go at the end of the month. In the circumstances, I think it better if we are both away from Pemberley for a while until matters next door have calmed down.'

She stared at him for a moment and then moved away. 'I shall, of course, do as you request, sir. I think that you are quite wrong in your assessment of the situation. The rift between my dearest Jane and myself will only worsen in my absence.' She straightened her shoulders and it was as if an invisible wall had come down between them. 'Pray excuse me, sir, I have things to attend to elsewhere.'

She walked away and he wanted to call her back and explain his reasons but couldn't do so. They would depart next week, sooner if possible, not leave it until the end of the month. He must send a message to Georgiana cancelling the dinner engagement tonight. Better no one else knew about today's events.

He would go upstairs and talk to Lizzy when he had written the letter to his cousin. Hopefully she would have calmed down a little and be ready to listen to him by then.

An hour later he arrived at their shared apartment to find everything had changed. She had removed herself and her belongings from his bedchamber and the communicating door was firmly locked from her side. She could not have made it plainer.

He stared at the door and was tempted to go around to the other side and remove the key but thought better of it. Lizzy was upset and he didn't blame her. He would allow her a night to get over it before making the closed door an issue.

He loved her – she was his life – but this was his house and he would not be denied access to any of its rooms even by Lizzy.

* * *

Lizzy collapsed on the bed, expecting to hear her husband hammering on the communicating door at any moment. The knob turned. She held her breath but he did no more and she was relieved there wasn't going to be further confrontation.

One thing was certain: if he insisted that she accompany him to London she would never forgive him. She would always love him but things between them would never be the same. It was fortuitous he already had an heir as the way things were at the moment he was unlikely to have the opportunity to produce another.

A woman was, in law, considered a chattel of her husband's for him to do as he wished with. She believed there was even a statute that said a wife could be beaten with a stick no thicker than his finger. Fitzwilliam could demand his marital rights, indeed could take them by force, but however estranged they became she was certain he would never do anything like that.

The door between their rooms was locked. That would be enough to tell him he wasn't welcome in her bed until – well, until he agreed that they shouldn't go away before she and Jane were reconciled.

Her first task must be to send a letter to both the butler and housekeeper at Grosvenor Square, informing them they would not now be coming. It would probably be wise to also cancel the dinner engagement tonight as she had no desire to share her marital problems with anyone else.

It took several attempts to compose the necessary correspondence as her penmanship was all to pieces. Eventually she was satisfied and sanded the sheet, folded it, applied the sealing wax and pressed in the Darcy seal.

Her abigail had been arranging her gowns and underpinnings in the closet. She could take the letter down and make sure Peterson sent a footman to the village immediately. She glanced at the clock on the mantelshelf and saw to her surprise the time was only half past eleven. How could her world have fallen apart in so short a time? Returning to the nursery was not possible as the children would be taking their morning rest. She needed to clear her head and a long, brisk walk around the grounds would do exactly that.

The sun was out – a perfect day to be outside. She had never enjoyed riding; that pastime was left to her sister Jane. Thinking of her brought tears to her eyes and she blinked them away. She would not be a watering pot but remain calm and dignified and not allow her innermost feelings to influence her behaviour.

A warm cloak, gloves and stout boots were required for this venture. Suitably attired she hurried downstairs and slipped out through one of the many side doors without being seen by anyone. She took a little-used path that led past the home meadows where the house cows grazed.

Once she was a mile away from the house she began to relax, to enjoy the early spring sunshine and notice wildflowers growing in the hedgerows. This narrow track wasn't one she had taken before – but then this wasn't surprising as the grounds of Pemberley were so vast she doubted that even Fitzwilliam had traversed it all.

The sound of the birds singing was soothing and soon she was striding out enjoying the walk and able to forget about the catastrophic events that had taken place earlier. There was nothing she liked more than an invigorating walk in the countryside. Her lips curved as she remembered several years ago when she had walked across the fields from Longbourn to Netherfield. Caroline Bingley and her equally unpleasant sister Mrs Hurst had been so shocked by her appearance.

She paused midstride as something struck her. Jane would take Caroline's side – she could hardly do anything else when she was living under her roof. Perhaps things weren't as bad as they appeared and she might be able to speak privately to her sister and persuade her that the love between them was too important to be put at risk by Caroline Bingley.

The walk had done her good and she was ready to return. This was the first time since her marriage that she and Fitzwilliam had fallen out. It must not be allowed to continue, so she would do her best to reach a compromise with him before things escalated.

After the vigorous exercise she was hungry and more than ready for her midday repast. That her skirt hem and petticoats were an inch deep in mud bothered her not one jot. She was mistress here and could be as dishevelled as she wished and nobody was in a position to comment.

The route she had taken brought her out just below the ha-ha. She ran up the steps and began the long trek across the grass to the terrace. A movement in one of the windows on the ground floor of the east wing caught her eye. Was that someone waving to her? She was in a quandary, not sure if she should respond. If it was Caroline then she had no wish to acknowledge her – but if the person waving was anyone else living in the house then she must respond.

Perhaps she could pretend she hadn't noticed – yes, that was the best option. She continued on her way keeping her eyes lowered as if admiring the daffodils and crocuses blooming around the trees.

'Mrs Darcy, I beg your pardon, but could you spare me a few moments of your time?'

Her head shot up. Mr Forsyth was bounding towards her and she had no alternative but to stop and talk to him. She nodded but didn't speak, uncertain what to say to the betrothed of the woman whose malevolence had caused the rift between herself and her beloved sister.

He slithered to a halt beside her and half-bowed. 'My Caroline is desperately upset about what happened between you. She considers Pemberley almost like a second home as she has spent so much time here over the years. Also, Mr Darcy is more than a friend to her…'

She had heard quite enough of this nonsense and interrupted him mid-flow. 'Mr Forsyth, Miss Bingley has never been more than the sister of his close friend, Mr Bingley. She was an acquaintance allowed to visit because of her relationship to my husband's closest friend. I believe you have been sadly misled on this subject.'

She set off towards the house indicating that the conversation was over, but he followed her and had the temerity to grasp her elbow.

'Mrs Darcy, I beg you to reconsider your position and apologise to Caroline so matters can be put right between you.'

This was the outside of enough. 'I have no intention of discussing this with you. You are a stranger to me.' She was about to step around him when he laid his hand on her arm.

'If you do not do as I ask, then you will lose your sister. She will not go against her husband's wishes.'

# 7

Lizzy shook off Mr Forsyth's hand. 'I think, sir, that you and Miss Bingley must leave Pemberley at once. When I speak to Mr Darcy I can assure you he will not be pleased. Making an enemy of him will be something you will both regret.'

She didn't linger to hear his response. Fitzwilliam must hear of this latest threat. Her heart was pounding and she was relieved to return to the sanctuary of her own abode. Once inside she leant against the wall for a few moments to recover her equilibrium.

How had it come to this? Was it possible that the elopement had just been a ploy to get Charles to invite the couple to Pemberley? Why would the wretched woman have given Mrs Hurst the route she intended to take unless she wished to be found by her brother?

Fitzwilliam would be able to make sense of this. The fact that they had parted on bad terms an hour or so ago made no difference. She must speak to him immediately. His study was empty. She sent for Peterson and the butler told her that her husband had gone out.

She would wait for him here – he would be informed of her whereabouts when he returned and they could be guaranteed privacy in this room. Pacing the carpet only made her more distressed. She slumped onto a chair and sat watching the flames flickering, hoping these would calm her. Her eyes slowly closed and she drifted off into a light doze.

* * *

Darcy returned from his ride, determined to put matters right between him and Lizzy immediately. He tossed the reins of his hunter to a waiting stable boy and strode into the house.

He was accosted by the butler. 'Mr Darcy, Mrs Darcy is in the study waiting to speak to you.'

Thank the good Lord! She too had decided this rift could not be allowed to continue a moment longer. His study door was ajar and he stepped in. She was curled up in a chair fast asleep. He walked softly to her side and dropped to his knees. 'Lizzy, my love, we must talk.'

Her eyes opened and she sat up immediately. 'I've been waiting this age, Fitzwilliam. There's something I must tell you.'

She pointed to a chair opposite and he did as she suggested. This was not to be the rapprochement he had hoped for – but any communication was better than none.

'What is it that has caused you so much agitation?'

He listened with incredulity to her story. 'I should have realised that a young lady taking part in a genuine elopement would never reveal their destination, let alone the exact route she intended to take.' There was something else that had been said that was pertinent. He frowned in concentration and then remembered what it was. 'Forsyth told me he reaches his majority next month. All he had to do was remain incommunicado until then. There was no need for the two of them to make a dash for Scotland and involve both Bingley and I in this charade.'

'The whole escapade was a ruse to get Miss Bingley to Pemberley. She knew that Charles and you would immediately ride to her rescue and would invite her here.' She stood up and shook out her gown.

'Good God, Lizzy, look at your skirts! You should have changed and then come down here.'

Her expression changed from friendly to aloof. 'I beg your pardon, sir, for offending your sensibilities. I shall go at once and change into something that meets with your approval.'

'I didn't mean...'

'There's no need to apologise. I have said what I came here to say and will now leave you to take whatever action you think appropriate.' She stalked to the door but he called her back.

'There's little I can do, as Bingley has as much right to entertain his family next door as we do. I cannot dictate to him on this matter. However, you can be very sure they will not set foot here. Neither will they marry in the chapel.'

'Even if matters between Jane and I are restored, I shall not leave here whilst they are still in residence. So if you intend for me to accompany you to London you had better come up with a way of removing them.'

Then she was gone. He snatched up a ledger from his desk, was about to hurl it at the wall, but managed to restrain himself in time. God's teeth! She was pushing him too far. He was master here and she should not issue him with an ultimatum.

There was no option open to him, apart from sending a message to Bingley in the hope that he wouldn't ignore it. His friend was well aware of his sister's shortcomings – after all, had not her interference caused his beloved Jane untold heartache before they were finally reunited?

He slammed his hands down on the desk, making the inkpot and documents jump into the air. At that time he had behaved far worse than Caroline Bingley and had persuaded his friend to abandon Jane as he'd considered the whole family beneath his notice.

He thought his proud behaviour behind him. Falling in love with Lizzy had opened his eyes to a better way of doing things. Why then was he reverting to his previous character?

He eyed the decanter of brandy on a side table and was sorely tempted to pour himself a large measure. Drowning his sorrows wasn't a sensible option – he must keep a clear head and come up with a solution to these apparently insoluble problems.

As he was writing the note to Bingley, he changed his mind. He would go next door himself – the staff there had been employed by him before they'd moved into the east wing. They would not refuse him entry – whatever Bingley or his wife might think.

His boots were muddy, his breeches not much better; he had better smarten himself up before he left. His valet had already laid out an array of clean raiment and soon he was ready to venture out on his mission.

The communicating door was still locked. No doubt it would remain so until this matter was resolved. If he was going to persuade Bingley to eject his sister and her paramour then he must come up with a reasonable alternative. There was a small estate presently unoccupied as his tenant had died the previous month. This would be ideal. The fact that sending them to live together without the benefit of clergy would be considered scandalous was of little import.

Caroline and Forsyth had already stepped outside the rigid rules of society and would be ostracised if they appeared in Town at the moment. After they had been married for a year or two, the *ton* would have moved on and their behaviour would be forgotten.

It would be better if he made his approach formal so he sent a footman ahead of him to announce his arrival at the front entrance to the east wing.

He stood a few yards from the door where he was clearly visible to anyone who cared to look from the drawing room window. The door opened and a brief conversation ensued between the servant and Bingley's butler. Darcy strode forward and marched in as if he owned the place – which technically he still did.

'Darcy, come with me to my study. It wouldn't be wise for the ladies to see you here.' Bingley grabbed his arm and all but dragged him from the entrance hall.

'Enough. Please release my arm, Bingley.' He spoke quietly but it had the desired effect.

'You shouldn't have come here; it will only exacerbate matters when Caroline discovers I've spoken to you.'

'I don't intend to hold a discussion in the passageway. Shall we keep our thoughts to ourselves until we can be private?'

They walked in uncomfortable silence until they were safely ensconced in the study. He didn't wait for Bingley to speak again but immediately told him what he and Lizzy had concluded about the elopement, as well as telling him how Forsyth had accosted her on the terrace.

'I didn't think things could get any worse, but they have. I don't know what Caroline was hoping to gain by her machinations. Is she so jealous of our happiness that she wishes to destroy it? I don't wish her to remain here any more than you do, but I can hardly send her packing with no destination.'

'I have a solution for you.' Darcy explained about the estate and Bingley looked less fraught by the time he'd finished.

'If the place has been empty for several months, it will hardly be fit to live in. How long do you think it will take your people to make it ready for occupation?'

'A few days at the most, I should think. I will have to find extra staff as most of those who were employed by my tenant have now retired. There are but a handful taking care of things at the moment.'

'Although Caroline's reputation is already in tatters, I'm reluctant to make matters worse by sending her without a chaperone. I shall write immediately to my other sister and ask her and her husband to go there.'

'If you send a letter by express they will have it tomorrow and can set out the next day. This means they will be there within the week. That will be ample time to prepare the house. Although the estate is small, the house is handsome enough and might well do as a permanent home for Forsyth once they are wed. I'd be prepared to sell it to him.'

His mission accomplished, he stood up to leave. 'I'm relying on you to speak to Jane. I shall expect her to visit Lizzy this afternoon and put matters right between them.'

He nodded and Bingley reciprocated. Satisfied he'd set things in motion to bring this unpleasant incident to a close Darcy returned to his side of Pemberley. Perhaps it would be the best if the east wing was returned to him – things would never be quite the same between him and his erstwhile friend.

* * *

The afternoon dragged by and even the pleasure of spending time with her precious babies couldn't raise Lizzy's spirits. Being at odds with her beloved wasn't something she enjoyed and she was now regretting the fact that the dinner party tonight had been cancelled. It would have been so much easier to spend the evening with Fitzwilliam if Georgiana and Jonathan had been present.

Changing for dinner had been abandoned, unless they had guests, so there was no need for her to return to her room before going downstairs. Would this evening be an opportunity to mend fences or would things get worse?

The drawing room was unoccupied. She looked at the clock and saw she was five minutes past the appointed time and he was always here before her. She wandered around disconsolately, picking up objects and putting them down again.

Then the sound of raised voices alerted her. Fitzwilliam was arguing with someone on the terrace. She hurried to the long windows in order to see who he was talking to. Not wishing to be seen, she remained out of sight behind the curtain.

The other voice was Mr Forsyth and he sounded most agitated.

'Look here, Darcy, that won't do at all. We are comfortable here and have no intention of removing to some dismal little estate of yours. Caroline will not budge until we are safely married and can buy a substantial place of our own.'

'Bingley wishes you both to leave, so it would be polite to do as he requests.'

'Bingley is a great fellow. He's not going to insist that his dearest sister goes if she isn't inclined to.'

'He might not, sir, but I do. Bingley is my tenant and must follow my instructions – if he doesn't intend to be evicted too.'

Lizzy clutched the curtain. Surely Fitzwilliam didn't intend to send Jane away as well? This must be an empty threat just spoken to push Forsyth into leaving.

Forsyth replied immediately. 'I've no desire to be at daggers drawn with you, sir, but I warned Mrs Darcy how it would be if things were not resolved...'

Fitzwilliam had obviously had enough and forcefully interrupted. 'I'll hear no more from you, Forsyth. If you and your future wife require to be accepted in any drawing rooms then you would do well not to make an enemy of me. You will leave Pemberley tomorrow morning at the latest. If you have not gone by the time I rise I shall send my men in to remove you by force.'

She staggered to the nearest chair and collapsed upon it. If her husband attempted to carry out his threat, then Charles could hardly stand by and do nothing. Her brother-in-law might barricade himself and his family into the east wing or he could take Jane and baby Charlotte away when his sister left.

Either option did not bear thinking of. A few days ago her life had been well ordered and without incident and now things were in ruination. The arrival of the hateful Miss Bingley, and her equally obnoxious betrothed, had smashed the family apart.

It wouldn't be long before the rest of the family was dragged into this appalling situation. Georgiana and Jonathan would naturally side with Fitzwilliam – but she wasn't sure if Kitty and Adam would do so as well.

Holding the summer house party would be all but impossible if things had not been resolved. They could hardly have an influx of guests if their own family refused to attend the event. The colonel would have to wait until next year to find himself a bride – he was five-and-thirty – but another year could hardly matter. It wasn't as if he was in his dotage or had a title and vast estate to protect.

She was still gathering her thoughts when Fitzwilliam strode in. As soon as he saw her huddled by the windows he understood that she had overheard his argument. His expression changed from grim to concerned and he was at her side before she had time to speak.

'Lizzy, I wish you hadn't heard that. Forsyth is an imbecile and has allowed himself to be manipulated by Bingley's sister. I cannot have them here – you must understand that.'

'Of course I do, but it would have been better if you hadn't threatened to manhandle them from the premises if they refuse to go. Imagine the fuss that will cause. Charles and Jane will have no choice but to go with them and I shall be devastated if my sister leaves under such circumstances.'

His eyes glittered; he was as moved as she. 'I'm sorry, my love, but I will not go back on what I said. Pemberley is mine and I will not have my authority challenged.'

'Is the place you offered them so awful?'

He shook his head. 'Absolutely not. Although not as big as Netherfield it is far larger than the Old Rectory where King and your sister live quite comfortably. They could not buy anything as substantial with what Caroline brings to the union.'

'In which case I shall not cavil at your decision. I just pray that Jane can talk sense into Charles and he can persuade Miss Bingley to leave peaceably tomorrow morning.'

He held out his hand and she took it. He pulled her gently to her feet, his smile sad. 'If it comes to the use of force, Lizzy, then Miss Bingley and Forsyth will rue the day they pushed me to this. They will not be received by any respectable family – I shall make it my business to let everybody know of their elopement and subsequent behaviour.'

There was no opportunity to reply as Peterson appeared to announce that dinner was served. The only positive aspect of this episode was the fact that now they could not possibly go to London. Fitzwilliam would be far too busy protecting the Darcy name.

# 8

Darcy did his best to turn the conversation away from anything controversial. Lizzy ate very little and everything he put in his mouth tasted the same. They were both relieved when the final cover was removed.

'I have the headache. I am retiring immediately. Goodnight, Fitzwilliam.'

He stood, as was expected of him. 'We need to talk, Lizzy, but as you are feeling unwell this will have to wait until tomorrow morning.' When she was at the door he added a final comment: 'I shall not importune you this evening but I expect to be able to do so if I should so want.'

She continued as if he hadn't spoken and he didn't intend to exacerbate matters by saying more on this difficult subject. He would send his valet in to remove the key when she was elsewhere. He had no intention of going in uninvited, but it was a matter of principle that all doors should be open to him.

He retreated to his study and made steady inroads into the decanter of brandy that always stood waiting on the bureau.

Despite the quantity of alcohol he consumed, his mood did not improve. The adage that one could drown one's sorrows was patently incorrect. He was as miserable in his cups as he had been sober.

The clock struck midnight. Too late to send for a refill – Peterson would have retired and he could hardly drag the old fellow out of bed. He might as well do the same. The last candle had been snuffed and the fire was safely guarded. Picking up his candlestick he turned to leave the room when something banged on the window.

He dropped the heavy silver candlestick on the floor and the study was plunged into darkness. What the devil was that? He swore under his breath at being as startled as a child by something as innocuous as a night-time noise.

There was sufficient light from the fireplace for him to recover his candle and as he was doing so there was a second loud bang. Somebody was trying to attract his attention. The house would be locked for the night so whoever was outside would have to scramble in over the windowsill.

'Wait a minute – I'll be there directly.' Quickly he reignited half a dozen candles and then drew back the curtains and opened the shutters. A ghostly white face pressed against the panes and for a shocking moment he thought one of the Pemberley spectres had returned to haunt him.

'Darcy, let me in. I need to talk to you most urgently.' Bingley's voice was muffled by the glass.

'I'll open the window and you can climb in.'

Once his friend was safely inside, and things restored, he gestured towards one of the leather-covered armchairs by the fire. Bingley sank into one and immediately dropped his head into his hands and groaned.

There could be only one explanation for his behaviour – Forsyth had passed on his ultimatum.

'Do you require me to find some brandy? I finished this decanter.' He was a trifle unsteady and hastily sat opposite his visitor before his inebriation could be noticed.

Bingley looked up. 'Like you, old friend, I've already consumed far more than is good for me. I couldn't visit until everyone was abed and both houses quiet. Jane is distraught at the thought that you would evict us from our home.'

'I don't want to do so – of course I don't. Lizzy would never forgive me if that happened. However, I cannot allow your sister and Forsyth to remain at Pemberley.'

'I wish to God we had not found her. It would have been far better if she'd continued on her way to Scotland.'

Darcy shared his views on this matter and his friend was at first incredulous and then accepted the whole thing had been deliberately planned.

'This upset is not good for Jane. Her health is precarious at the moment and I fear she will miscarry the baby if things don't calm down.'

'Have you told your sister and Forsyth that they have to leave?'

Bingley shook his head miserably. 'There was so much screaming and crying I hid in my study and left them to it. They will leave. I shall instruct my staff to pack their trunks at first light. I give you my word, Caroline and Forsyth will be gone before breakfast.'

'I can hardly allow them to use my property after their behaviour. They will have to resume their journey to Scotland and take the consequences.'

'I shall ensure they have sufficient funds to travel there.'

Bingley yawned and stretched out his legs towards the fire. 'I'm wondering if any of their story is true. Do you think his family actually objected to the union and are looking for them?'

'I care not either way, and neither should you. Wash your hands of them – in a day or two she will no longer bear your name and I doubt that the scandal will reach here.'

Bingley looked longingly at the empty decanter. 'I need a stiff drink...'

'What we both need is coffee so we can clear our heads and be ready for the morning.'

* * *

Lizzy was on edge waiting to hear Fitzwilliam moving about next door. She must have fallen asleep, because when she woke she was disorientated and the candles had burned out. There would be no more rest until she was sure he was there.

Even the fire had gone out and the room was unpleasantly chill. Hastily she pulled on her bedrobe and pushed her bare feet into her slippers. This was done by touch alone; what she needed was to find the tinderbox and light a candle, but she doubted she would locate what she needed in the darkness.

She kept her eyes closed and edged her way across the carpet, her hands outstretched, hoping she would arrive safely at the communicating door. She managed this without mishap and quietly turned the key. The door opened inwards and, holding her breath, she carefully inched it open.

The room was dark and cold. She knew immediately that he wasn't there. In all the years since they had been married he had never failed to come to bed if he was at home. He wasn't given to staying up all night drinking himself into a stupor. Something untoward had taken place and she would go downstairs to ensure that he was safe.

This couldn't be done without a candle to guide her. She would have to reverse her steps and try and find the dressing room where the fresh candles and tinderbox were kept. She'd left the door open and slowly moved in what she hoped was the correct way. Her sense of direction was normally excellent and she had no doubt she would reach her destination safely.

Then her right leg collided with something solid and she lost her balance. She had walked into the bed. As she fell her hands grasped at the covers but, instead of preventing her fall, they added to the chaos by slithering from the bed and entangling her within their suffocating folds.

She thrashed about in panic trying to dislodge the material and twice her slippered toes connected painfully with the bed frame. Then she was hoisted from the carpet.

'Sweetheart, stand still and let me untangle you.' Fitzwilliam, as always, had come to her rescue.

The choking coverlets were removed and she was able to breathe again. The room was still dark, but not as black as before, as there was a faint light flickering from next door.

'I was looking for you. Where have you been?'

His answer was to sweep her from her feet and carry her into his room. 'You cannot sleep in there. You must have my bed.'

She was placed on her feet and he stepped away, making it clear he had no intention of joining her unless invited. He appeared a little unsteady on his feet and for a moment she thought he was unwell. Then she realised he was a trifle bosky.

Her lips curved. 'I think you can rest next door, as I doubt you will notice the disarray of the covers the state that you are in.'

He raised a hand in salute. 'I have been drinking with Bingley.

We have resolved our differences and his sister and Forsyth will be leaving tomorrow.'

'I'm pleased to hear you say so. Thank you. I'll not ask how Charles came to be drinking with you – you can tell me in the morning. You will need to take a candle with you.'

'How perspicacious of you, my love. I shall take this one so you had better get into bed before it goes.'

He stretched out to pick up the candlestick and his hand missed it entirely. He was a danger to himself.

'Fitzwilliam, I will light other candles so we can both see what we are doing.' She proceeded to do just this whilst he swayed dangerously in the doorway. 'Come along, I can help you disrobe. You will have a shocking headache tomorrow and I shall have absolutely no sympathy for your suffering.'

'I intend to sleep in my boots, my dear. It will be a novel experience.' His smile disarmed her. 'And I can assure you it's not one I intend to repeat anytime soon.'

She placed a light on the bedside table and then quickly gathered up the scattered covers from the floor. By the time she had done so, he was spreadeagled on the sheet and snoring loudly. Once he was safely tucked in she retreated to his bedchamber.

She left the door ajar in case he cast up his accounts in the night and needed her assistance. As she drifted off to sleep in the marital bed she couldn't help thinking that her decision to sleep apart from him had somehow been circumvented.

Whilst she was in his domain, he had every right to be beside her. This was the first time since she'd known him she had seen him the worse for drink. It should have disgusted her, but on the contrary it made her love him more. The man she had met all those years ago at the assembly at Meryton would have been too proud to have allowed himself to be seen in such a state.

He had changed and for the better. They would go to London as planned. She was almost looking forward to the visit, even though it meant leaving the children behind. Spending three weeks alone with him would be delightful, despite the fact they must attend a variety of social events.

At dawn she was awakened when the bed dipped and her husband slid in beside her. For an appalled moment she thought he'd got into bed with his boots on, but then his naked thigh touched hers and she forgot she was cross with him.

They arrived at the breakfast parlour at the same time as Charles and Jane. 'Lizzy, they have gone. I can't tell you how relieved I am this unpleasantness is over.'

Her sister ran towards her and they embraced fondly. 'I hope this is the last we ever hear of them.'

'Oh, I hope so too. I cannot bear to think that dreadful woman will come here a second time to cause trouble between us. I should never have allowed myself to be taken in by her and supported her against you and Darcy.'

Charles took his wife's arm. 'You were not to blame for that, my dear. It was I who was gulled by her. You must not fret; it's bad for you in your delicate condition. All you need to know is that they have gone from here. What might happen in the future is something we shall not dwell on at the moment.'

Lizzy felt a trickle of apprehension slither down her back. Charles thought his sister might cause trouble at a later date and she feared he might be correct.

* * *

Darcy took Bingley to one side whilst the ladies were talking fondly together. 'Did they leave without a fuss?'

'They had no option as I sent my staff in to pack their belongings whilst they were still asleep. By the time they had both got up it was a *fait accompli.* I didn't speak to either of them. They were escorted from the premises whilst I skulked in my study until they had gone.'

'Presumably they will continue on their journey to Scotland if they are genuinely determined to be married away from their family. However, my friend, I think if we bothered to check we would find that they are returning to London. There will be a notice of their nuptials in *The Times* in a few weeks and you can forget about them.'

Had Forsyth told Bingley of his threat to have his sister and her future husband ostracised? Perhaps it would be better not to bring this subject up, but to let time pass before he mentioned it. As far as he was concerned the matter was over, unless Miss Bingley caused further trouble.

'When do you depart for Town?'

'Next week. We shall not be gone long and rely on you and Jane to ensure my children are well in our absence.'

'Absolutely. Why not move them into our nursery for the duration? Their nanny and nursemaids can accompany them so they will not feel neglected.'

Lizzy and Jane drifted over to join them and he broached the suggestion.

His wife was delighted to accept. 'I shall be so much happier knowing they are under your care, Jane dearest.'

Darcy was aware that his sister-in-law looked less pleased about having her niece and nephew in residence. Did she think Fabian and Amanda might bring sickness to her own child? He knew little about such things but was well aware his offspring were far more robust than little Charlotte.

He put his arm around Lizzy's waist. 'I was thinking it would be a good notion to send word to our respective sisters and invite them to dine, but then I recalled that Kitty cannot travel. Perhaps we could go to the Old Rectory instead?'

'I should like that. As we are now intending to leave in a few days' time it had better be tonight or the next day. I'll write a note immediately and then Kitty can send word to Georgiana and Jonathan.'

They were now far enough away from Jane and Bingley for him to explain his concerns about moving their children next door.

'I believe that you're correct in your assumptions. It is perhaps a little irrational on her part, but I think I would be over-protective if either of our children were so delicate. I shall tell her Fabian has the snuffles and it would be best if they remained where they are.'

He left his wife to deal with this domestic matter. Darcy suggested to his friend that after they had all broken their fast together the two of them rode over to Bakewell with the message instead of sending a groom.

After the message was delivered it was decided they were to dine the next night with Kitty and King, and then he and Lizzy would depart from Pemberley the day after. The discord between him and his beloved was gone, as if it had never happened, and they were as happy together as they had ever been.

The babies were too young to understand their parents were going to be away from home for a few weeks, but Lizzy insisted on a tearful farewell anyway. He and Georgiana had rarely seen their parents and he believed that he had not suffered unduly from this arrangement. He thought that being apart from the twins would be good for his wife. He was determined to persuade her to spend less time in the nursery in future and more time with him.

As soon as this wretched war, with the upstart Bonaparte, was over he intended to take her to Italy. She would love the architecture and the churches as much as he had done when he'd made his grand tour with his tutor many years ago.

The morning of their departure arrived. The baggage had set off ahead of them along with his valet and her abigail. The house in Grosvenor Square was always in readiness for their occupation. The butler, Gregson, and the housekeeper, Watkins, made sure of that. They would have added sufficient temporary staff to the permanently employed servants so that their every need would be met.

The weather was clement for the end of March and the roads reasonably dry. With luck they should reach their destination with only two overnight stops. Their accommodation had been reserved, a fresh team sent ahead, and he expected the journey to be uneventful.

They had been travelling for an hour in companionable silence when Lizzy spoke from the other side of the carriage. 'I have been thinking about Miss Bingley and Forsyth. Did Charles tell you where they were going? Although she behaved despicably, I cannot help but be concerned for her welfare, and her reputation, after she was sent away so abruptly with no apparent place to go.'

'He didn't speak to her. He gave her one hundred guineas to cover her travelling expenses. Extravagant as she is, that should be enough to take her wherever she wishes to go.'

'I'm still puzzled as to why she wished to come to Pemberley. Did she hope to gain status by marrying there?'

'Possibly. I think it more likely she hoped to be included amongst our acquaintances again and could think of no other way of doing this. I certainly had no intention of inviting her to stay with us and I doubt that Bingley would have done so either, apart from the extraordinary circumstances.'

She sighed. 'In which case, my love, she was foolish to antagonise us all. If she had remained pleasant she would have achieved her aims and in a few weeks might even have been living close by.'

'Then it was fortuitous she behaved as she did. We would have been obliged to include her in our circle if she was residing in the neighbourhood. Now – let us talk of something else. I never want to hear that wretched woman's name again.'

# 9

By the time they eventually arrived at Grosvenor Square at dusk on the third day, Lizzy was heartily sick of the journey. Despite the fact that she and Fitzwilliam had enjoyed being together, they had both run out of conversation. She was already regretting leaving the twins at Pemberley. Would they forget their mama in the three weeks she was going to be away?

Her husband had become more distracted the closer they got to the capital. No doubt he was dreading the next few weeks as much as she was. Neither of them enjoyed mixing with strangers in overcrowded drawing rooms. They both preferred the comfort and privacy of their own home.

On entering the vestibule, they were greeted by the housekeeper and butler. Gregson bowed deeply.

'Sir, madam, everything is ready for your arrival. I thought you would prefer a supper tray upstairs tonight.'

'Thank you, we shall eat in our sitting room. Bring any correspondence and cards that have arrived for me at the same time.' Lizzy nodded and, picking up her skirts, headed for the grand staircase.

'I shall join you shortly, my love, but first I must attend to my own letters. I am expecting something from my cousin.'

The trays arrived before he did and she had them set out on the side table and dismissed the staff who had fetched them up. She would wait until Fitzwilliam arrived before investigating what had been sent. It was bound to be excellent as the cook here was as good as the one they employed in Derbyshire.

She sorted through the invitations and ranked them in order of suitability. Where there were two on the same evening she selected the one that might be expected to have a dozen or so suitable contenders for the position of Mrs Fitzwilliam. She was disappointed that there weren't more to select from.

Not all the important families had returned to London – the main events of the Season took place in April, May and June. Fortunately there were some taking place next week, which would hopefully allow them to investigate the young ladies who were on the marriage mart.

The door swung open and Fitzwilliam strode in. 'Excellent, you have waited for me before you began your supper.'

Whilst they ate she showed him the choices she'd made and strangely he rejected two and replaced them with the less prestigious affairs.

'The first party is in two days, which gives us ample opportunity to settle in and start receiving visitors. Are there any particular places where you intend to pay a morning call?'

Lizzy pointed to three of the cards that had been left. 'I shall go to these tomorrow and will send footmen out to deliver our cards announcing we have arrived. I'm anticipating there will be other soirées and musical evenings, as well as the ones we have here.'

'We must draw up a list of families we intend to invite to the house party in July and send them invitations before we leave.

My cousin is coming to supper tomorrow night, so you will be able to quiz him on his exact requirements.'

'I shall do no such thing. He's not the sort of gentleman one could discuss such things with. He is almost as formidable as you are, my dear.'

'Do you have plans for the morning, Lizzy?'

'I intend to visit Hatchards and purchase some books. No doubt there will be other emporiums I shall go to as well. The afternoon will be taken up with morning calls, so I doubt that we will meet until we change for dinner.'

He smiled his toe-curling smile. 'I'm relieved you didn't suggest that I accompany you on either of those expeditions. I have one or two business matters to attend to myself.' He stood up and held out his hand. 'I know it's early to retire, but will you join me in our bed?'

* * *

Darcy left Lizzy asleep and completed his ablutions without disturbing her. His valet dressed him efficiently and he was ready for the first of his business meetings by eight o'clock. Today he must forego his breakfast as he doubted that Mr Perceval, the prime minister, would take kindly to being kept waiting.

His cousin was outside ready to speak to him when he emerged from his brief appointment. 'Anything new to report?'

'Not really. The prime minister just wanted to reiterate how much importance he attaches to this mission. It would seem that there are factions within our own government who are against the war – he is besieged from all sides and wants this particular thorn to be removed as speedily as possible.'

'I think you must hold your house party at the beginning of

May, not July. I'm sure no one you invite would refuse such a prestigious invitation.'

'Lizzy will have to be told the real reason behind this. I've no wish to continue to deceive her. There has been more than enough discord in our lives recently.' When he had finished telling his cousin about the unpleasantness caused by Bingley's sister, he understood the need to be honest with Lizzy.

'You must tell her everything. I'm sure anything she learns will remain secret. I have an appointment at Horse Guards so must leave you here. It would appear that Count Duvall, the devil who is transporting the documents to Bonaparte, has been seen and I'm tasked with setting one of my men to follow him. I look forward to joining you this evening.'

Hugo marched away – even out of uniform one would immediately know he was a soldier. Darcy pulled out his pocket watch and thought that if he made haste he might be in time to accompany his wife to the bookshop.

The carriage was waiting outside his house in Grosvenor Square and a footman was about to fold up the steps and close the door. In two strides he was beside it and jumped in.

'Good heavens, Fitzwilliam, where did you come from? Is something amiss?'

He ignored her comment and gestured to her maid that she remove herself. Once they were alone he was able to explain his sudden appearance. Her reaction to the information was quite unexpected.

'How exciting! I should have guessed you would never allow yourself to become embroiled with anything so mundane as a search for a bride for your cousin. Of course we must bring forward the house party – I shall send word at once to Pemberley so they can start preparing all the guest rooms.'

She looked at him as if seeing him for the first time. 'Imagine my mother's reaction if she was ever to discover that her most revered son-in-law is a government spy.'

'I'm not an agent, merely a civilian who offers my assistance in whatever way I can. The colonel is an intelligence officer, so I suppose one could say that we do have a spy in the family.' He stretched out his legs and relaxed against the squabs, feeling happier than he had for months.

'I hated having to deceive you, my love.'

'There's no need to apologise. I understand completely. I never thought I should be grateful to Caroline Bingley for anything, but I don't believe I would have been taken into your confidence if she hadn't caused so much trouble.'

'Now that you know the names of the families we must include in the invitation, we should be able to conclude the matter in a few of days. We shall announce that our children are unwell and we have to return to the country immediately.'

'Yesterday I would have been delighted by your suggestion. However, I am quite content to remain here for the allotted time. I intend to visit the opera and theatre more than once.' She was counting ominously on her fingers. 'There are three museums and a variety of exhibitions we must also attend.'

For an awful moment he thought her speaking truly but then she laughed at his expression of horror. 'Good God, Lizzy, I was quaking in my boots at the thought of having to accompany you to so many tedious places.'

'I've no more inclination to go to the theatre or opera than you, but I should like to visit one or two exhibitions before we return. I am quite happy to attend without you.'

Hatchards was bustling with like-minded ladies intent on purchasing the latest novels, and he retreated to the far side of the shop where he could lurk with other gentlemen. Lizzy had said she had more errands to complete and as he had intruded on her morning plans he could hardly complain.

Half an hour later she arrived at his side with a brown paper parcel held triumphantly before her. 'I have everything I came for, Fitzwilliam. We can go home so we can settle on a new date for the house party. It's fortuitous I hadn't invited my parents, as my mother would no doubt have found the change of date an interesting topic of gossip amongst her friends.'

Much as he enjoyed her company, he politely declined to go with her on her morning calls that afternoon. Instead he walked round to his club where he hoped to learn more about the Sinclair and Hall families.

* * *

Lizzy returned to Grosvenor Square delighted with what she had accomplished that afternoon. She had met half a dozen young ladies doing the rounds as well as two older women, one a widow and the other working as a companion. If Colonel Fitzwilliam was in genuine need of a bride then both these candidates would be a suitable match for him.

Her husband was not the only one who could keep secrets. She was determined to find his cousin a wife – even though he thought this search to be a false one. If she had her way, by the end of the house party the last member of the Darcy clan would be betrothed.

She made a list of those she wished to invite and made sure that the families of the candidates she had met that afternoon were included. It was unlikely that either her husband or his cousin would take much interest in the list as long as the two suspect families were on it.

Making morning calls had never been a pleasure until today.

Having an ulterior motive for visiting had made the experience so much more enjoyable. She was almost looking forward to the next week of musical evenings and informal supper parties.

When Fitzwilliam strolled in to change for dinner he looked more relaxed than he had recently. 'Good, I'm glad to see that you haven't yet changed. Hugo won't have time to return to his lodgings to put on his evening rig.'

She put down her pen with a smile. 'We don't change at Pemberley any more unless we have guests so why not do the same in Town?' She picked up the list and handed it to him. 'I have four families already. With the two that must be invited, we almost have a houseful.'

He scrutinised the paper and nodded. 'Excellent. We shall meet them at the first two events we attend. I just hope they are not impossible. If they are indeed traitors then they will be suspicious if they get an invitation from someone who is known to be highly selective in his acquaintances.'

'I'm sure Cousin Hugo is well aware how high in the instep you are. He wouldn't have suggested this ploy unless they are acceptable. Remember you considered my family to be beneath your notice when you first met us. By the by, the Gardiners will be coming to our house party as well as Mrs Collins and her impossible husband.'

His eyebrows vanished beneath his hair. 'I beg you, my darling, do not invite the Collins family. I doubt I could survive the experience.'

He was so easy to tease. 'Don't look so alarmed, I would never willingly have Mr Collins under my roof. The last time I heard from Charlotte Collins she was in an interesting condition again so couldn't travel anyway.'

'Don't look so sad. There will be more children to fill our nursery in good time.' His smile was wicked as he continued. 'I give you my word, sweetheart, I shall make every effort to achieve this end.'

Hastily she got to her feet and fixed him with her sternest look. 'Your cousin will be here at any moment so do not think I shall tumble into bed with you right now.'

'In which case I guarantee that neither of us will have much sleep tonight.'

Hand in hand they made their way to the drawing room; the colonel was announced a few minutes after they arrived. Fitzwilliam went forward to greet him, leaving her to view the two of them together. They were remarkably similar in build and features and could easily be mistaken for brothers rather than cousins.

'Good evening, Hugo. Thank you for agreeing that I should be taken into your confidence. I have already sent word to my family that the house party will take place in the first week of May. I have also informed the staff at Pemberley so that they may begin to prepare every guest chamber for the invasion.'

His smile was warm as he came over and half-bowed to her. 'Darcy was right to insist that you knew everything. I believe you already have a list of families to invite.' He held up his hand as she was about to show him. 'I rely on your good judgement. There's no need for me to know who you've decided to include.'

The evening passed pleasantly enough but the speaking looks she exchanged with her husband made her pulse race and she was relieved that their guest took his leave as soon as the meal was over.

'Don't expect to see me at any of these social events – I never attend – so to do so now would draw unnecessary attention. I shall call round at the end of the week in the expectation that you will have made the acquaintance of the suspected traitors.'

Hugo strode off and Fitzwilliam turned to her. 'I have one

letter to compose and then will join you upstairs.' He trailed his hand across her cheek on his departure, leaving her pulse skittering.

Recently they had spent more time making love than they had in the past few months. The surge of joy made her catch her breath. She was convinced that by the time they returned home to Derbyshire she too would be expecting another infant.

* * *

Lizzy was dressed in her most elegant evening gown and her beloved was resplendent in black. They were to attend what was called 'an informal supper party' where they expected to be introduced to Sir Robert and Lady Sinclair and their progeny – Miss Annabel Sinclair and Mr Richard Sinclair.

When they were in the carriage Lizzy had a question. 'Do you think that Mr and Mrs Hall and their children will be present, Fitzwilliam? From what you've told me they are only on the fringe of society and might not have gained an invitation.'

'I doubt it. I think you will have to pay a morning call on Lady Sinclair in order to make their acquaintance.'

She settled back on the squabs, enjoying the intimacy of the darkness and the feel of his shoulder pressing against hers. An unexpected bubble of laughter escaped, sounding loud in the confines of the carriage.

'What has amused you, sweetheart?'

'I was thinking that I almost hope it takes another year for me to conceive if we are to spend more nights like the last one.'

He took her hand and raised it to his mouth. Even through the fabric of her glove she felt his kiss. 'I love you, Elizabeth Darcy, and intend to demonstrate how much as often as I can.'

His voice was gruff and his fingers closed over hers in a grip that was almost painful.

'And I return the sentiment, dearest Fitzwilliam. Although we have drifted apart in the past months I believe that is all behind us.' She should have stopped there but something prompted her to speak what had been in her heart. 'I know why there was this distance between us. You were unhappy with the amount of time I lavished on the twins and felt neglected.'

He released her hand as if it had become repellent to him. He moved so there was distance between them before he spoke. 'Are you, by any chance, suggesting that I am jealous of my children?'

His tone had changed from loving to icy. She bitterly regretted her remark and wished the words unsaid, but they hung between them. Either she could apologise and deny his suggestion or support her words with evidence. She chose the latter – she was never one to avoid a difficult situation.

'What else was I to think when you moved from the marital bed? When you spent as much time away from home as you did in it? Nothing else had changed so what other conclusion could I draw than that the arrival of our children was the problem?'

His anger filled the carriage. Too late for regrets. She must deal with the consequences of her rash remarks and pray that he would realise she was right once he had recovered his temper. Of one thing she was certain – she would not allow herself to be crushed by his disapproval. She was made of sterner stuff than that.

# 10

No one would have been aware that Darcy was enraged. He escorted his wife inside the venue, smiled, nodded and occasionally half-bowed when required. Tonight he had a duty to perform and must put his anger aside.

Lizzy wasn't fooled for a minute – she knew there would be a reckoning once they were in Grosvenor Square. The host's idea of an informal supper party did not coincide with his own view on the matter. The place was uncomfortably full, with scarcely elbow room in the first reception chamber.

'It should be less unpleasant away from the crush. I have seen the Sinclair family and you must make an effort to become acquainted with Lady Sinclair.'

'As you have failed to inform me of the appearance of this person, how do you expect me to recognise her?' The words were spoken civilly but he knew her well enough to be able to detect the disdain in her response. Although others would not have noticed, she was aware of his ill humour towards her.

He forced a smile but it failed to convince her. She remained aloof and raised an enquiring eyebrow. 'I am waiting, sir – do you intend to tell me what these people look like or not?'

'Lady Sinclair is wearing a hideous ensemble in what could be described as puce. She has a matching turban with feathers – one would have to be blind not to see her.'

'And Miss Sinclair?' She tapped her foot and he barely bit back what would have been an inappropriate response to this provocative gesture.

'The young lady in question has russet hair and her gown is pink. Is that sufficient information for you?'

She removed her hand from his arm and nodded regally. 'Indeed it is, Mr Darcy. No doubt speaking to Sir Robert is beyond my capabilities, so I will leave that difficult task to you.'

She walked away and he could not help but be aware how many gentlemen turned to watch her progress. She was a diamond of the first water and however much he might wish to strangle her at the moment he could not deny that to him she was the loveliest woman in the room.

There were to be cards played so there must be a room set aside for this purpose. As neither young Sinclair nor his father were visible, he must suppose they had already made their way there. The description he had given her of these two gentlemen was equally explicit. Sir Robert was a man of middle years with grey hair, which he wore fashionably short. He was tall and thin and had a penchant for lurid waistcoats.

His son was of similar stature but with broad shoulders. His hair was the same colour as his sister's. Having so distinctive a feature made finding them amongst the crowd much easier. He shouldered his way to the card room and immediately saw his quarries about to sit at a table set out for four. He reached the final chair and placed his hand on it possessively a second before another gentleman.

'I hope I may join you. This is the only safe place to be tonight – and here I intend to remain until my wife allows me to leave.' He nodded at the three men around the table and sat down. 'Darcy, at your service.'

Sinclair introduced himself and his son, and the fourth member of the group grunted an unintelligible response. This did not bode well. The man was already in his cups and might disrupt his plans by his behaviour.

'What are we playing tonight, gentlemen? Loo, vingt-et-un or piquet?' All three were gambling games as he doubted that his companions would wish to play something as tame as whist.

'Loo, but we can change to one of the others later on if you require,' Sir Robert said.

His son and the anonymous player nodded. Darcy had come prepared and had both coins and flimsies with him and was ready to lose it all if necessary. He was an expert card player so expected to leave the table better off than when he sat down.

After an hour things were even between him and Sir Robert. The fourth person had stumbled off and his place had been taken by a jovial gentleman who failed to introduce himself. Despite this man's bluff appearance, he was sharp-eyed and an expert player.

They had been supplied with mediocre claret, which the others had drunk in quantity. He still had a half-full glass beside him.

When the current hand was completed – he had been the winner – he stood up but left his winnings by his place. 'Excuse me, gentlemen, I'm going to find a decent wine. This should not take overlong. I cannot play all evening with only this revolting stuff to drink.'

Young Sinclair immediately stood up. 'I'm with you on that, sir. Pa can watch your winnings, can't you?'

'Delighted to do so, old fellow. Now you come to mention it, this claret is filth. Make sure you bring sufficient for all of us.'

Darcy waylaid a footman with his request. He slipped the man a guinea and was instantly assured that from this point forward a plentiful supply of the best claret available would be served to them.

'We shall not go in for supper, so have some brought to us on a tray.' Mr Sinclair had watched this exchange with admiration.

'I say, sir, that was capital. Best to have food when one is drinking.'

'Is your father a hardened gambler?' This was not a comment likely to endear him but something about this young man made him think he could not possibly be involved in anything nefarious.

'I fear so. Despite the substantial estates he owns, and his more than adequate income, we are constantly hiding from the bailiffs – we never know from one quarter to the next if there will be the wherewithal to pay the tradesmen's bills.' He smiled confidingly. 'However, six months ago our fortunes changed as a business venture of Papa's paid out handsomely. I don't like to gamble myself, nor drink to excess, but I promised my mother to remain with him and see he didn't lose too heavily tonight.' The young man pulled a face. 'Mama believes me to be of the same ilk as my father, but I accompany him about Town in an effort to prevent him from destroying the family.'

Darcy patted Sinclair's shoulder. Normally he was averse to physical contact but believed this gesture would help the relationship progress. 'I give you my word that anything I win from your father will be returned. I've never ruined anyone and don't intend to start doing so tonight.'

* * *

Lizzy watched Fitzwilliam make his way through the crowd. She couldn't help but be aware how people stepped aside for him as if he were royalty. Was it the fact that he was so tall or just because he carried an air of authority about him?

He would accomplish his objective, so she must do the same. As she was only of medium height she could not see over the heads of the milling crowd. However, the puce feathers on Lady Sinclair's turban acted as a beacon. All she had to do was keep her eye on those and then she should have no difficulty finding the two ladies she wished to become acquainted with.

She could hardly walk straight up to them and introduce herself, as that would seem odd. She must contrive an incident that would make it possible to speak to them. The woman's strident tones carried clearly across the chamber. Lizzy was sure the space around the Sinclair ladies was a direct result of the string of complaints the woman was directing to anyone who was foolish enough to pause in her vicinity.

Perhaps a collision of some sort would serve the purpose. Lizzy backed out of the crowd as if escaping from someone she wasn't inclined to speak to and deliberately walked into Miss Sinclair. The girl was standing a yard or two away from her mother, looking as if she wished she wasn't related to her.

'I beg your pardon, did I tread on your gown?' Lizzy apologised.

'No, ma'am, you did not. Although I would have been pleased if you had so I could retire to have it mended.'

Lady Sinclair was still in full flow and had now moved on to the poor quality of the wine being served. She was obviously under the impression that her daughter was standing beside her and listening to her, whereas she was in fact apparently talking to herself.

Several ladies were already nodding and smirking and Lizzy

decided she would intervene. She placed her hand on Miss Sinclair's arm. 'I am Mrs Elizabeth Darcy – to whom am I speaking?'

'I am Annabel Sinclair and that is my mother, Lady Sinclair.' The girl almost shuddered as she looked towards her parent.

'Then, my dear, you must introduce me to her.'

Annabel's expression of relief and gratitude made Lizzy wish she didn't have to dissemble.

'Mama, I have just met Mrs Darcy and she would like to make your acquaintance.'

The garrulous lady stopped in midsentence and turned. She was immediately aware she was talking to a member of the *ton* and nodded regally. 'I'm delighted to meet you, Mrs Darcy. Would you be related to the Darcy family from Pemberley in Derbyshire?'

Lizzy returned the nod. 'I am married to Mr Fitzwilliam Darcy of Pemberley, Lady Sinclair. It is a sad squash in here. Shall we find somewhere more comfortable to converse? Darcy has abandoned me to play cards, so I doubt I will see him again until it is time to leave.'

'Sir Robert is of a similar disposition, Mrs Darcy. I dislike cards of any sort. Annabel, is that an empty table behind the pillar over there?'

'It is, Mama.' The girl dashed off, leaving Lizzy and her new companion to follow at a more sedate pace.

As they crossed the chamber, she spied a footman and beckoned him. 'I should like champagne and orgeat to be brought to the table over there.' She slipped the man a coin and he bowed and set off on his errand.

Once they were comfortably settled, her ladyship became less acerbic and the hectic colour along her cheeks began to fade.

'Mrs Darcy, I cannot tell you how much I dislike these over-crowded parties.'

Lizzy hid her smile behind her hand. She, and anyone in the vicinity, had already heard more than enough on that subject.

'I become anxious and know I say too much, and most of it things better left unspoken. I apologise if I might inadvertently have offended you.'

'My lady, I share your aversion to crowds. I only came because my husband insisted that I accompany him. We shall do much better here together where it's quiet.'

The footman returned and placed the glasses on the table before vanishing. They sipped their drinks in silence for a few minutes. Lizzy thought she might have misjudged Lady Sinclair.

'Do you intend to dance later, Miss Sinclair?'

'No, ma'am, I don't intend to. Like Mama I'm not comfortable in company.' The girl blushed and lowered her eyes.

Lady Sinclair patted her daughter's hand affectionately. 'I despair of you, my love, and believe I shall never find you a husband you can be comfortable with.' She turned to Lizzy. 'My son, however, is a man about Town and has no interest in the estate. The good Lord did not see fit to give me progeny who would conform to what one might expect.' She sighed sadly. 'If only Sir Robert would accept that his daughter has no need to make an advantageous marriage, or his son to spend his time in the country, my life would be so much less fraught.'

'No doubt I shall have the same dilemma when my children are grown. I have twins but they are not yet a year old, so I have many years before needing to deal with a similar problem.'

'Which do you prefer, Mrs Darcy? The countryside or the city?' Miss Sinclair asked eagerly.

'I much prefer to remain in Derbyshire and have people visit me. We are having a house party in May. Would you care to join us at Pemberley?' Lizzy would not have invited strangers so readily to her house under normal circumstances and she hoped they would not think it odd of her to have done so, so soon in their acquaintance.

'How kind of you to ask us when we have only just met. Are you quite sure Mr Darcy will not object?'

Oh dear! Fitzwilliam's character was obviously known to Lady Sinclair. 'He leaves such matters to me, my lady. He does not concern himself with domestic details. Indeed, Pemberley is so large if we had a hundred visitors he could still remain apart from them if he so desired.'

'In which case, my dear Mrs Darcy, I'm delighted to accept your kind invitation on behalf of myself, Sir Robert and my children. It will be a pleasure to get out of the smoke and smell of London for a week or so in the middle of the Season.'

'Mama, do you think that Papa and Richard can be persuaded to leave Town just as things are becoming more lively?'

This was something that Lizzy would like the answer to as well. She drained her glass of champagne and stood up. 'Perhaps you could call tomorrow and let me know your answer? I can then give you a card with all the necessary information. We are in Grosvenor Square – I'm sure your coachman will know which house.'

'How fortuitous! We too are residing in the same place. I'd no idea you would be our neighbours.'

Lizzy shook out her skirts, nodded and smiled. Mission accomplished. Well, half completed as she had yet to meet the Hall family. Tomorrow it might be possible to turn the conversation around to any friends Lady Sinclair might have in Town and then somehow include them in the invitation.

* * *

Darcy made sure he didn't win too much from anyone, but Sir Robert continued to lose heavily to the other gentlemen at the table. Sinclair had willingly relinquished his seat an hour or so ago and disappeared to join his cronies.

The man must have lost a small fortune already if the pile of vowels accumulating in front of the other players was anything to go by. He was thankful when supper was brought to them on a tray. He noticed that only two other tables were being served in this way – everyone else had left their cards and gone to find their food in the dining room.

In order for the food to be placed in front of them, the game had to stop. The gentleman, although this was a misnomer as he was an uncouth individual, who held the vowels scooped them up and rammed them in his pocket.

'I expect your debts to be paid by the end of the week, Sinclair. You know where to find me.' The man pushed back his chair and shoved his way out of the room, leaving an uncomfortable silence behind him.

The third player pushed the chits across to Sir Robert. 'Playing for the fun of it, old chap – tear these up.' He too got to his feet and strolled off, leaving Darcy alone with his quarry.

He poured two glasses of claret and pushed one across. 'Drink this. You look as if you need it.'

'I do, Darcy, dipped too deep as usual. Don't have the wherewithal to settle – will have to take a repairing lease until I'm in funds again.'

Sir Robert helped himself from the selection of cold cuts and pasties. His losses hadn't affected his appetite. The food was surprisingly palatable considering the quality of the wine they had been served earlier.

After both plates were empty Darcy snapped his fingers and the table was cleared immediately. 'I've no wish to play any more.

I must find my wife. She will be eager to leave as she doesn't enjoy these evenings. I suggest that you do the same.'

The man scowled at him. 'It's all very well for someone like you, someone with deep pockets. It wouldn't matter how much you lost, you would always have enough to cover your debts. I need to recoup and I ain't leaving until I've done so.'

'You are already in over your head. Don't make it worse. You could lose your estate if you carry on this way.'

'It's none of your business. I'll do as I damn well please. We're strangers – why should you care if I'm ruined?'

Darcy stood up. 'I don't have an opinion either way, Sir Robert. I was merely offering you sound advice.' He turned as if to go and then turned back. 'Think of your wife and children, sir. Do they deserve to be destitute because of your gambling?'

He made his way into the next chamber, which was now far less crowded than before. Presumably the guests had drifted away to find their supper. He looked at his watch and was shocked to see how much time had passed. Lizzy had been left to her own devices for far too long.

He checked throughout the reception rooms and was unable to find her. Eventually he sent a footman to enquire if his carriage had already been called for. It had – his wife had gone home almost two hours ago, leaving him to walk.

This was the outside of enough. She was well aware he didn't have his cane, or a male servant to accompany him. Although the journey home was less than a mile, and did not require him to walk anywhere unsafe, it was unwise for any gentleman to be abroad on the streets late at night.

To add to his annoyance it started to rain heavily halfway home. By the time he reached his destination he was drenched to the skin and chilled to the marrow. He took the stairs two at a time. What he had to say to her could not wait until the morning.

# 11

The clock in the sitting room of their apartment struck midnight as Fitzwilliam thundered down the passageway. She'd been regretting her decision not to ask the carriage to return for him since the rain had started half an hour ago. Making her husband walk home was one thing, obliging him to get soaked was quite another.

He was going to be very cross indeed and she hoped she could defuse his anger by telling him the good news about Lady Sinclair. The fire was burning merrily and the room was pleasantly warm. He had dismissed his valet earlier, so he would have to disrobe without help.

She was already in her night attire but had remained awake so she could talk to him. There was a decanter of brandy waiting, a pot of coffee keeping warm in the grate and a plate of assorted pastries on the side table. Hopefully this would be enough to soothe the savage beast before she was given a severe set-down.

From the noise in his bedchamber he was removing his wet garments and getting into his nightshirt and bedrobe. The door was ajar – but she had no candles lit so perhaps he didn't realise she was in here. Did he believe that she had retired to her own bed?

Then he burst in, his hair on end and his expression alarmed. 'Thank God! When I looked next door and your bed was empty I almost had an apoplexy. I thought you had not returned.' In two strides he was beside her and she tumbled into his arms.

'I am so sorry, my love. I should have sent the carriage back...'

'We'll discuss that later, sweetheart. Now I have better things to do.'

This was the first time they had made love on the floor but despite the obvious disadvantages she very much enjoyed the experience. A delightful and satisfactory time later she sat up.

'I have refreshments waiting.' She attempted to wriggle free of his embrace but he tightened his hold, pulling her back against his chest. They were now both propped up against the *chaise longue*, their limbs entangled and the only covering their discarded nightwear.

'That is exactly what we need. However, I have yet to talk about my lack of carriage and the fact that I had to walk back unescorted in the pouring rain.' He sounded fierce but she knew he was teasing.

'I believe that you have been amply recompensed for your unpleasant experience, sir, so I will hear no more about it.' She glanced up at him and he was smiling down at her, his eyes alight with love.

'In which case, madam, your penance shall be to fetch me sustenance. And no, you cannot reclaim your nightgown in order to do so.'

After scampering about the room with no clothes on at all, she was relieved to slip back under the warmth of the night-gowns and bedrobes.

'Here is your brandy and pastries – you are quite capable of pouring your own coffee. It should still be warm enough to drink, even though it's been standing there for hours.'

Whilst she had been skipping about the room, he had made their nest more comfortable by gathering up the cushions from the chairs and collecting the blanket that had been folded neatly at the end of the *chaise longue*.

Now they were sitting on some of the cushions covered with their night garments and leaning on the others. He tossed the rug across their legs before handing her a cup of coffee. She sipped and settled back with a sigh of contentment. 'You have put the brandy in the coffee. It hardly matters that the drink is not as hot as it should be.'

'How did your conversation with Lady Sinclair progress?'

She told him what had transpired and he regaled her with his own exploits at the card table. 'From what you have said, Fitzwilliam, it would appear that only Sir Robert is involved in traitorous activities. It will go hard with his family when he is exposed.'

'That is hardly your concern, Lizzy. I can assure you that although they will be ruined socially, I shall make it my business that they do not lose their estate. I believe that Sinclair will be relieved to give up his racketing about Town.'

'I have invited Lady Sinclair to call this afternoon and shall give her an invitation card when she comes. Tomorrow I shall visit her in the hope that I'll be introduced to Mrs Hall. I misremember exactly where we are to be this evening. As I have already achieved my goal, could I not remain at home?'

He yawned and ruffled her hair, which was now floating around her shoulders. 'If you are suggesting that I parade around Town on my own, then you are in for a sad disappointment, my love. We shall suffer together. Is that not what a devoted couple should do?'

The clock on the mantelshelf whirred, clicked and then struck three times. 'We must go to bed at once. I'd no idea it had got so late.' She was on her feet before he could protest and dashed into the master bedroom, wishing she had her nightgown to cover her nakedness.

There was sufficient light from next door for her to scramble into bed. The sheets were icy. She should have run the warming pan through before getting in.

'Here, darling, put this on. I can hear your teeth chattering from here.'

She emerged from under the covers and regained her feet. He dropped the garment over her head. She noticed he was similarly attired in his nightshirt, and had the missing bedrobes slung across his arm. These he placed carefully across the end of the bed before walking round to his side and climbing in.

The candle was extinguished and he gathered her into his arms so they could share their body heat and sleep in comfort.

* * *

Darcy slept fitfully and put this down to an excess of alcohol. He got up before Lizzy was awake and removed himself to the study to read the newspaper and consider his next move. It was of paramount importance that he made the acquaintance of Mr Hall, as he had a feeling that this man was up to his neck in the treachery even if Sir Robert was not a willing participant.

His cousin was pleased with their progress and agreed with his findings. 'We don't know a lot about Hall. He has a modest estate in Hertfordshire and several business interests in the city. His only connection to Sir Robert is that they are both investors in a shipping line.'

'Is he a hardened gambler as well?'

'Not as far as we can discover. He has expensive tastes and a desire to be accepted in the best houses, but I hardly see that as a reason for him to betray his country.'

'Do you know which clubs he attends? It might be easier to make his acquaintance there rather than rely on bumping into him at one of these wretched evening events.' Darcy was as eager as Lizzy to avoid attending any further routs and parties if possible.

'He is a member at Boodle's. I am too, so perhaps we should go there this afternoon and see if we can contrive a meeting.'

'I shall leave word for Lizzy that we're going to St James's Street. She will be occupied with calls all afternoon.'

The weather was clement, all sign of yesterday's rain departed. It would be a pleasant stroll to Piccadilly and into St James's Square. He enjoyed his cousin's company and counted him amongst his closest friends. Bingley, of course, was also a good friend, but he lacked the perspicacity and sharpness of wit that his cousin had.

He wasn't familiar with Boodle's and couldn't recall ever having visited this club before. They signed the visitors' book and made their way into the noisy interior. Despite the earliness of the hour the place was busy and most of the members were involved in some sort of card game. This club was renowned for the amount of money that changed hands in wagers; sometimes a huge stake would be bet on the most trivial of outcomes. There had been an occasion when one hundred guineas had been placed on which spider would finish its web first.

Hugo introduced him to several members but the gentleman they sought was not present. However, a crony of his cousin said he was certain Hall was attending a prize fight that was taking place somewhere in the East End.

'I've no desire to follow him there, cousin, but would do so if you think I should.'

'I've no liking for this sport either but will go along. There's no immediate urgency as you have already established a connection with the Sinclair family. It's possible that your wife has had more success at one of her morning calls.'

They parted company and agreed to meet up at the end of the week when Darcy hoped he would have more favourable news to impart.

As he made his way back to Grosvenor Square he thought he saw his family carriage bowl past but he was mistaken. This brought back to mind the disagreement between himself and Lizzy, which hadn't been discussed last night. The incident had been ignored by both of them as if nothing untoward had taken place.

This just added to his slight unease about their relationship. It might be his imagination but he believed he detected a distance growing between them. He didn't know if it was of his making or hers. He had no intention of dwelling on such issues. Emotional matters were best left to the ladies. No doubt Lizzy would speak to him if she thought there was something pertinent to say.

His lips curved as he recalled the delightful interlude last night in front of the fire. What did it matter if a man and his wife were no longer sharing every thought as long as they still loved each other? However much Lizzy might annoy him, he found her irresistible and whatever her misdemeanours he would always forgive her.

There was a row of carriages outside the house. Devil take it! He had quite forgotten there were to be callers – he had no intention of being dragged into them. He would enter by the side door that led from the stables. With luck he could slip past any beady-eyed matron and find refuge in his study until the house was their own again.

Unfortunately just as he emerged into the entrance hall the front door opened and the Sinclair family came in. He was surprised to see Sir Robert had accompanied his wife. He could hardly vanish now without appearing appallingly uncivil.

He nodded to both and she curtsied and her husband half-bowed. Richard Sinclair smiled warmly but his sister kept her eyes lowered and would not look at him.

'Good afternoon, my lady, Sir Robert, what a pleasant surprise to see you here. I shall take you through to join the other guests in the drawing room.' He shook his head at the footman waiting to announce each new arrival.

Lizzy was circulating amongst the dozen visitors, and he recognised none of them. Two parlourmaids were handing out tea and almond biscuits. His appearance caused a noticeable reaction to ripple around the assembled company. An uncomfortable silence fell and all present turned towards him.

* * *

'Good afternoon, my dear, what an unexpected pleasure to have you come in to meet my guests.' Lizzy recovered from the shock of seeing her husband and walked over to greet him.

'I'm afraid I cannot remain above a few minutes. But as Sir Robert and his family have just arrived I wished to bring them in myself.' He pulled a comical face, nodded politely to the circle of interested spectators and retreated before he was obliged to speak to anyone else.

'Lady Sinclair, welcome indeed. Allow me to introduce you and your husband to those you do not yet know.'

In some drawing rooms a bell was rung every quarter of an

hour to remind the guests that the allowed time for their visit was over. Lizzy did not like this practice and relied on her visitors to remove themselves without prompting.

She was awash with tea after sharing so many cups with her guests and was relieved when she was finally alone. Tomorrow she would have to return these calls and dreaded spending her entire afternoon traipsing from house to house.

Although she had not had much opportunity for private conversation with the Sinclairs she had been able to hand her ladyship the invitation card to the house party just before she left. Sir Robert had obviously come under protest and had remained at the far end of the room and not spoken to anyone. His son, however, had circulated and drawn his quieter sister into several conversations. Lady Sinclair had been more subdued than the previous evening, which had possibly endeared her to the other guests.

Fitzwilliam wandered in. 'I see your afternoon was a resounding success, sweetheart. Mine was less so as my cousin and I failed to locate Hall.'

When he explained where the colonel expected to find Mr Hall she was not surprised her husband had refused to accompany him. He abhorred such pastimes as prize and cock-fighting.

'I have sent a note around to Lady Arnold tendering our apologies for being unable to attend her rout this evening. If I manage to meet Mrs Hall and her daughter tomorrow I shall endeavour to discover at what events they are likely to appear, so we can further our acquaintance. With luck we shall have achieved our objective in the next few days and will be able to return home.'

'We must arrange for a letter to arrive by express – my cousin can see to that. If we just depart our staff will talk. However loyal, one's staff gossip still travels faster below stairs than it does above.'

'How true. I shall spend a quiet evening alone as I assume you will go to one of your clubs.' He looked somewhat shocked at her suggestion but she couldn't imagine why. He was not accustomed to spending time with her in Grosvenor Square as she never came to London with him.

'I had not intended to go out again today.'

She was about to congratulate him on his good sense, and say how much she was looking forward to having him all to herself, when he continued.

'However, I shall do as you suggest and dine elsewhere. Do not wait up for me. I shall sleep next door tonight.'

He raised a hand in farewell and left her alone, wishing she had held her tongue. They were constantly at daggers drawn nowadays and stumbled from one misunderstanding to another. What had happened to the closeness they had shared until last year?

Tears spilled down her cheeks and she brushed them away. She had become a veritable watering pot these past few days and it was not like her to give in to her emotions. Then she recalled the last time she had cried at the slightest thing. It had been when she was increasing.

Her monthly courses were always somewhat erratic so she had given up trying to keep track of them. She always had sufficient warning to prepare herself and had so far not had any embarrassing incidents. When had her last one been?

With all the excitement of the last few weeks she had quite forgotten about such things – she was almost sure it was more than six weeks. She leapt to her feet and ran after Fitzwilliam. She was determined to stop him before he went out in order to give him the good news. A physician could not confirm her diagnosis for another month or more but there were sufficient signs for her to be almost sure.

Then she stopped halfway up the staircase. From the outset of her previous pregnancy she had been unwell, unable to keep down all but the smallest, plainest meals. If she was indeed with child she would be suffering from the same unpleasant symptoms.

Her happiness and excitement fizzled out. She was mistaken – a longing for another child had made her misinterpret the physical signs. No doubt there were a myriad of other reasons why her monthly flow was delayed. There was not enough evidence to raise Fitzwilliam's hopes.

Her tears could also be attributed to a wife's natural concern that her relationship with her beloved husband was not as it should be. The answer would be clear one way or the other in a few weeks, so she would bide her time and keep this to herself.

She wandered disconsolately from one room to the other, unable to settle or think of anything to occupy her time. Perhaps she could go through the list of possible guests for the house party and write out invitation cards.

Coming to London, she had hoped, would repair the rift in her marriage but the opposite was true. Had he always been so quick to take offence or had she become shrewish over the past few months? Had her disappointment in not conceiving another child soured her?

Tears marred the card she was writing and she swallowed the lump in her throat.

# 12

Darcy silently endured the ministrations of his valet until he could stand it no longer. 'Enough, Dawson. It will do. I can tie my stock myself. You are dismissed – I shall not need you again this evening.'

'Very well, sir.'

He stared with disfavour at his image in the glass. When had he become so bad-tempered? What the devil was wrong with him? He tossed the crumpled strip of material aside and jumped to his feet. He could not be content if he was at loggerheads with his darling Lizzy.

Still in his shirtsleeves he dashed from the room and went in search of her. Eventually he located her in the study sitting at her escritoire, which faced out over the garden. Her back was to him; she didn't hear his entrance.

He walked soft-footed until he was standing directly behind her and then he realised she was crying. He was a brute to have brought her so low.

'Sweetheart, please don't upset yourself. Here, take my handkerchief and dry your eyes.' He pushed the cloth into her unresisting fingers and then picked up the chair with her in it and turned it round so he could see her.

He dropped to his knees and gently placed a hand under her chin and raised her face. She looked as wretched as he felt. This would end now – they would remain here and talk until the root of the problem was discovered and things were put right between them.

Obediently she blew her nose and wiped her face but she did not seem inclined to explain what had overset her. 'Lizzy, what's wrong? Come, we shall sit by the fire and talk things through.'

He regained his feet and reached out to take her hand, but she shook her head. Were things so bad between them that she couldn't bear his touch? Then she smiled and he breathed again.

'Where is your stock? And more importantly your topcoat? I can't remember seeing you in such disarray before.'

He offered his hand a second time and she took it. He pulled her to her feet and led her across to the large sofa before responding to her question. 'I was in the process of getting ready but decided I must speak to you instead.' When she was settled he took her hands again. 'I'm yet to receive an answer to my question.'

When she had revealed her worries he was horrified. 'How can you think I had become bored with you and the children? You are my world – all three of you. I admit I have been undertaking tasks for the prime minister that I would not normally have accepted. This was to allow you to spend as much time with our babies as you wished without feeling obliged to attend to my needs.' He smiled and her eyes lit up in response. 'Fabian and Amanda must come first with you whilst they are so small and vulnerable.'

'How ridiculous I have been,' Lizzy said. 'I should be grateful not to be increasing so soon and not fretting about this and imagining that you had lost interest in our marriage.'

'Bingley isn't overjoyed that Jane is increasing so soon. Although she had a healthy pregnancy and easy delivery little Charlotte has been a constant worry to them both.'

'I am tardy with my monthly courses, Fitzwilliam, but on reflection I do not think I am expecting another baby. Either way, I shall no longer think about it but rejoice in what we already have.'

'I cannot remain down here dressed as I am. Shall we spend the evening upstairs and have our supper sent up?'

'I should like that. There is something that I've been meaning to mention about the reason we are supposed to be in London. If we are meant to be searching for a suitable bride for your cousin, then surely he should be accompanying us? I cannot believe that any gentleman would leave such an important decision to someone else.'

'Exactly so. I've been trying to tell him this but he avoids the question. I believe we have an invitation to the first important ball of the Season to be held in two days' time. He must accompany us and be introduced to those you have already chosen.'

'I just hope he doesn't break the heart of any of the girls we invite to the house party. He is a handsome man and there will be no shortage of young ladies willing to become his wife.'

They strolled hand in hand through the house and to their private sitting room. He repaired to his dressing room to find a coat whilst she sent word to the kitchen. It hardly seemed worthwhile getting smartened up, as they would be remaining up here. He shrugged on his dressing robe instead.

Lizzy was curled up on the daybed and he joined her there. 'I know Lord Rochester – it's his daughter the ball is for. I shall see him and make sure he sends invitations to the Sinclairs and Halls. If Hugo pays particular attention to the Hall girl then it will not seem strange to include them in the house party.'

'I agree. Have you any idea what Miss Hall is like? You had an excellent description of the Sinclair family.'

He frowned, trying to recall what he'd been told. 'She is an outdoor type, not in the common way, but my cousin said she's an intelligent girl but somewhat outspoken.'

'She sounds ideal for the purpose. As long as she's not an antidote I believe our scheme will work.'

'In which case, Lizzy, I shall make sure the letter supposedly sent from home arrives on Saturday morning. We should be back at Pemberley by the middle of next week. This will allow you no more than a week or two before your family arrives. Will that be sufficient?'

'Fitzwilliam, it's kind of you to think of me in this way but as the invitations have already been sent to friends and family there is no option but to be ready in time.'

He laughed and joined her on the *chaise longue*. 'To tell you the truth, sweetheart, I cannot think how having the two families under my roof is going to make it easier for my cousin to discover if they are indeed traitors.'

'I had thought the same, but didn't like to say so. We must assume he has some scheme in hand to which we are not privy. Regardless of the circumstances, I am actually quite looking forward to entertaining a large number of guests.'

'I shall endure it for your sake and for my cousin – but I can assure you I shall be glad when this nonsense is over. I don't intend to do anything else for Mr Perceval but I am afraid I have no option but to do as he wishes, as long as he is prime minister.'

* * *

Lizzy took her maid with her when she set out on her round of morning calls. This was not strictly necessary but she hoped Sally would be able to glean some extra information below stairs about the families she intended to include in the house party. As far as staff and everyone else was concerned, this was a genuine search for a wife for the colonel.

'Sally, remember to be discreet in your enquiries. You will learn more from listening to the gossip than adding to it. I require to know anything that might help with this venture.'

'Yes, ma'am, I know what to do.'

Lizzy had arranged things so that she called in at the establishment that was the greatest distance away and then would make three further calls on her return journey. The first that the carriage pulled up outside was a smart house in a quiet cul-de-sac just off Hanover Square. She had spoken briefly to Lady Stonham the previous evening and had been delighted to learn she numbered both Lady Sinclair and Mrs Hall amongst her acquaintances.

There were two other carriages waiting outside so she would not be the only one present. She hoped that one of the carriages had brought Mrs Hall and her daughter. The door opened as she arrived at the top of the steps and she was bowed in by a butler who enquired politely as to their names.

The sound of voices echoed from the open doors across the black and white chequered vestibule. Sally slipped away to the servants' hall and Lizzy stepped into the drawing room as her name was called out loudly.

Lady Stonham was overjoyed to see her. 'Mrs Darcy, come in, come in. Let me introduce you to my other guests.'

The first matron and her stout daughters were of no interest to Lizzy, but the second was the family she wished to meet.

Mrs Hall was unremarkable in every respect, modestly dressed and softly spoken. Her daughter, on the other hand, was quite startling. She was a head taller than her parent, had hair the colour of a raven's wing. Her sharp features were redeemed by green eyes that sparkled with intelligence. Lizzy liked her immediately.

'Mrs Hall, Miss Hall, I'm delighted to make your acquaintance. Are you remaining in Town for the whole Season or just visiting?'

Mrs Hall almost smiled. 'We are not here for more than a week or so, Mrs Darcy. My husband has business interests in the city and we stay just long enough for him to attend to those. We are not here to participate in the entertainment.'

'I hope to see you both at one or two parties before you leave. Miss Hall, is this your first Season?'

The girl laughed. 'I don't believe in any of that nonsense, madam. I'm here under sufferance. I much prefer to be in the country looking after my horses. We have a successful stud, you know. My brother and I run it together.'

'I share your dislike of large social occasions, Miss Hall, but I am on a mission. Colonel Fitzwilliam, my cousin, is hoping to set up his nursery and has asked me to find him a selection of young ladies from which to choose. Would you care to be included on the list?' She said this with a straight face and someone less intelligent might have taken her seriously.

To Lizzy's astonishment Miss Hall nodded. 'I would indeed, Mrs Darcy. If I have to be married one day I would much prefer it to be to a soldier. I believe I could enjoy following the drum.' She drew Lizzy to one side. 'What sort of man is he? Do you think we would suit?'

This was an extraordinary conversation to be having with a young lady she had only just met but Lizzy answered without hesitation. 'If Cousin Hugo is genuine in his desire to find a wife, then I think you would be ideal. He is in his thirties, above average height and although not as handsome as Mr Darcy, in my opinion, they are often mistaken for brothers.'

'I am not considered a beauty, but neither am I bracket-faced. Is he looking for an heiress? If he is then he will be disappointed as I have no more than a modest dowry. My maternal grandfather is a baron – but my mama is considered to have married beneath her.' The girl smiled and when she did so her face changed from plain to beautiful. 'There, you have the whole truth. Do you still wish to add me to your list?'

'I certainly do. We are having a house party in three weeks' time, which I would like to invite you and your family to. However, I think it would be best if you met the colonel before you decide if you want to come.'

'We have no invitations to any events at which he might be present. We are not part of the same social strata as yourself, Mrs Darcy.'

'I shall make it my business to have an invitation to the Rochester ball sent to you. I know that my cousin will be there to see if he approves of my choices. Would it be in order to send it to Lady Sinclair? Then you can be sure that you will be attending the event with a family that you are already familiar with.'

'That would be absolutely splendid. Annabel Sinclair is a friend of mine and her brother Richard is a crony of my brother Thomas. By the by, my given name is Jennifer in case you wished to include this on the invitation.'

The fifteen minutes allowed for a morning call had passed too quickly. Lizzy would have liked to get to know this lively girl a little better. She hated to deceive her, but at least the family would have the opportunity to mix with the *ton* and who knew where that might lead.

Sally had little of interest to report, which gave Lizzy time to reconsider her plans. She banged on the roof of the carriage and it rattled to a halt. A face appeared at the window.

'I have changed my mind and need to return to Grosvenor Square immediately.'

The under-coachman touched his forehead and disappeared. There was no need now for her to visit anywhere else and make meaningless conversation with complete strangers. She had accomplished her task. All that remained was for her to explain to Cousin Hugo that he must ensure he danced at least once with Miss Hall at the ball.

* * *

Darcy listened with growing incredulity to his cousin. 'Let me get this straight – not only am I to hold a house party in order to allow you to investigate these two families but also to host a private meeting for those in favour of the war effort at the same time?'

'You have understood perfectly. Sir Robert and Hall will think the event a cover for this meeting and not suspect the real reason.'

'Do these men know they are being invited as a ruse to trap the traitors?'

'No, they do not. Only you, the prime minister and I are aware that Sir Robert and Hall are suspects. I require these guests to be kept separate from the rest – is that possible? Those that I am inviting would expect to be private and not part of a social gathering.'

'I see. This whole thing is becoming deucedly complicated.

I'm fairly sure that anyone who knows you is aware that the last thing you need is a wife in tow. The prime minister told me he is concerned that he's losing support to the naysayers.'

'Our thinking is that the two suspects won't be able to resist spying on us. I do actually intend to discuss the problems facing our soldiers on the peninsula. The committee needs to have a united front in parliament; coming up with a strategy should be a deal simpler away from the distractions in Town.' His cousin seemed uncomfortable as he explained his reasons. No doubt this was because he had added a dozen extra uninvited guests to the house party.

Hugo showed him the list of names. 'We have more than enough invited to fill Pemberley to bursting. Make sure you arrange for the letter, supposedly from Pemberley, calling us home, brought round to us the morning after the Rochester ball.'

'I shall contact these people myself, if you have no objection.'

'They can go in the west wing – the ground floor can easily accommodate half a dozen visitors and their servants without impinging on the main part of the house.'

The colonel departed, leaving Darcy with much to think about. This whole charade was becoming more involved by the day. A proportion of the guests, those with eligible daughters, were coming in the hope that his cousin might select one of them to be his bride. Those from the army thought their presence was required for a secret meeting. The family were the only ones who knew the truth.

This was a recipe for disaster. He vowed this would be the last time he allowed himself to be involved in such matters. His family home had suffered from ghosts, scandal and now spies. If he had got things straight in his head then Hugo and he would be spying on Sir Robert and Hall; these two would be spying on the war committee. No doubt the interested mamas would also be spying on each other to see which of the young ladies present was likely to be chosen.

He was interrupted in his letter writing by the arrival of his wife. He tossed aside his pen and went to greet her. 'My love, I did not expect you home for another hour or so. Is something wrong?'

'Not at all, but I have something pertinent to tell you and saw no need to make further calls.' She explained about her meeting with the Hall family.

'That's excellent news, Lizzy. My cousin was unable to scrape an acquaintance with Hall at the prize fight so you have done his job for him.' There was something else she wasn't telling him and he was determined there should be no further secrets between them.

'What are you keeping from me?'

She looked a little disconcerted but then smiled. 'I've decided that Miss Hall is the perfect match for the colonel. It matters not if her father is involved in something nefarious…'

'Stop right there, my love. However delightful this young lady is my cousin can never marry her once her father is exposed as a traitor. They will no longer be received in society – they will be tainted by association.'

Her expression told him she was unconvinced by his statement. 'In which case, Fitzwilliam, let us hope that Cousin Hugo has mistaken the matter and neither family are sending secrets to the French.'

There was little point in saying that his cousin wouldn't be going to such lengths if he wasn't already certain of his facts. He explained about the extra guests.

'What a muddle! And don't forget, my dear, that added to this volatile mix will be my parents and my sister Mary. All we need is for Caroline Bingley to return and cause more trouble and this will be a house party remembered for all the wrong reasons.' She shook her head. 'Despite the size of our home I cannot believe that the presence of the military gentlemen will remain unnoticed by the other guests. How are we to explain their presence?'

# 13

Colonel Fitzwilliam was to travel with them in the carriage to the ball. Lizzy had insisted because, unless he was firmly at her side, she thought he might renege. She was determined, whatever her husband said to the contrary, to promote a match between Miss Hall and Cousin Hugo.

She wouldn't ostracise a family because one of their members was a traitor, so neither should anyone else. It would be punishment enough for the relatives to lose their loved one in this way without being obliged to moulder in the country for the rest of their lives.

In her opinion there were too many rules governing society. Another thing that she thought wrong was that if the head of the household committed suicide this was enough to ruin the reputation of the rest of the family. Indeed, it would seem that if a person did anything beyond the pale then all their relatives were obliged to suffer as well.

When her sister Lydia had run away with Wickham and lived with him without the benefit of clergy, her mother had fallen into a decline. Only when her sister's marriage had been arranged by

Fitzwilliam was Mama's health restored. Papa had been reluctant to receive his daughter even though she had been respectably married and he had never really forgiven her. Wickham was now dead and Lydia is in far-off India.

Lizzy had made a special effort this evening and was wearing a new ball gown in yellow silk with a gold chiffon overskirt. Her hair was dressed formally and she was wearing the Darcy parure. She had only had the opportunity to wear this once before and was looking forward to seeing her husband's reaction when she appeared dressed like a queen.

'Sweetheart, you look staggeringly beautiful. I don't recall seeing that ensemble before.'

She curtsied. 'Now you know why I requested that you wore your gold waistcoat. With this tiara and my heeled slippers I am almost as tall as you tonight.'

He had his white gloves in one hand and with the other he cupped her face and kissed her. 'You will outshine them all, my love. Hugo is waiting downstairs and he's wearing his dress regimentals. I was almost blinded by the plethora of gold frogging on display.'

Sally held out the matching evening cloak and Fitzwilliam took it. He swirled it around Lizzy's shoulders and they were ready to leave.

With her gloved hand resting on his arm, he escorted her down. The carriage was already outside and it did not do to keep the horses waiting. The colonel was resplendent in red jacket, skintight white breeches and black boots.

'You look wonderful, Cousin Hugo. You will be surrounded by eager young ladies – for there's nothing they like better than a man in uniform – especially one as handsome as you.'

He snapped his heels together and bowed, his shako clutched to his chest. 'Thank you, ma'am, I aim to please.' He grinned, making him look even more attractive. 'Might I be permitted to say, Cousin Lizzy, that splendid as I am, I am outshone by yourself.'

Fitzwilliam snorted inelegantly. 'If you two have stopped ogling each other, shall we get on? The sooner this wretched business is over the happier I shall be.' He looked down his aristocratic nose at her, but with a twinkle in his eye. 'No doubt you will expect me to stand up with you tonight.'

She couldn't prevent her giggles escaping. Hardly a suitable reaction for a woman married for several years and the mother of two children. 'At least tonight you cannot turn your nose up at me for being less than attractive. I well remember overhearing your rude remarks at the Meryton assembly several years ago.'

'Baggage! I thought you promised never to mention that regrettable occasion again. I shall honour you with three dances but do not suggest I parade around the floor any more than that. No doubt you will not lack for partners.'

'I've no desire to dance with anyone else but you.'

Cousin Hugo interrupted their conversation. 'That will not do at all; you must stand up with me. It will raise my position in the eyes of the *ton* to be seen with the most beautiful woman at the ball.'

'Very well, I agree to dance with you, but no one else.'

It hardly seemed worthwhile taking the carriage as the journey was no more than ten minutes, but the wait to disembark was three times as long. Eventually they negotiated the welcome party and made their way into the ballroom.

'Fitzwilliam, can you see Mrs Hall and her daughter? I must introduce your cousin immediately.'

From his prodigious height he was able to scan the chamber. 'They are at the far end, close to the quartet. There are still empty chairs by them, so it will not seem odd that we make our way there.'

Lizzy made the introductions and watched closely to see if either Hugo or Miss Hall seemed interested in each other. He bowed, she curtsied. Then she overheard him invite the girl to stand up with him in the first set and she accepted.

'Mrs Hall, are your husband and son not with you tonight?'

'They are to join us later. I must thank you for arranging our invitations as I know we would not have received one but for your good offices.' She gestured to the splendid floral decorations that festooned the walls. 'I must own that we have never attended anything so grand. It will be something to remember when we return to our home in the country.'

'Sir Robert and Lady Sinclair have also been invited. I look forward to renewing my acquaintance with them too.'

Fitzwilliam was becoming restless and she touched his arm affectionately. 'My dear, why don't you escape to the card room? I doubt there will be any dancing until all the guests have arrived.'

He nodded at Mrs Hall and smiled at her. 'Remember, Lizzy, I shall return to lead you out when the first set is called.'

His cousin and Miss Hall were no longer in sight. This was a breach of etiquette and would do neither of them any favours. She glanced around and her fists unclenched when she spotted them no more than a few yards away and both behaving impeccably.

Mrs Hall had seen her staring. 'Colonel Fitzwilliam is a fine figure of a man, Mrs Darcy. My Jennifer was beside herself with excitement at the thought of meeting him tonight.'

Lizzy smiled inwardly. She hoped Cousin Hugo would fall in love with the girl as she was perfect for him. He must know that for him to be showing this partiality his companion could only draw one conclusion – that he was genuinely interested in her.

He was an honourable man, like her husband, and would not deliberately mislead this young lady.

* * *

Darcy threaded his way through the press of people, expecting to find his cousin at his shoulder, but when he reached the double doors that led to a less populated area of the house discovered Hugo had not followed him.

Where the devil was he? Darcy stared over the heads of the milling crowd and immediately spotted the errant gentleman. It was hard to miss the scarlet regimentals. Hugo was deep in conversation with Miss Hall – this rang warning bells. Hadn't Lizzy suggested the two of them would make an ideal match?

He had told his wife a relationship with the daughter of a traitor wouldn't be considered by any member of the *ton*. Was it possible she had been correct in her assumption that the two of them would instantly form an emotional attachment?

The Darcy name must not be dragged down by such an association – he must do his best to discourage the girl. There was little point in speaking to his cousin on the matter, as once his mind was made up Hugo would not change it. They were similar in more than appearance.

This was a damnable business and he wished he had not allowed himself to be involved. He had never thought to fall in love with any woman until he met Lizzy. Although it had taken them a year or more to overcome her prejudice and his pride, he had known from the moment he had set eyes on her that she was the one for him. He was a better man for marrying her.

How could he deny his cousin the same experience? His lips curved. Good God! The two had only just been introduced and here he was already thinking that they had fallen in love. Such fanciful imaginings were better left to young ladies who were of a romantical nature rather than a serious gentleman like himself.

What he needed was a stiff drink and a conversation about sensible things like the price of corn or the cost of keeping horses in London.

He returned to the ballroom in a better frame of mind and was relieved to see his wife dancing with his cousin – there was no sign of Mrs Hall or her daughter. After an interminable time of skipping and bowing Lizzy was finally returned to him. He was unperturbed that she hadn't kept her first dance for him.

'At last, sweetheart, I have come to claim my dance.'

'Would you mind very much if we sat this one out, Fitzwilliam? I find myself quite breathless after all that exercise.'

'I shall dance with two other young ladies from your list, Lizzy, then I shall escape to my club.' Cousin Hugo gave her a warm smile. 'I was much taken with Miss Hall and would have danced with her a second time if she had not been called away to some emergency or other.'

His cousin strolled off. 'I am concerned about what might have happened to take the Halls away when both of them were so obviously enjoying this experience. Mrs Hall told me so herself. I must see if I can be of any assistance in whatever disaster has overtaken the family. I don't suppose you heard anything whilst you were in the card room?'

'I didn't. Neither Hall nor Sir Robert was present and neither were their sons. I shall come with you in case I might be needed.'

They wandered through the building peering into rooms but found no sign of the missing couple. She made enquiries in the ladies' retiring room but to no avail. Whatever it was that had taken her new friends away was not to be revealed that night.

'I think it must be something to do with Sir Robert and Lady

Sinclair, as they haven't come this evening and I'm sure they would have been eager to do so.'

'In which case, Lizzy, shall I call for our carriage or do you wish to remain and dance with me?'

'I'm quite content to return to the tranquillity of our own establishment. Tomorrow I shall call at the abode of Mrs Hall…'

He interrupted her. 'No, you must not interfere. I'm sure we will hear the reason for their disappearance soon enough.'

In the time it took for a footman to run round to Grosvenor Square and summon their carriage, they could have walked home twice over. Darcy was glad to leave the overcrowded rooms to those who enjoyed such occasions.

Once safely inside the carriage and rattling over the cobbles he was able to relax.

'When is this supposed letter from home to arrive? I do so long to go back to Pemberley and the children.' She spoke from the darkness.

'It should arrive tomorrow morning, so we will be able to set out for Derbyshire the next day. With luck one or other of us will be able to discover what drama took our quarries from the ball tonight.'

'I have no intention of coming to London again for a very long time. I dislike the unpleasant aromas and long for the fresh air of the countryside. I cannot think why some prefer to live here all year round.'

He found her hand and took it into his own. 'I too have had more than enough of the city in recent months. This shall be my last assignment. In future I shall devote myself to my family and estates and be glad to do so.'

* * *

Fitzwilliam remained at her side all night and they were both in bed when there was a thunderous knocking on the door that led into the passageway.

They both sat up and she was about to tumble from the bed in order to answer but he restrained her. 'Remain where you are, Lizzy. Let Dawson or your girl see who it is.'

'But it's scarcely dawn – they won't be up. It can't be the letter we're expecting as your cousin wouldn't send it at this ungodly time. You must see what's wrong.' She gave him a none too gentle push and he threw back the covers. 'Fitzwilliam, put on your nightshirt, you cannot parade around as you are.'

His laugh was loud in the darkness. 'I'll do so, if I can find it.'

She heard him rummaging about on the carpet and then the rustle of material as it slid over his head. As he strode to the door, apparently unbothered by the fact that he couldn't see where he was going, the person outside knocked loudly for a second time.

Her heart was pounding – her mouth dry. It must be a dire emergency for a member of their staff to bang so frantically.

The door opened and she tensed, straining to hear what was said. The chamber was so large whatever was said was indistinguishable from her position in bed. Her husband was suddenly illuminated by the light of a candle. His face was grim and her stomach roiled.

'What is wrong? Tell me at once. Has something happened at home?'

'The message is from Hugo. He's downstairs awaiting me. Thomas Hall has been abducted. I must get dressed and see how I can assist in this matter.'

She knew better than to offer her help. He was quite capable of dressing himself when required. In a remarkably short time he was back. 'I shall get up as well. I'm wide awake now. Would you mind very much if I joined you downstairs as soon as I am ready?

I could go to Mrs Hall and her daughter and offer her comfort at this difficult time.'

'Remain where you are, Lizzy. Mr Hall can take care of his family without our interference. My cousin and I will do what is necessary to find the young man. God willing he hasn't been murdered.'

'This has to be in connection with the other business, doesn't it? You will be careful, won't you? You are not a soldier like Colonel Fitzwilliam.'

'I can take care of myself if needs be. Don't fret, my love; I shall come to no harm.'

Then he was gone, leaving her to worry about his safety. She was at a loss to understand why Mr Hall's son had been kidnapped. She shuddered. It couldn't be for ransom as the family were not especially wealthy. The poor fellow must have been taken in order to pressure his father into further treachery. His mother and sister must be beside themselves with worry.

Good heavens! The redoubtable Miss Hall would not sit back and let others investigate – she would already be involved and could be in deadly peril. Lizzy was certain neither Mrs Hall nor her daughter were aware that Mr Hall was involved in anything untoward. The girl could not possibly know why her brother had been abducted, not for money but for a more sinister purpose.

She flung back the comforter and ran to her dressing room. Finding the necessary underpinnings was simple enough, as was putting on her stockings. All she had to do now was discover a warm, practical gown that did not require the assistance of her abigail to put on.

Her many ensembles were carefully folded on the shelves in the closet but she couldn't recall which of them would slip over her head, or had buttons at the front rather than the back. The moss green cashmere caught her eye and she pulled it out for inspection.

It had all the requisite features. The house would be cold as the servants would not be up to light the fires so early in the day. She must find a shawl and put on her boots rather than her indoor slippers.

There was no time to do an elaborate arrangement for her hair. She quickly braided it and pinned it in a coronet around her head. Satisfied she'd done the best she could, she collected the candlestick and hurried through the silent house praying that her husband and his cousin had not already departed on their errand of mercy.

As she reached the head of the stairs the two of them appeared in the hall. They were both wearing riding capes so must be heading for the stables. 'Fitzwilliam, please wait a minute. There's something I must tell you before you leave.'

He tore up the stairs two at a time. 'I asked you to remain in your chamber. I don't want you involved in this.'

Quickly she explained her theory about Miss Hall.

'I can't believe she would take matters into her own hands. However, we shall go to their house first and make sure the girl has done nothing foolish.'

With that she had to be content as he didn't stay to reassure her further. The longcase clock in the drawing room struck four. She might as well return to her apartment until the house was awake.

'Madam, would you care to go into the yellow drawing room. There will be chocolate and pastries brought to you shortly. The fire is already alight.'

Lizzy spun round in shock to find the butler, more or less correctly dressed, standing behind her. She had quite forgotten someone must have been roused from their bed in order to answer the front door.

'I shall do that. There's no need to wake the household so early. If the room is warm I shall be quite happy to wait until Cook and her staff are on duty as usual.'

The chamber was pleasantly warm – far more comfortable than her apartment – so she decided to remain there. This room faced the garden at the rear of the house and was peaceful; no noise from the street reached here.

She hadn't been there for very long when Gregson rushed in clutching a letter. He had been so disturbed by this second unusual event that he had failed to place it on the silver salver before bringing to her.

This was the letter purportedly from Pemberley telling them that some domestic crisis needed their immediate return. She took the folded square and broke the seal, knowing that this letter was no longer a welcome excuse to leave Town, but a further complication.

# 14

A sleepy groom had his horse waiting when Darcy arrived at the stable yard. He nodded his thanks and mounted the rangy bay gelding. 'If we cut through the park it will be quicker.'

'I'll take your word for it – not the way I would choose – but as we can gallop, the extra distance should be no obstacle.' His cousin was already astride his own mount and ready to depart.

Fortunately the moon was full and gave sufficient light for them to canter over the cobbles. No doubt the sound of the hooves would alarm many of the residents in this smart residential area. This was of no matter; they needed to get to the Hall household as soon as possible.

As soon as they were in the park he pushed his horse into a gallop and they thundered across the greensward, sending roosting pigeons into fluttering panic. He knew the general direction, but not the exact location. He would have to rely on his cousin for directions when they emerged at the other side of the park.

He drew rein as he saw the exit gates approaching. 'Where to next?'

'Turn left, and it's the third turning on the other side of the street.' Hugo pushed his horse alongside. 'I'm damned if I know why Hall should have sent for me. I've never met the man and am barely acquainted with any member of his family.'

'Are you suggesting he knows that you're leading the investigation into his activities?'

'It's possible, but unlikely. But I can't think of any other explanation.'

They had reached the street they wanted and crossed the thoroughfare. There was no need to ask which house it was. A substantial dwelling halfway down the crescent was the only one with light streaming from the windows – all the rest were in darkness, the residents in peaceful slumber.

'I think I might know. Miss Hall was much taken with you and you are no doubt the only soldier of her acquaintance. You were the most obvious choice to ride to the rescue.'

Darcy ducked his head as he guided his horse under the archway that led to the rear of the building. They were expected and a stableboy and groom were waiting to receive their mounts.

They took the path from the yard, which led towards the house. The side door was flung open before they reached it. As he had suspected it was Miss Hall who rushed out to greet them and not either of her parents.

'Thank you so much for coming, Colonel Fitzwilliam.' She seemed somewhat surprised to find Darcy standing outside the door. She recovered quickly. 'Also, thank you, Mr Darcy, for accompanying the colonel. Please come in – you will find the house in disarray. My mother is beside herself and my father has yet to come home.'

She led them to the drawing room, which he was surprised to find unoccupied. 'Mama is too distressed to speak to you. She is in her bedchamber being attended to by her maid.'

The fact that this young lady was entertaining two gentlemen before daybreak without a chaperone was not lost on him, but his cousin seemed unbothered by this monumental breach of etiquette.

'My dear, you must tell us exactly what transpired. How do you know that your brother has been abducted and is not in some den of iniquity with his cronies?'

The girl pushed a piece of paper into his hand. Darcy had not noticed she'd been carrying this. Hugo quickly scanned the contents and handed it to him.

The note was unequivocal:

*We have your son. If you want to see him alive again then you will deliver the package as instructed.*

*You have until eight o'clock.*

'Where is your father?' Hugo asked.

'He is out of town, sir, and not expected home until tomorrow. He had business to attend to with Sir Robert.' The girl appeared more angry than upset. 'This note was delivered more than an hour ago. The person who brought it was not a pleasant man, which is why I opened the letter myself even though it was addressed to my papa.'

Hugo nodded. 'You did the right thing. Have you any idea as to the whereabouts of the package that is referred to?'

She almost stamped her foot. 'Of course I don't. If I did I would have sent it round immediately and not have involved you in this family matter.'

Darcy felt obliged to point out something they both appeared to have overlooked. 'There is no direction on the note so, even if we had the item they refer to, we would have no notion where to send it.'

This was obviously related to both men's involvement with the French. They could hardly discuss this in front of the girl. 'Miss Hall, take us to the study. We shall begin a thorough search. You must look in your father's apartment – we can hardly do that ourselves.'

She pursed her lips and he thought she was going to object to his issuing her with orders. Then she nodded. 'We have only four hours to discover what they require. God willing, when we do find it the parcel will already have the address written on it.'

The study was at the rear of the house and had convenient access to the outside. It would be the ideal place for a clandestine visit. A person could come and go without being seen by anyone else in the house.

The butler handed them candles from which they ignited several others once they were safely inside the study. 'This has to be to do with what you are investigating, Hugo. For some reason Sir Robert and Hall failed to pass on whatever their paymasters were expecting to that damned count. Do you think they have made a bolt for it?'

'I'm beginning to suspect as much. Another thing, I believe that Miss Hall might well know more about this matter than we suppose. She didn't question the demand for a mysterious parcel and was happy to search for it without asking what it might contain.'

'That's something we must ask her, but first we must endeavour to find what is required and send it…'

His cousin stared at him as if he was speaking in tongues. 'Send it? Have you taken leave of your senses? If it's treasonous material, as we suspect, then it cannot be put into the hands of those who ask for it, even if it means the death of the boy.'

If Hugo had punched him in the face he could not have been

more shocked by this reply. 'God's teeth! I'll not be party to a murder.'

'The matter is out of your hands. You are a civilian – this is a military matter and one of national security.'

'Then tell me why we are looking for this item so urgently if you don't intend to use it to ransom the boy?'

This was a hit direct. 'You're correct – I appear to be saying one thing and doing the contrary. Shall we search this room or stand about talking and wasting valuable time?'

They worked methodically, looking in and under every piece of furniture to no avail. They pulled out all the books and the bookshelves and found nothing untoward behind them. Even the chairs and desks were upended and the undersides carefully examined.

'This has been a fruitless exercise, Darcy. I'm beginning to suspect they took what we're looking for with them when they left London.'

The room was cold but Darcy had his riding coat on and the vigorous search had been sufficient to keep him warm. It wasn't looking hopeful for young Hall. If they didn't find the documents then it was academic, as they wouldn't have anything to exchange for him.

Then he heard the girl approaching at a run and she burst into the room holding a brown paper parcel tied with string and liberally covered with red sealing wax. She waved it triumphantly above her head. 'I have it – Mama recalled him putting this in one of her hat boxes last week. Eventually she realised that I might be looking for it.'

'Does it have an address on the front?' Darcy asked immediately.

'It does, but it's not somewhere I recognise. You must set out immediately and take it to them, there's not a moment to lose.'

He exchanged a glance with his cousin. If Hugo didn't explain the circumstances then he would.

Hugo had removed the package from the girl and was examining it closely. 'Miss Hall, you don't seem surprised by this eventuality. Do you know what's in here by any chance?'

'I think I might do – I believe that my father and Sir Robert are blackmailing someone important. This package must contain whatever incriminating material they had. Now it has to be returned to its owner in exchange for my brother.'

'What makes you think so?'

'A few months ago we were struggling to pay our bills and then from nowhere there was sufficient to clear our debts and for us to come to London. I thought until tonight that my father had been lucky at the gaming tables but now I know the money came from a far worse place.'

'I shall take care of this, my dear; I suggest that you return to your bed and leave things to us. I give you my word Thomas will be home by the time you rise.'

The girl ran across and threw herself into his cousin's arms. Hugo stiffened but after a few seconds he responded by embracing her. 'I thank you, sir, for coming to our rescue. I knew I could rely on you to help. I shall do as you suggest, but I'll not go to bed but sit with my mother and offer her comfort.'

She curtsied to Darcy and then they were alone again. 'You must be as relieved as I that Miss Hall is not aware of the truth, cousin. I assume that as you have given your word you will fetch her brother home safely that you don't intend to keep these papers.'

'I've a plan that I hope will suffice. We must unpick this string, remove the contents, and replace them with other material. Then rewrap the package, making sure it is identical in every way to the one I hold in my hand.'

This was not an easy undertaking, but between them they made note of exactly how the string was tied and the position of each blob of sealing wax. Hugo examined the first document. Then he began to flick through the rest of the papers.

'There's no information here of national importance, just things anyone could discover from reading the journals. We can give them these papers. I can't believe my luck – sending the original parcel means things can go ahead as planned. Sinclair and Hall will not be exposed and I still have a chance of catching the perpetrator.'

'Why would whoever it is send papers that are of little worth? Surely the count will not be happy.'

'Perhaps the traitor was unable to smuggle out anything of value this time. It doesn't mean he won't obtain information that is damaging to the war effort in the future.'

They carefully rewrapped and sealed the papers.

'This looks and feels the same as it was before. It will have to do as there's no time to do any more. You will have to deliver this, Darcy. I cannot take the risk that they might recognise me as an officer.'

'I sincerely hope that you will be at my back with your weapons at the ready. I can hardly go to this rendezvous with a loaded pistol in my pocket.'

'Presumably you have a stiletto secreted in the top of your boot?'

'No I don't. I've never seen the necessity to carry one as I rarely travel alone. I must pray that whoever we are giving this package to does not have the authority to open it.'

The parcel fitted snugly into an inside pocket of his riding coat and was indiscernible once he arranged the folds about his person. He considered himself a courageous man, but he lacked the ruthlessness of a soldier and he feared this might be his undoing.

Fresh horses were waiting in the yard and this time they were to head in the opposite direction towards a less salubrious part of London. His cousin led the spare mount intended for the young man they hoped to rescue. It was now full light but the streets were more or less deserted, apart from the sprinkling of servants running errands for their masters or mistresses.

He had had no notion where the dwelling they sought was situated, but Hugo had elicited information from one of the stable lads. No doubt there would be speculation in the yard as to why they should need to visit such a place.

'We're approaching the street. We've been observed for the past ten minutes.'

Darcy swallowed the lump in his throat and straightened his shoulders. He would not show these miscreants how scared he was. Not for his own safety, although that was of some concern, but because the life of young Hall rested on his shoulders.

'I'm ready. Make sure the horses are facing in the right direction. I've not vaulted astride since I was a stripling, but I think I could manage it if my life depends on doing so.'

They clattered to a halt outside a grimy building where there were a further couple of scruffy individuals lolling about on the steps. The air was thick with soot and the smell from the gutters made him gag.

He dismounted with as much of a flourish as he could manage and strode to the front door. It opened as he arrived. He remained outside and spoke to the shadowy shape lurking in the gloom behind it.

'I have the package asked for in the letter. Mr Hall is away, and it took some time for us to locate it at his house, which is why we did not arrive earlier.' He waited for a response but there was none. 'You will have the item when the young man is free.' He removed the package from his inside pocket so they could see that he did in fact have it with him.

Why hadn't the two thugs moved up behind him and pushed him through the door? He swivelled slightly so he could see Hugo from the corner of his eye. His cousin had his pistols pointed at these men and this was holding them at bay.

'Hand it over first – you'll not see the little bastard otherwise.'

Darcy's mouth was dry but he managed to reply. 'I told you my terms. Mr Hall out here in exchange for the package I have in my coat. If he is not forthcoming by the time I count to ten the deal is off – we will keep the item, which presumably is of considerable value, and you can do what the hell you like with Hall. I've never met him and I'm just doing a favour for a friend of my wife's.'

He began to count loudly, glad his voice sounded firm and confident. He had reached seven and nothing had happened. His heart was thudding painfully. Had he made a disastrous error and signed the death warrant of the poor boy?

Then there was a scuffling and the door half-opened and a dishevelled young man was ejected. Immediately he tossed the parcel through the door, grabbed Hall's arm and hurtled back down the steps. 'We have seconds to get away. No time to talk.'

He vaulted into the saddle, almost going over the horse's ears, but somehow he kept his balance. He kicked the beast into a flat gallop whilst his feet still dangled and the reins were barely in his hands. They thundered down the street and at any moment he expected a hue and cry to start – for the watchers to block their path.

Instead they reached a more salubrious area without pursuit and he was able to ram his boots into his stirrups and check that the other two were beside him.

'I say, sir, that was capital fun. Thank you for coming to my rescue.'

'I'm glad to be of service, Hall. I think we can reduce our pace now. Colonel, I suggest we go to Grosvenor Square.' It would be better to question the young man away from the vigilance of his sister. It was still possible he was involved in his father's activities.

'Excellent idea, Darcy. Your staff will be up and can supply us with a much-needed breakfast.'

The return journey took longer as they were travelling at a more decorous pace. An adjacent church clock struck seven as he led the way through the arch into his stable yard.

He was met by his butler. 'Have breakfast served immediately, Gregson. Is Mrs Darcy downstairs?'

'Madam is in the yellow drawing room, sir. A letter arrived by express some time ago and madam asked for your trunks to be packed.'

'Thank you, that will be all.' He waited until the butler had gone about his business before turning to the two gentlemen beside him. 'Hugo, take Hall to my study. I expect there are things you need to ask him and you don't require my assistance to do so. Join us in the breakfast room when you are done.'

# 15

Lizzy ignored the expectant face of the butler who was obviously desperate to know the contents of the letter that he believed had arrived so unexpectedly. As she was about to toss it aside she realised she must open it and pretend to be concerned.

In fact the paper was empty – Hugo had not even bothered to write a message purporting to be from someone at Pemberley. She slid the missive into her sleeve as it would not do to leave it lying around in case one of the staff picked it up.

The door had been left ajar and she heard the rattle of crockery approaching. Gregson brought in her tray and placed it on a convenient side table by the fire.

'Mr Darcy and I have to return to Derbyshire as soon as possible. Would you inform the stables that we shall require the carriage at dawn tomorrow? Also, have word sent to my maid and Mr Darcy's valet to have our trunks packed. They will need to leave later today.'

He bowed. 'I shall do so at once, madam. We shall be sorry to see you depart so soon. Might we have the pleasure of your company later on in the Season?'

'I fear not, but I believe friends of Mr Darcy are to bring their family here later in the Season. Therefore, do not dismiss the temporary staff; have them employed in refurbishing and cleaning.' This was pure fabrication on her part, but those servants had been taken on for a month and it would be unfair to dismiss them after little more than a week.

Despite the earliness of the hour she was surprisingly hungry and demolished everything that had been sent to her. Her appetite hadn't been diminished by the worry of having her husband and his cousin gallivanting about the place in an effort to rescue young Mr Hall.

She stretched out her legs on the sofa and covered them with a rug. She would sleep for a while in the hope that when she awoke Fitzwilliam would have returned safely.

She was roused from her slumber when he pressed his cold lips against hers. Instinctively she reached out and encircled his neck, pulling him closer. His kiss deepened and she responded eagerly. It was him who broke the embrace.

'My darling, much as I would like to make love to you here, we must not as we could be interrupted at any moment.'

'You are back safely. I'm so glad to see you.'

He chuckled and moved her legs so he could sit down with her. 'That is self-evident. The young man is safe and my cousin is interrogating him.' He pointed to the empty tray. 'I take it you will not be requiring breakfast.'

'I ate a prodigious amount, but I believe I still have a small corner to fill. No doubt Gregson told you the letter arrived.'

He yawned widely and the gesture was catching. 'We shall eat and then retire for a few hours.' The wicked glint in his eyes made it quite clear that sleep was not uppermost in his mind.

'Tell me what happened – did you have to hand over state secrets?'

By the time he had regaled her with his exploits a footman tapped politely on the door and announced that breakfast was served.

'I'm glad everything turned out well, Fitzwilliam. I was afraid that this business might delay our departure. As Miss Hall was promised that her brother would be safely back by the time she got up, it's imperative he departs soon.'

'In future I intend to leave matters in the capable hands of my cousin so this must be his decision. We shall hold the house party as planned, but that will be the last of my involvements with the intelligence service.'

'I am relieved to hear you say so, my dear. Listen, I can hear voices. The others are there before us.'

Both Mr Hall and Cousin Hugo stood up as she entered but she waved them back into their chairs. The room was redolent with the smell of fried ham and her mouth watered despite the fact that she'd eaten not so long ago.

'Good morning, gentlemen. Pray continue your meal.' They resumed their seats and continued to eat with gusto. 'Just ham for me, Fitzwilliam, thank you. I shall help myself to coffee.'

She took her place at the table and poured herself a cup from the silver jug on the table. The atmosphere was relaxed; obviously the young man was not a suspect.

'Mr Hall, I hope that you, your mother and sister will come to Pemberley next month, even if your father is unable to join us.'

He swallowed his mouthful before answering. 'Looking forward to it, ma'am. We seldom get the opportunity to rub shoulders with the rich and powerful of this land. I've heard much about your country estate – the finest in Derbyshire I believe.'

'We like to think so. We must return there tomorrow as our children are both unwell.'

'I sincerely hope that it's nothing serious.' He put down his cutlery with a clatter. 'If you will excuse me, Darcy, Mrs Darcy, I must return to my house and reassure my family that I'm well. We too will be leaving Town as soon as may be and will remain on our country estate for the foreseeable future.' His expression was serious. He must have been told about his father's traitorous activities.

He was at the door before he spoke again. 'If you wish to withdraw your invitation, Mrs Darcy, we will fully understand.' He bowed and walked out, looking older than his years.

There were no servants present so they could converse freely. 'I assume that he knows what was in that package. Surely this means the house party is now unnecessary? You have proved that his father is culpable and the fact that Sir Robert has left Town with him must mean he is fully implicated too.'

The colonel wiped his lips on his napkin. 'I wish it was as simple as that. The young man still believes this was to do with blackmail, not treason. I have told him I've no interest in this matter and don't intend to report the incident to the authorities. My mission is to discover the paymaster and also from whom these documents are coming.'

Fitzwilliam interrupted. 'Surely you already know that it's this Count Duvall fellow.'

'Duvall is not the paymaster. He's another go-between and merely transports what he receives to France.'

'Hall and Sir Robert are merely intermediaries as they have no connection to Horse Guards.'

Lizzy put down her cup, her interest in her second breakfast gone. This was a conversation to which she should not be privy. 'If will excuse me, I'm going to retire. No one had much sleep last night and we leave for the country at dawn tomorrow.'

* * *

Darcy watched her go and wished he could accompany her. 'Do you have any inkling of who else is involved?'

'Obviously someone who has access to these secrets, and this person must be someone I know.' Hugo scowled. 'It will be one of the inner circle, one of the gentlemen invited to Pemberley.'

Finally, the truth had been revealed. The house party had never been to entrap Hall or Sinclair, but to uncover the traitor at Horse Guards. He had been manipulated by his cousin. 'Sir Robert and Hall are merely bait, are they not? Your real quarry has always been someone from the army.' He stood up, making it plain his cousin was no longer welcome at his table. 'This is the last time I'll be embroiled in your machinations. I don't appreciate being made a fool of.'

He placed his hands on the table and leant over so his face was inches from his cousin's. 'And neither do I appreciate my family being involved. When this is over, you will not be welcome at Pemberley.'

'I understand, but for me King and Country must always take precedence over family. I will not apologise for doing my duty.' He stood, bowed as if to a stranger, and marched out.

Darcy slowly straightened, wishing he could have handled it a little better, had not let his fury alienate his cousin. He and Hugo had been close friends since they had attended school together and now his intemperate words had severed the connection.

Lizzy would think him a fool and rightly so. One did not cut off one's relations because one's pride had been hurt. There was nothing he could do to mend matters now. He must rely on the genuine affection between them to mend the rift at the house party in May.

He headed for his apartment, knowing that his wife would have something pertinent to say on the subject. His lips curved and his chest tightened. Maybe he would leave this discussion until later as he had something far more interesting in mind.

His valet helped him disrobe. After his exploits this morning he was mud-spattered and sweaty, and could hardly get into bed as he was. For decency's sake he pulled on his bedrobe after his ablutions, dismissed Dawson and headed for the bedchamber.

The room was dark, both the shutters and curtains still closed. Naked, he climbed into bed expecting to find Lizzy similarly unclothed. However, his questing hands encountered the material of a voluminous nightdress. Whatever his intentions, hers had been made quite plain by donning this hideous garment.

He slid in behind her and put his arms around her waist. Once she was comfortably settled within his embrace he drifted off to sleep. Lovemaking and political discussion would have to wait until they were both fully rested.

When he opened his eyes he was alone. From the banging and raised voices coming from next door the maids were busy packing the trunks ready for their departure tomorrow. He ran his hand across his bristly chin – he would have to shave before he went down.

Once he was ready he went in search of his missing wife. The hour was now almost midday; he couldn't remember the last time he had remained in bed so late. He heard Lizzy talking to someone in the drawing room and made his way towards her.

He paused outside, not to eavesdrop, but to ascertain with whom she was speaking. Good God! He recognised that voice.

'Hugo, I didn't expect to see you here again today.'

His cousin smiled as if nothing untoward had taken place

between them. 'You look better, Darcy. I hope you have recovered your temper because there's something you need to know.'

Lizzy tried to hide her smile. She obviously knew about his crass behaviour. 'Do not dawdle in the doorway, my dear, but come and join us. You will be as astounded as I was to hear Cousin Hugo's news.'

With a resigned sigh he took the seat beside her on the *chaise longue* and raised an enquiring eyebrow.

'Things have moved on apace since we spoke earlier today. Young Hall has taken his family to the country but Sir Robert and his father have returned and are behaving as if nothing out of the ordinary has occurred in their absence.'

'Presumably they are aware of the abduction and the fact that their precious package was given in exchange?'

Darcy leant back and closed his eyes. There was something he couldn't quite grasp – a vital piece of information was eluding him.

He sat up and punched his right fist into his other hand. 'I have it. Those two must have known what they were handing over wasn't valuable – that's why they didn't pass it on. This means they knew the contents.'

'You might be right. Let me think for a minute. The only explanation that makes sense is that their usual source failed to produce the required material this month. Therefore they cobbled together something and wrapped it up, but then got cold feet and left Town rather than pass it on.'

'So once the item had been handed over there was no need for them to remain absent from Town.' Darcy's heart thumped heavily behind his waistcoat. He believed his cousin could unmask the traitor without involving his family. 'The traitor must have been out of the country for the past few weeks and unable to pass on any secrets. If you check who was missing from the war cabinet you will have the man you seek.'

Hugo nodded. 'I'll certainly do that, but unless there was only one man missing we will still be guessing.'

* * *

Lizzy was reluctant to join in this conversation but as he had thought fit to discuss the situation with her she was emboldened to speak. 'But you will have narrowed down your search – and further investigation might reveal facts about these men that will identify the traitor.'

Both her husband and his cousin agreed there were unlikely to be more than two or three absent at the same time. His cousin left to continue his search and said he would be arriving in Derbyshire several days before most of the guests.

Fitzwilliam then sheepishly explained what he had said to his cousin last night and they laughed about it. He would always be a proud man. Why not – after all, was he not the biggest landowner in Derbyshire and one of the warmest men in the country? Since he had known Lizzy he was now prepared to admit his faults and make amends for them.

He was pleased with her small deception that would mean the temporary staff maintained their employment. 'I was thinking that I might lease this house for the remainder of the Season – possibly for every year as it's prohibitively expensive keeping it open when we so rarely use it.'

'I applaud your reasoning, my dear. Why not make a proviso in the lease that if you require to come to London on business whoever is living here must be prepared to accommodate you in a guest chamber?'

'I'll see my lawyers today, before we leave for home. It's

remarkably fine today – why don't you accompany me? I know you don't like to ride, but we could take the carriage and stroll about Green Park either before or after my meeting.'

'I should like that. I'll fetch my bonnet and reticule whilst you send word to the legal gentlemen that you will be arriving imminently. As they are situated in Bond Street, why don't we forego the carriage and walk there?'

After a pleasant afternoon they returned to the house to find Lady Sinclair and her progeny waiting to speak to them. Gregson had shown them into an anteroom and they had been served with refreshments.

'I shall leave you to speak to them, Lizzy. If you need me I shall be in my study.'

A lurking footman was sent to fetch the Sinclair family. He would direct Lady Sinclair, her son and daughter to the drawing room. Lizzy remained on her feet ready to welcome the uninvited guests.

'Mrs Darcy, I do apologise for descending on you unannounced. I cannot tell you what an uproar there is at my house. We have come to throw ourselves upon your mercy and ask if I can accompany you to Derbyshire immediately with Richard and Annabel – and not wait until the date stated on the invitation?'

Whatever she had been expecting the lady to say, this was not it. 'Please take a seat, all of you, then you must explain what has so distressed you.'

The lady burst into noisy tears and Annabel Sinclair took her parent's hands and offered what comfort she could. Mr Sinclair drew Lizzy to one side.

'Thomas Hall came to see us before he left and explained what our fathers have been doing in order to supplement their legitimate income. I cannot tell you how shocked we are. I knew him to be a hardened gambler and drinker – but a blackmailer?

Mama has stormed out in high dudgeon and is refusing to return. But we have nowhere else to go. She has a reasonable annuity but that won't be sufficient to keep us.'

'I can't see that this is any of my business, sir. We are barely acquainted after all.'

The young man looked quite wretched. 'I know that, Mrs Darcy, but my mother would not be dissuaded from coming to ask you. Just tell her that you cannot help and I'll take her home.'

Now was not the time to tell him that his father's sins were far worse than blackmail. She needed to speak with Fitzwilliam urgently. If the family were separated then Sir Robert would not come to the house party. She wasn't sure if that mattered any more.

'I am sorry for your troubles, sir, and will at least speak to my husband before giving your mother a response. Pray excuse me whilst I go and find him. I promise I'll return as quickly as I can.'

She hurried from the room, her thoughts in turmoil. She wasn't sure that even her clear-thinking husband could come up with a solution to this conundrum.

# 16

Darcy listened to what Lizzy had to tell him. 'Let me think – we can hardly take Lady Sinclair and her family to Derbyshire as that would be condoning her behaviour. I think we must persuade her to return to her husband.'

'How will that help your cousin with his mission? What if we tell her she can come to Pemberley immediately as long as she is reconciled with Sir Robert first?'

'Then he can still join her the following week and nothing will be out of place. This is a miserable business. I can't see this poor woman and her family, or Mrs Hall and hers, facing anything but financial and social ruin when it's done.'

She stood on tiptoes and kissed him. 'Thank you, my dear, I shall go at once and tell her. I believe that all she needs is time to come to terms with the knowledge. I'm sure she is well aware she cannot survive apart from Sir Robert.'

When she got to the door she paused. 'We can still leave at dawn tomorrow can't we?'

'We have no choice, my love, as my lawyers already have tenants ready to move in the following day.'

'How can that be? You only visited your lawyers yesterday.'

'It was fortuitous. Another client of theirs are unhappy in the lodgings they had found the Season. The gentleman concerned had only just left their offices.'

Whilst he had been talking his mind had been on the other problem. He could think of no way for the families of the traitors to extricate themselves from this coil. The Crown would be within its rights to confiscate their estates and leave the wives and offspring destitute. However, perhaps he could use his influence with the prime minister, such as it was, to be satisfied with the lives of the miscreants themselves.

Over dinner he learnt that Lady Sinclair had accepted their offer and would be setting out for Derbyshire as soon as she could arrange it. 'They will arrive at the same time as Mr and Mrs Bennet and Mary. I rather think that your mother and Lady Sinclair might be bosom bows before the visit ends.'

Lizzy smiled. 'They are certainly of a volatile disposition and have a tendency to say rather more than one would wish on any subject. I hope your prediction is correct, for the matter could go in either direction. It would be decidedly uncomfortable for all of us if they were constantly at daggers drawn – especially with everything else that will be going on besides.'

'Have you arranged any entertainment for our guests apart from shooting, fishing and riding?'

'Fitzwilliam, you are quite impossible. I hardly think that the ladies will participate in any of those pastimes. We shall take drives into the countryside to admire the views and we shall also invite our neighbours to a garden party in the grounds.' She raised her hand and began to count on her fingers. 'There will also be a musical evening, a theatrical evening, dancing after dinner most nights as well as a grand ball to round off the proceedings.'

He shuddered. 'If you expect me to be involved in charades then you are sadly mistaken, madam. I might be persuaded to attend the musical event and ball.'

She leant across and rapped him sharply on his knuckles with her fork. 'It is you, sir, who are deluded if you think you can escape any of these events. I shall require your full cooperation at all times. Have I made myself quite clear?'

The fork was poised, this time with the tines down as if she intended to impale him on the prongs. He shook his head in defeat. 'Desist, you termagant. I shall do as you ask. By the way, will any of our guests be bringing children?'

'Have you run mad, Fitzwilliam? I deliberately excluded them because of the reasons behind us having a house party. I intend to have Fabian and Amanda removed next door for the duration so they will be at no risk from anything that might transpire.'

His amusement vanished to be replaced by something else entirely. 'I should never have agreed to this. It's not too late to cancel it...'

'It's far too late. Arrangements have been made and my family will be setting out in a day or two and are no doubt looking forward to seeing their grandchildren. They haven't seen any of them since they came for the Christmas festivities. Mama intends to stay for a week or two with Kitty and Adam at the Old Rectory before she returns to Longbourn. No doubt my papa will want to remain with us so he can spend time in our library as he did before.'

'With luck the man who is leaking the secrets will be uncovered quickly and we can send the rest of the unwanted visitors about their business.'

His words were said to reassure his wife. He was well aware it wasn't going to be as simple as he pretended. The spy had remained undetected for months and was hardly likely to reveal himself by his behaviour. The house party was planned to continue for three weeks and it could well take that long for the matter to be resolved.

'I intend to retire now, my dear, as we must be up before dawn. I shall not remain for dessert.' She folded her napkin neatly and placed her cutlery on top.

'I have no desire to remain here alone. We shall go up together.' He touched her hand and her cheeks coloured. He had no need to say anything else. She was as eager as he to tumble into bed and make love.

* * *

The journey to Derbyshire was accomplished without mishap and as the carriage turned onto the drive Lizzy smiled across at her husband. 'Fitzwilliam, are you not as excited as I am to be returning here? You certainly don't look particularly eager to be back.'

He frowned but then shrugged as if shaking off his malaise. 'I beg your pardon, my love, I have been wool-gathering these past hours. I'm not sanguine this house party will be a pleasant experience for any of us. The young ladies invited are going to be sadly disappointed – and two families are going to have their lives ruined.'

'You are refining too much on this, my dear. Even if this were a genuine search for a bride for your cousin, the young ladies might still have been disappointed. They and their families are coming because they hope to be entertained at one of the finest houses in the country at no expense to themselves. I think it highly unlikely any of them will be particularly upset when they are not chosen.'

'I concede defeat on that point. What about Lady Sinclair and

Mrs Hall and their progeny? You cannot believe there will be a happy outcome for them.'

'I don't think they will be particularly sad to see the head of the household removed from circulation. Neither of the gentlemen have been loving husbands or fathers. As long as you can persuade the prime minister not to confiscate the estates they will be better off in the long run.'

He looked at her as if she were an escapee from Bedlam. 'How can having their family name blackened beyond repair be an acceptable situation? The girls will never marry well and neither will the young men. They will not be received anywhere and it might be generations before the taint is gone.'

'You are right to say they will not be received by society, but where they are known and liked in their own neighbourhood I'm sure things will not change. It certainly would make no difference to us if one of our well-liked acquaintances was in a similar position.' She fixed him with her fiercest look. 'You won't refuse to entertain either of the families after Sir Robert and Mr Hall have been arrested, will you?'

His smile was warm and he looked like her beloved again and not a formidable stranger. 'Whatever my personal feelings on the matter, my love, as always I shall be guided by you.'

'Fiddlesticks! You only do as I ask if you do actually agree with me. We will be home very soon and I can think of nothing else but holding our babies in my arms.'

Their arrival would have been noted long before the carriage actually pulled up in front of the house, even if one of the outriders had not gone ahead.

Not only was Nanny standing outside with one of the nursemaids, each holding a baby, but Jane, Bingley and little Charlotte were also waiting to greet them.

'It seems an age since we saw our son and daughter and yet

we've been gone scarcely a sennight. Is it my imagination, or have they both grown in our absence?' His expression was of wonderment; his love for his children could not have been more obvious. How could she have ever thought him a delinquent father?

The door was opened and the steps let down but Fitzwilliam was out first and turned to lift her to the ground. Lizzy took his hand and together they ran up the flight of marble steps. Fabian was crowing with delight and holding out his hands to her. She snatched him from the nursemaid and her husband took Amanda from Nanny.

With her son on her hip she rushed across to embrace her sister and kiss her little niece. 'I cannot tell you how pleased we are to be back here. We have so much to tell you – are you coming in or shall we come to you?'

'I have asked the kitchen to prepare a repast for us all and it is waiting in the garden room.' Jane was positively glowing with health and Charlotte looked equally robust.

Lizzy turned to ask Fitzwilliam if he was content to go into the east wing but he had already set off after Charles in that direction. 'Nanny, we shall take the twins with us. There's no need for either you to accompany us.'

Charles had had the garden room built on when the east wing had been converted for him and Jane. It was a welcome addition and a pleasant place to sit – it was also a safe environment for all three babies.

Over their meal Fitzwilliam told them everything that had happened in London. He had decided that Jane should be included in the discussion as they would need her help when the guests arrived.

'We have ample room in our nursery for your two, Lizzy, and also for your nanny and head nursemaid. I think it wise to remove the children from any possible danger.' She shared an anxious glance with Charles. 'I was so looking forward to this event, to having three of my sisters and my parents here together. But now I'm rather dreading it. Do you think there will be violence when the traitor is uncovered?'

'You must not fret, Jane, my love – there will be half a dozen military gentlemen present and they would take care of any nonsense of that sort.'

'It is my intention to keep the two parties separate. They will be housed on the ground floor of the west wing. When Fitzwilliam's father was alive he was a stickler for etiquette and believed that single gentlemen should be kept as far away as possible from single ladies. The chambers have not been used for years as we prefer to have everyone upstairs at night.'

'Where have you put Mary and our parents?'

'They will be on our side of the house, of course, as they are family. Fitzwilliam, do you think that your cousin should be with us or with his comrades?'

He raised an eyebrow and she wanted to throw something at him. He saw the danger signals and hastily answered her very reasonable query. 'He must go in with us; after all, this whole farrago is – as far as everyone else is concerned – being held for his benefit.'

He turned to Charles with a sigh of resignation. 'I'm damned if I'm going to join in any theatricals – what about you?'

Lizzy laughed. 'Kindly moderate your language, my dear. I'm sure that Jane doesn't want to hear such things in her drawing room.'

'As we are not in that particular room, presumably I'm free to swear like a trooper anywhere else.'

'Now you're being quite ridiculous, Fitzwilliam. Apologise at once for your bad language.' She sounded stern but he clearly knew she was having difficulty containing her amusement.

He rose and bowed deeply to her sister. 'I beg your pardon, Mrs Bingley, I do hope you have it in your heart to forgive me.' He then clutched his chest in a dramatic fashion and quite ruined his apology.

He was irresistible when in this mood. This happy interlude was interrupted by Fabian falling flat on his face and screaming as if he was being murdered. His crying was contagious and soon all three were howling.

'Come, we must take our children back to the nursery. They are overdue for their afternoon nap. Thank you for a delicious luncheon, Jane. I have matters to attend to this afternoon, but we must spend time together tomorrow morning.'

* * *

The next two days passed in a flurry of activities into which Darcy was dragged whether he wished to be or not. Lizzy required him to oversee the preparations for the bachelor rooms, agree to her itinerary and even make a list of suitable activities to entertain the Bennets and the Sinclairs who were due to arrive today. Their luggage had come first thing and their servants had said the others were not far behind.

They met for luncheon – a repast he didn't always indulge in – and she posed a question that had been bothering him too.

'Do you think that the Hall family will come? Thomas Hall removed his family immediately he was returned from his kidnapping and I've no idea of their address in the country.'

'Hugo will be aware of the circumstances and no doubt will have arranged matters to his satisfaction.' She pursed her lips and he laughed. 'I know, Lizzy, that's of absolutely no use to you. I should assume that they are all coming and not allocate their rooms to anyone else.'

'That's as I thought. Although I have some concerns about both the Sinclairs and the Halls attending. Is it possible word might have got around about the reason for his abduction?'

'Nobody should know. I'm sure the family won't have talked of it and those who received the parcel of useless information would not need to speak of it either. I expect they are hoping they will receive something more useful next time.' She seemed satisfied by his answer as she changed the subject.

'It is fortunate indeed that the musicians are willing to stay at the local inn – at our expense of course – as I don't know where we would have squeezed them in otherwise. I have been obliged to employ extra staff and there will be several outside men masquerading as footmen for the duration of the house party.'

'I can't remember Pemberley ever being at capacity before even when my mother was alive and we used to entertain. No doubt the ghostly occupants of the east wing had much to do with that.'

He helped himself to another slice of the succulent, pink ham. 'I gather from Bingley that Kitty is now able to travel without casting up her accounts. Does that mean she and Adam, and Georgiana and Jonathan will be here tonight to welcome your parents?'

'Yes, they will. That will make fourteen sitting down to dine. I've told Cook to serve only one course but plenty of removes, plus desserts. I'm sure nobody will require anything elaborate. Three of the ladies are in an interesting condition and the others will have been travelling for several days.'

This was the first time Lizzy had mentioned that her sisters were increasing without looking sad. Had she come to terms with the fact that she wasn't in that happy condition herself?

'Fitzwilliam, you mustn't look so worried. I'm quite content with the family we have and if the good Lord decides at any time that we shall have more children then that will be soon enough.'

He took her hand and raised it to his lips. 'As long as we can continue as assiduously in our efforts, then I am content also.'

Her cheeks coloured. He was glad he could still make her blush.

'Behave yourself, sir; you are incorrigible and insatiable. Now, if you'll excuse me, I am going to spend time in the nursery. I know we agreed to move the children next door, but I shall miss them dreadfully.'

'I must speak to my factor. I'll join you there when I'm done.'

They left the small dining room together and were just traversing the central passageway when a parlourmaid appeared. The girl curtsied.

'Sir, madam, Mr Peterson asked me to tell you that there are three carriages approaching. They will be here within a quarter of an hour.'

'You had better make your meeting brief, my dear, and I've just enough time to repair my appearance before our guests arrive. I wonder why there's a third carriage. Do you think it is your cousin?'

'I doubt it as he prefers to ride – however great the distance. We shall discover the occupants of the mysterious vehicle shortly. I do think it strange they should be arriving simultaneously.'

# 17

Lizzy hurried to the nursery to make sure the twins would be ready to be admired by their grandparents. Satisfied everything was as it should be, she flew to her apartment in order to check that her hair was tidy and her gown uncreased.

Not a moment too soon she arrived in the grand entrance hall just as the first carriage pulled up outside. Fitzwilliam strolled up to join her. 'The mystery visitors are about to be revealed.' He leant down and kissed the top of her head. 'Have you any suggestions as to who they might be?'

'My best guess is that it's Georgiana or Kitty – but why should they come here twice in one day? Surely coming to dinner this evening is sufficient?'

The butler and the housekeeper had gone out to greet their guests so there was no need for either Fitzwilliam or herself to do so. They would wait inside and greet the arrivals as they always did in the Great Hall. Several footmen would already be unloading any small items of baggage that had travelled in the carriage.

She exchanged a smile with her husband. 'I can hear Mama so the first carriage held my family.'

'I'd forgotten just how piercing Mrs Bennet's voice is. You will forgive me, my love, if I find something urgent to do with Mr Bennet.'

The front door was open and her mother surged through. 'Mr Darcy, Lizzy, how glad I am to be here. I cannot tell you how unpleasant the journey was. We have been travelling for hours and I have the most frightful megrim.'

Fitzwilliam nodded and Lizzy did the same. 'Welcome, Mama, I'm sorry you're feeling unwell. I'll have a soothing tisane sent up to you immediately. I have put you in the same chambers you stayed in at Christmas so I'm sure you can find your way. Would you like to see Fabian and Amanda?'

'I'm far too unwell. Possibly tomorrow morning when I'm feeling more the thing.'

Her father wandered in with Mary close behind. Her sister hadn't been included in the last invitation after her disgraceful behaviour in London, so this was the first time she'd seen her for over a year.

'Papa, I'm so glad you have come.' He raised a hand in a vague salute but again they did not exchange embraces. This omission was hurtful as Lizzy had always considered herself close to her father.

'Mr Bennet, I have acquired several interesting volumes since you were here last. I've put them out in the library for your perusal,' Fitzwilliam said.

'Excellent, excellent. Good to see you, Darcy, Lizzy. I'll go and look at them now.' He vanished leaving Mary standing forlornly on her own.

This time Lizzy ran forward and put her arms around her

sister. 'I'm so pleased to see you, Mary. Kitty and Jane will be here this evening and are eager to hear all your news.'

Mary had remained rigid in her arms and stepped away as soon as she was released. 'Thank you for inviting me, Mr Darcy, Lizzy. If you will excuse me I shall follow Mama and take care of her. I don't intend to come down for dinner, so please don't lay a place for me.' With a whisk of her skirts she too was gone.

'That didn't go well. I might have forgiven her, but she obviously hasn't forgiven me.'

'After her behaviour in London last year she is fortunate indeed that either of us is prepared to receive her at Pemberley.'

'I suppose that is correct. I had hoped she would be more forthcoming now the rift is repaired.'

'Although her manner has not improved, sweetheart, I could not help but notice she looked very smart. If she would only smile she would be a remarkably pretty young lady.'

'That will be two less at the table as presumably my mother will not come down either.'

There was no time to discuss this as the occupants of the second carriage were ushered through. As expected it was Lady Sinclair and her son and daughter.

'Mrs Darcy, Mr Darcy, thank you so much for inviting us stay at your wonderful home. I declare it has taken us more than half an hour to travel from your gate to your front door.' She drew breath to speak but Lizzy stepped in quickly to forestall the next gush of words.

'I hope you had a reasonable journey, my lady. My housekeeper will conduct you to your rooms. Miss Sinclair, Mr Sinclair, welcome to Pemberley.'

A few more pleasantries were exchanged and then these three also disappeared up the grand staircase. 'Where are the other travellers, Fitzwilliam? Surely they should be coming in by now.'

He walked to the window and looked out unperturbed that he might be seen. 'I've no inkling as to who these people might be. They are strangers to me. I sincerely hope they are invited guests. There are two young ladies and an elderly woman plus a young gentleman with shirt points so high he can scarcely turn his head. Does that ring a bell?'

'Oh dear! It must be the Dowager Countess of Finsbury and her grandchildren. I've never met them but they were on the list that your secretary supplied. I'm sure their invitation had the same date as everybody else's, so why have they arrived a week early?'

He stepped away with a rueful smile. 'We are about to find out. They are on their way in. She looks a formidable old lady.'

The dowager sailed in, the egret feathers on her turban bobbing wildly. The three young people walked a few paces behind her and looked extremely uncomfortable.

'Mrs Darcy, you must be astonished at my arriving a week ahead of time. We have been visiting relatives in Scotland and the journey back took far less time than I anticipated.'

No apology was offered and Lizzy wasn't sure if she was affronted or amused. 'Fortunately, my lady, your rooms are ready.' She smiled and beckoned the nervous trio over. 'We dine at six o'clock. This will give you ample time to recover from your travels.'

The two girls curtsied and she realised they were identical twins. The young man bowed. Lizzy was amused at his purple and gold striped waistcoat.

Her husband had beaten a strategic retreat, abandoning her to deal with these unexpected guests. Peterson came at her gesture. 'Please have her ladyship and her grandchildren taken to their chambers.'

The butler snapped his fingers and two footmen appeared. Lizzy waited until this quartet was on the way up the stairs before turning away. She supposed she should really go to her mother and see how she was, but she would be unwelcome there.

Jane would be agog for news of the visitors so she would go next door and spend an hour with her sister before her children were brought down to the drawing room.

* * *

Darcy persuaded Mr Bennet to play a game of billiards and they were joined by Richard Sinclair.

'Please say if I'm intruding, sir, but your butler directed me here. This is Lord Finsbury. I met him lurking about in the passageway.'

'Come in, both of you. Here we are safe from interruption.' Darcy flicked open his pocket watch. 'We have an hour before we need to change for dinner. Mr Bennet, your wife and Mary will not be joining us but I hope that you will.'

The older man nodded, not bothering to enquire why his travelling companions were not coming down. 'I wouldn't miss it for the world, Darcy – you set an excellent table. I doubt that Mary will come, but Mrs Bennet will recover from whatever ails her and be down in good time.' He chalked the end of his cue. 'I'm sure it has not gone unnoticed that my wife enjoys her food.'

Sinclair looked shocked at such plain-speaking but Darcy knew his father-in-law merely tolerated his wife – there was no affection left between them.

'Whatever Mrs Bennet decides, I'm sure Lizzy will have matters in hand.' After one game he nodded to both gentlemen.

'If you will excuse me, I must go to the drawing room as my children will be coming down. Do you wish to accompany me, Mr Bennet? You will be astonished at the changes in your grandchildren since you saw them last.'

'I shall see them tomorrow. I'm not one for infants, sir; they hold no appeal for me however endearing they might be to the ladies.'

Darcy left them to their game. He found his in-laws sadly lacking as parents and grandparents – he vowed he would never be so dismissive of his children, however many he was blessed with.

Miss Sinclair, Lady Sinclair, Jane and Bingley were with Lizzy, as well as the three babies tumbling about on the priceless carpet. There was no sign of the dowager or her granddaughters.

'I hope you're comfortably settled, my lady. I'm sure that my wife has told you that anything you require needs only to be requested.'

Instead of joining Lizzy on the sofa, he dropped to the floor and welcomed all three toddlers into his open arms. Who was more surprised by his behaviour it would have been hard to tell. Bingley laughed and dropped to his knees as well.

After a delightful period the nursemaids collected their charges and he was able to scramble to his feet. 'I fear this jacket might never recover from the experience. However, I wouldn't have missed it for the world.'

Her smile was radiant. 'It's time to change for dinner, my love, so you may remove your besmirched garments. Fabian, Amanda and Charlotte have had a wonderful time playing with their papas.'

Once in the privacy of their rooms he asked if she'd had word from Mrs Bennet. 'No, I've heard nothing but knowing my mother as I do, I wonder if I should tell Peterson to lay a place for her.'

'What do you think of the Sinclair family? I must say I quite like them – even the garrulous Lady Sinclair.'

'As do I. The daughter is as quiet as the mother is noisy but neither of them are in any way unpleasant. I'm looking forward to having all my sisters here this evening, but I do wish Mary was more forthcoming. It's as if she has decided to spend the remainder of her life at Longbourn and is making no effort to find herself a suitable husband. After your generous gift she has a sizeable portion and I'm sure would have no difficulty finding a partner if she applied herself to it.'

'Do you think that all young ladies should aspire to a good match? Is there no place for spinsters?'

'I know; it's hardly fair that a woman is expected to marry well or is considered a failure. Whereas a gentleman can remain a confirmed bachelor and nobody casts aspersions at him.'

'I just require her to be as happy as I am. I cannot believe she's content living at home with my parents.' She pulled a face at him. 'It seems a pity to waste this opportunity to matchmake. If I cannot push your cousin into matrimony then maybe I can find my sister someone of whom we can all approve.'

He raised his hands, indicating his surrender. 'I would not dream of interfering. Exactly how many eligible young men are we expecting?'

'Almost as many as there are young ladies – it's a perfect opportunity for a young gentleman to get to know a possible bride. During the Season there might not be the chance to do more than dance a few times, speak for a few moments at a morning call, or possibly ride or drive out together. A house party is quite different.'

'In which case, sweetheart, do we count this event a failure if there are not at least two betrothals announced before it's over?'

* * *

As expected Mama came down to dinner but Mary didn't appear. Lizzy introduced her parents to the other guests. Her father nodded vaguely to all as was his wont, but her mother was obviously delighted to meet not one, but two titled ladies.

'Let's hope that Mrs Bennet still wishes to keep up the acquaintance with Lady Sinclair when she knows the full story,' Fitzwilliam said quietly.

'That matters not – as long as they are civil to each other whilst they are here I shall be content. I think I can hear Kitty and Adam arriving. This is the first time she has been here in an age – I'm going to greet her as I doubt that she'll have time to speak to me once she's in the drawing room with everyone else.'

Lizzy slipped out, confident she would not be missed. Richard Sinclair and Lord Finsbury were talking to Charles, and Jane was attempting to engage the three young ladies in conversation. The dowager, Lady Sinclair and Mama were deep in conversation and oblivious to everyone else.

'I'm so happy to have arrived here without casting up my accounts, Lizzy dearest.' Kitty rushed forward and embraced her whilst Adam spoke to Fitzwilliam.

'You look much better than you did last time I saw you. Georgiana and Jonathan have yet to arrive and Mary is sulking in her room. I think you will like the Sinclairs.'

As they were talking, Georgiana and Jonathan arrived and there was a further pleasant interlude of introductions before dinner was announced.

The evening was most enjoyable and even Miss Sinclair

managed to utter a few sentences when the tea trolley was brought in later. Everyone retired early with the promise that they would gather again in the morning for an excursion to Bakewell village. Georgiana and Kitty were to meet them there and then they would all go back to the Old Rectory for midday refreshments.

'Do you really intend to accompany us, Fitzwilliam? I would have thought you would prefer to do something with the other gentlemen.'

He looked relieved. 'If you are quite sure, my love, then I will happily forego the pleasure. I doubt that Mr Bennet will emerge from the library to do anything, but the young gentlemen can accompany me if they have the inclination to do so when I ride over to see how my new tenant has settled in at Whitecross Farm.'

'We do not expect any further arrivals until Saturday, so we will have ample time to get to know those who are here already. I do hope that Mary decides to join us tomorrow and doesn't intend to remain in her room for the entire visit.'

'Hugo will be here tomorrow unless something occurs to delay him. No doubt he will be much scrutinised by the dowager. I can't wait to see how he deals with that redoubtable old lady.' Fitzwilliam smiled.

'That reminds me, Lady Sinclair has assured me her daughter is no longer considering putting herself forward as a suitable wife for your cousin. The poor lady is expecting news to arrive here about her husband's perfidious actions. Imagine her horror when she discovers the true nature of his misdemeanours.'

'My cousin's cronies are due to arrive later next week.'

'I don't expect we can keep their presence secret for the duration of the house party. What am I to tell our other guests if anyone asks who is residing in the bachelor quarters?'

'Shall we face that problem when it arises, Lizzy? I've spoken to Peterson and he has the matter in hand. If all goes to plan no one, apart from ourselves, will realise they are here.'

'Apart from the staff, of course, as they will be the ones to wait on them. It will be very difficult to keep this quiet as servants always gossip and word will spread upstairs.'

'Until Hugo arrives tomorrow and explains his plans, I've no more idea what's going to happen than you do, my love. God knows how he intends to expose the traitor – but I can assure you I've no intention of becoming personally involved.'

'I should hope not, Fitzwilliam. I've no wish for you to become embroiled in violence of any sort.' A horrible thought occurred to her. 'Do you think fisticuffs or firearms might be involved?'

'Possibly. If things escalate I shall stay well clear and leave those trained in such matters to take care of it. It's quite possible those concerned will come and go without any of us ever knowing what happens...'

'I'm sorry to interrupt, but you're forgetting about Sir Robert and Mr Hall. This house party was set up in order to unmask these two gentlemen. I thought the idea was for them to try and steal further secrets by eavesdropping on this meeting, and for you and Hugo to catch them.'

He refused to meet her eye and she knew there was more to this than he'd revealed. 'Fitzwilliam, I must know the whole. I will not be fobbed off with some Banbury tale.'

When she had heard how the colonel had misled her husband she was incensed. 'I don't understand. Are you saying that Sir Robert and Mr Hall are no longer going to be arrested?' She didn't allow him to reply but continued, too angry to listen. 'This whole charade is for nothing? The inconvenience, the expense, the deceptions and the trip to London were unnecessary?'

'I was as furious as you when I discovered his true reason for involving us. However, we have no option but to see it through. Although, why he couldn't have completed his mission elsewhere I've no idea.'

'You didn't answer my original question. Are the other two gentlemen to be allowed to go scot-free?'

'No, of course they aren't. They will be arrested at the same time as the other traitor.'

He took her hand as if intending to take her into the bedchamber and put an end to this conversation. Discussing matters of state with one's wife was a most unusual enterprise and she ought to be glad he treated her as an equal, so decided she should discontinue the conversation.

She stepped aside, determined to ask one more question. 'Has it not occurred to either you or Colonel Fitzwilliam that the traitor and the other two are already known to each other?' She had no need to continue. He understood immediately what she meant.

# 18

Darcy shook his head in disbelief. 'How could we be so stupid? It's perfectly possible they are already acquainted.' All thoughts of bedroom sport vanished from his mind. 'If the traitor has got wind of this house party, and knows who has been invited, then he will know it's a trap.'

'I think that's unlikely as the people I invited are not known to each other – apart from the Sinclairs and the Halls of course. What about the person who is paying for this information? Not the French count – but the Englishman. Have you any inkling who he might be?' Lizzy curled up in a chair and waited for his response. He should not be discussing government business with her, but she already knew so much to continue to do so would make no difference to the security of the country.

'Hugo intends to interrogate the traitor in the hope that he will reveal the name of his paymaster.' He sat in the chair opposite hers in front of the cheerily burning fire. 'Maybe this is not such a disaster after all. Perhaps my cousin planned it this way – if the three are known to each other he might well intend to drop into the conversation that Sir Robert and Hall are on the premises in the hope that this information will cause the traitor to inadvertently reveal himself.'

'This has become even more convoluted than it was before. Exactly who is the bait?' She frowned. 'Tell me, my dear, if these spies are to be arrested at Pemberley, who is to do the arresting? Are we to expect a brigade of soldiers to appear?'

'I should never have allowed myself to be inveigled into this, Lizzy.' He closed his eyes, trying to see an option in which they could all come out of it unscathed. Then, to his surprise, she laughed. He jerked upright and stared at her.

'Your cousin has a lot to answer for and I will make him pay for his misuse of your relationship. He will not leave here without becoming betrothed to one of the young ladies. He might not wish to be married but that will be his just deserts for involving us in his intelligence work.'

He returned her smile. 'If anyone can work this miracle, then it's you, sweetheart. But I must point out to you that it won't be only my cousin you are punishing. What about the unfortunate young lady who will be obliged to marry him?'

'Whatever I might feel about Cousin Hugo, he will make an excellent husband. He is wealthy, the grandson of an earl, and a very handsome man. I can assure you that not all young ladies desire to hang on the coat-tails of their husbands – many would be delighted to be left in peace. Not everyone is like us, Fitzwilliam.'

'Then I will not interfere in your plans. Now, it's getting late – shall we retire?'

* * *

He rose early and discovered the other gentlemen, apart from Mr Bennet who never appeared before noon, were already in the breakfast room. They stood up politely at his entry but he waved them back.

'Good morning, are you intending to ride out with me? It's not obligatory, and the ladies will be elsewhere most of today, so you would be perfectly safe remaining here.'

'We have just been discussing exactly that, sir, and would be delighted to come with you. Derbyshire is relatively unknown to me and I should enjoy seeing the countryside more closely,' Finsbury said as he resumed his breakfast.

Sinclair held up the silver coffee jug and Darcy nodded. 'Yes, thank you. I prefer it to small beer. You are outnumbered by young ladies at present, but I can assure you we expect the numbers to be more even by the time everybody arrives at the week's end.'

'I have to admit, sir, that I was dragged along unwillingly by my grandmother,' Finsbury said. 'She refuses to travel without me in tow as protection for my sisters. However, having got here I'm delighted that I came. Pemberley has to be one of the finest houses in the land.'

They munched away companionably and he was the first to put down his cutlery. He addressed the two young men. 'Join me in the stables in half an hour – I'll have a footman conduct you. I fear you could be wandering around this place for days unable to find your way.'

He wanted to speak to Bingley before he went out to ensure his friend didn't inadvertently reveal what he knew to any of the guests. Jane was the soul of discretion and could be relied on to keep things to herself.

Bingley was in the study engrossed in a newspaper. He looked up and greeted him. 'A fine day for a long ride, Darcy. Jane has decided not to accompany Lizzy on her jaunt as she's feeling unwell this morning. Nothing to worry about, a normal side effect of her condition.'

'Is that yesterday's *Times*? What were you reading so avidly?'

'There's an announcement that caught my eye. My sister has married David Forsyth. His parents must have come round so they could obtain a special licence.'

'I wish her no ill will as long as they don't return here.' From his tone he made it clear that Bingley wasn't to invite his sister and her new husband even to his side of Pemberley.

'Don't worry, old fellow, I've no intention of seeing her again – either here or anywhere else. I have my family around me and have no need for anyone else.'

'Do you intend to ride with us this morning? I thought I'd take my guests up on the moors whilst the weather is clement.'

Bingley shook his head. 'I have business to attend to, but I'd much prefer to come with you. I believe everyone is dining here tonight. Come to think of it, I reckon Jane's indisposition has been brought on by the necessity to organise this dinner party. It will be the first time we've entertained on such a grand scale.'

'But not the first time that you have, Bingley. I well remember the ball at Netherfield. The white soup was the talk of the neighbourhood for weeks.'

* * *

When Mary didn't appear for breakfast Lizzy decided to intervene. Her sister couldn't be allowed to moulder in her room a moment longer. The gentlemen had already eaten and left for their ride. She made sure the remaining guests were comfortably settled before excusing herself.

Mary didn't have her own sitting room, but her bedchamber was sufficiently spacious to allow for a third of it to be furnished for sitting. Lizzy hesitated for a second, wondering if she should walk straight in or knock and wait to be invited.

Instead she tapped on the door and then opened it. 'Good morning, Mary, you will no doubt be aware that no tray has been fetched to you. If you want to eat you must come down and join us.'

The girl had been staring morosely out of the window – but was elegantly attired and quite ready to descend if she so desired. She turned and scowled at Lizzy. 'I didn't ask to come here; I know I'm not welcome. Mama insisted and Papa has closed the house so I had no choice.'

'What happened last year must be forgotten. I require you to understand something, Mary – you were not invited to attend our Christmas festivities for that reason. However, Fitzwilliam and I want to include you in our family again. I can promise you no mention will be made of the events in London when you betrayed our trust and caused Georgiana to be abducted by Wickham.'

'Even if you do not speak of it, everyone else will do so and I shall be ostracised.'

'That's fustian and you know it, my dear. You look very smart – it would be a shame to waste that gown by remaining closeted in here.'

There was no point in continuing this conversation. She had said her piece and even if her sister wasn't hungry she certainly was. If she continued to eat at this pace she would be the size of a whale by the end of the summer.

'We are going to see Kitty and Georgiana after a visit to Bakewell. The gentlemen have gone out for the day and we will not be together until we meet before dinner in the drawing room.' Lizzy didn't wait for a response but turned and left the room.

She was almost at the stairs when Mary joined her. 'I shall come, but only because you are determined to starve me if I don't. I don't intend to enjoy my stay here; I would much prefer to be at home with my music and my writing.'

This last comment caught Lizzy's attention. 'Writing? Have you decided to become an author? What an excellent idea, for it's an ideal occupation for a spinster.'

Her teasing remark had the desired effect. 'Spinster? Please don't call me that. I'm not at my last prayers yet as I've not reached my twentieth anniversary. Do you think I might find myself a husband one day?'

'Dearest Mary, you have blossomed into a lovely young lady. You are intelligent, accomplished and an heiress. I'm sure you will receive more than one offer whilst you are here, but only if you are prepared to join in and enjoy yourself.'

The girl at her side smiled and for the first time looked happy. 'I beg your pardon for being so curmudgeonly, Lizzy. Tell me at once which of the young gentlemen you've invited you think might be suitable for me.'

'Good heavens, I cannot tell you that. You must make up your own mind once you have met them.'

Mary squeezed her arm. 'At least I know that all the gentlemen will be eligible and come from good families or they wouldn't have been invited to Pemberley.'

Lizzy could hardly contradict this erroneous statement. Neither Thomas Hall nor Richard Sinclair would do. Her parents would never allow their remaining unmarried daughter to wed the son of a convicted criminal.

'Mama is in high alt having Lady Finsbury and Lady Sinclair to converse with. I doubt that she'll have another of her sick headaches on this visit.'

On the way down she told Mary about Caroline Bingley's visit and her sister was suitably horrified.

* * *

They set off in two carriages at the appointed time and everyone declared the day a success on their return. There was barely time for them to retire and change before going to the east wing for dinner.

Lizzy hoped to find her husband in their apartment and was not disappointed. 'Fitzwilliam, did you have a pleasant day? We did, and I'm delighted to tell you that our guests are all getting on famously.'

'Yes, most satisfactory, thank you. My cousin arrived half an hour ago and will be joining us for dinner next door.' He didn't look particularly pleased about this prospect and a flicker of unease ran through her.

'I have some worrying news as well. Will you hear mine before I hear yours?' She quickly explained about Mary's determination to find herself a husband and the risks that entailed.

'We will face that obstacle if and when it occurs. You're right to say I have had disturbing information. Hugo believes there might be more than one involved in this treachery. After his investigations as to who might have been out of Town last month he discovered that there were only two members of the inner circle missing, distant cousins, and they had gone together, supposedly to visit a sick relative.'

'Surely that means it will be much easier to prove their treachery? All he has to do is keep them both under surveillance and catch them in the act. There is no longer any need to have the officers here and we can just enjoy the house party.'

'I'm sorry, I didn't explain it properly. The two he suspects are close friends of his and it's quite likely he could also be implicated. Who better than an intelligence officer to have contact with the French? He's frequently abroad and could well have set this in motion.' She was about to protest but he shook his head and she held her tongue.

'I said to him that nobody could possibly suspect the man who was leading the investigation as, by uncovering the traitors, he would find himself arraigned as well. Hugo disagreed with my assessment of the situation. If he was the instigator, then who better to keep his involvement secret whilst revealing the others?'

* * *

Darcy wished he'd not shared this particular piece of information with Lizzy as she had more than enough to contend with keeping all the guests content. Instead of being distressed she smiled ruefully.

'By insisting that we keep no secrets from each other I've had my comeuppance. I'd much prefer not to know your cousin's plight so I intend to forget you told me. Like an ostrich I shall bury my head in the sand and be the perfect, charming hostess whose only objective is to facilitate a betrothal between Colonel Fitzwilliam and a suitable young lady.'

'An excellent solution. We must change if we intend to be downstairs to escort our guests next door. As it takes me half the time it takes you to get ready, I'll go ahead. I can introduce Hugo to those who arrive before you.'

His valet had hot water waiting. He completed his ablutions and was dressed and on his way whilst Lizzy was still in her undergarments. He poked his head around her dressing room door but she waved him away.

Whilst they had visitors he and Lizzy had returned to using

the grand staircase. This led into the entrance hall whereas the smaller, more ancient wooden stairs didn't necessitate this detour, but led directly to the centre of the house.

He paused at the gallery to admire the magnificent carvings of animals and other mythical beasts that intertwined the balustrade. They rarely used the vast reception rooms that stood either side of the hall; they much preferred the more intimate atmosphere of the drawing room.

No doubt the whole place would be festooned with flowers, ribbons and other such frivolities when Pemberley was thrown open for the ball that would be the grand finale of the house party. He frowned. Whether this event took place or not must depend on what happened next week when the war committee arrived.

Hugo was before him and greeted him with enthusiasm. 'Good evening, Darcy, I'm glad you have arrived first, for I've no desire to be obliged to make idle conversation with complete strangers.' He waved his brimming glass of brandy, sending droplets of golden liquid onto the priceless carpet.

'A bit early for that, isn't it, cousin?' Darcy nodded at the glass.

'I consider myself a soldier, rather than a member of the *ton*, my friend. Therefore I drink when I want to. Remarkably fine cognac, I must say. Is it French?'

'I'm sure it is – but it was purchased legitimately many years ago by my father.'

There was no time for further conversation as he could hear people approaching and from the volume of noise he was certain it must be his mother-in-law, and possibly Lady Sinclair as well.

'Good evening, Mr Darcy, Colonel Fitzwilliam, we thought we were tardy, but obviously not.' Lady Sinclair made no further comment and Mrs Bennet said nothing at all. If these unusual circumstances were to remain Darcy thought he might almost enjoy the evening.

He nodded to the ladies as did his cousin. 'Is Miss Bennet to join us tonight?'

'Indeed she is, sir. She's quite recovered from her bilious attack. Will my other daughter and her charming husband be coming?'

'I imagine so, ma'am. Ah! I believe I can hear the remainder of our party arriving.'

He and Lizzy escorted their guests next door where they found that Kitty and Georgiana and their husbands had already arrived. The unmarried members of the group congregated together at one end of the spacious drawing room whilst the Dowager Countess of Finsbury, Lady Sinclair and Mrs Bennet took centre stage. He could not help but notice Mary looked very fine and was attracting the interest of the two single gentlemen. The rest of them milled about by the door. It was strange that there was still no sign of his father-in-law.

'Is your father unwell, Lizzy? Do you think I should go and find him?'

'Would you do that? I cannot imagine what is keeping him so long and Jane won't have dinner announced until he's here.'

Darcy slipped away and entered his own domain by a side door. He found a footman and sent him upstairs to look whilst he checked the billiard room, study and library. Mr Bennet certainly wasn't downstairs. Peterson met him in the central passageway.

'He's nowhere on the premises, sir. I've had all the reception rooms thoroughly searched. I've sent someone to the stables to see if he's there.'

'Thank you. Continue to look. I'll speak to Mrs Bennet and see if she can explain the mysterious disappearance of her husband.'

# 19

Lizzy watched Fitzwilliam leave and could not help but be worried. Her papa was infamous for being late, but even for him this was unusual. He had impeccable manners and wouldn't dream of offending Charles and Jane.

'I think I must go and to speak to Mama. She might know where he is.' She addressed this remark to Kitty and Jane – Georgiana had moved away to join the more lively group at the far end of the room.

'I do hope Darcy finds him quickly as I've no wish for my first grand dinner party to be ruined by our father's tardiness. I shouldn't approach Mama, dearest – she's engrossed in her conversation.'

'I do hope he is not unwell or taken a tumble somewhere,' Kitty said.

'I should delay for another ten minutes and then have your butler announce dinner. I'm sure nothing untoward has taken place and they will all join us in the dining room very shortly.' Lizzy hoped she sounded calm when the very opposite was true.

She caught the eye of the colonel, who was talking to Charles, and he strolled across. 'Could this be anything to do with your business? Do you think my father might have...'

'My dear Lizzy, you are refining too much on this matter. Mr Bennet has probably fallen asleep somewhere and forgotten the time. Remember he is not a young man any more.'

'In which case why is it taking so long to find him and bring him here?'

'Pemberley is a vast establishment, my dear. It could take an hour or more to search every room.' He glanced over her head and his expression changed, then he was his usual charming self again. 'Forgive me, Fitzwilliam wishes to speak to me.'

Lizzy turned and saw immediately her husband was alone. She refused to remain in ignorance of the situation and followed to the far end of the room.

'I'm glad you came over, but you must keep smiling. I've no intention of alarming any of the ladies or ruining Jane's party.'

She placed her hand on his arm, feeling the tension beneath her fingers. 'What's happened? Has Papa taken ill?'

He addressed both of them. 'As far as I can ascertain he's no longer at Pemberley. The reason I've been gone so long was that I ordered every footman to search and there's no sign of him. His valet is certain he didn't put on his outer garments so he obviously didn't intend to go outside.'

Her heart thudded uncomfortably behind the restriction of her bodice. 'What shall we do? We can hardly...'

'We shall go into dinner and pretend that everything is as it should be. I've arranged for a search party to continue to look for him both inside and out. There are a dozen outbuildings that haven't been investigated yet. We will tell Jane and Mrs Bennet that he's had a bilious attack and retired to his room.'

The colonel interrupted. 'Will she not rush to his side?'

She and Fitzwilliam exchanged a glance but Lizzy left her husband to reply.

'They are not exactly a devoted couple. I doubt she will even notice his absence.'

He held out his arm and she placed a hand on it. 'There's been so much deception in our lives of late; I can't bring myself to lie to my sisters, so I'll leave it to you, Fitzwilliam.'

She didn't say she thought him better equipped to tell falsehoods as he'd been deceiving her for months about his so-called business trips. A flicker of annoyance crossed his face but then his lips curved and he marched across to Jane and Charles and told them without hesitation that her father was in his bed, when they both knew he could be anywhere.

The meal seemed interminable and Lizzy could scarcely eat any of the delicious food served to them that night. Neither Fitzwilliam nor his cousin seemed bothered and tucked into each remove with gusto. When Jane stood up to lead the ladies into the drawing room, Lizzy was heartily relieved.

Her sister had promised to play the pianoforte so that the younger members could dance. If Charles and Cousin Hugo were prepared to partner one of the single ladies, they would have sufficient to make up a set.

She drew Jane to one side as soon as they were away from the dining room. 'Forgive me, but I'm feeling unwell. You might have noticed that I was unable to eat anything tonight. Please make my apologies to your guests.'

'You do look rather pale, dearest Lizzy. Perhaps there is some ailment going around the family. After all did not Mary have a bilious attack today and now Papa? Don't worry, you run along. I must search out my music so I can play. I'm an indifferent musician, as you know, but I doubt the young ladies and gentlemen will notice.'

There was no need to ask for her cloak as Lizzy hadn't bothered to wear one. The night was fine and dry and they were only required to walk a few yards from one front door to the other. Not wishing to draw attention to herself, she exited via the side door and entered her own abode in a similar fashion.

She was greeted by Reynolds, the housekeeper. 'Madam, we have searched from top to bottom and not found Mr Bennet anywhere. The outside men have done the same for the outbuildings and are now going through the grounds.'

'Has the search been systematic? Have you checked the servants' quarters? The nursery floor? The attics?'

'None of those, Mrs Darcy – it didn't occur to me that Mr Bennet could be in any of those places.'

'Then please organise it now. I can't imagine he would have gone outside without his coat.'

The housekeeper wrung her hands. 'Do you think the ghosts might have returned and spirited him away like they did Miss Kitty?'

'No, I'm certain they haven't. There will be a much more reasonable explanation. I shall wait in the small drawing room. I require to know when each place has been searched.'

* * *

Darcy had no desire to linger over port – he wanted to return home and find his father-in-law. 'Bingley, forgive me, but I'm concerned about Lizzy. She didn't eat anything and I fear that she might be unwell.'

He didn't wait for permission to leave but stood up, nodded at the other gentlemen and strode out. He'd no need to go into the drawing room to search for his wife, as he was certain she would already have gone home.

Peterson almost ran to his side. In all the years he'd known the man he'd never seen him move so fast. 'Is Mrs Darcy here? Have you found Mr Bennet?'

'Mrs Darcy is in the small drawing room, sir. And no, we haven't found Mr Bennet.'

He was on his way to Lizzy when she appeared. Her skirts were gathered in one hand, and she looked like a lady on a mission. 'Fitzwilliam, I believe I might know where he is. I recall Papa saying he wanted to look in the wine cellar as you'd told him you had bottles dating back a hundred years.'

'Why on earth should he go down there tonight?'

'I think he wanted to find something extraordinary to take next door.' She smiled ruefully. 'I know, the wine is not his to give – but I'm sure he would have spoken to you first.'

'I'll speak to Peterson – I don't want to dash your hopes but I think it unlikely he's down there.' She put her hand in his and he raised it to his lips. 'Don't look so perturbed; I'm sure there will be a happy outcome to this mystery.'

Reynolds was nowhere to be found but a senior footman responded to his summons. 'Has the wine cellar been searched?'

The man looked puzzled by this request. 'I doubt it, sir – it's kept locked. Mr Peterson has the key in his pantry.'

'Fetch it to me.'

The man ran off, and a few moments later returned. 'It's not there. Unless Mr Peterson has taken it, I don't know where it is.'

Lizzy tugged at his arm. 'I told you, Fitzwilliam, my father took the key and has somehow got himself locked in there.'

'In which case I'll go and investigate. Remain here, Lizzy. It's cold and dark down there.'

'I'm not a ninnyhammer, Fitzwilliam. I'm well aware what a wine cellar is like. I'm coming with you.' She stared up at him with a determined look in her eye and he knew when he was defeated.

He snapped his fingers and the footman handed him a candlestick. 'You might as well lead the way; we shall follow close behind.'

It was some time since he'd been in the bowels of the building and he'd forgotten just how dark and unpleasant the cellars were. Lizzy moved closer to him and he put his arm around her waist. Fortunately the passageway was wide enough to allow them to travel side by side.

'It's dank and smells peculiar down here, Fitzwilliam. I'm surprised how high the ceilings are and how well constructed the archways and bays are. Is the wine cellar much further?'

'If I remember rightly it's that door ahead. Look, I can see from here that the key is in the lock.'

She shrugged off his hold and ran pell-mell to the door, dodging past the footman who had hesitated. Darcy followed her and heaved the heavy oak door open. Inside was pitch-dark.

'Papa, are you in here? Are you hurt?'

There was no answer. But he couldn't believe this was a wild goose chase. 'I believe he might be in here. It's a huge space full off alcoves and shelves. It's quite possible he dropped his candlestick and has become disorientated and unable to find his way back.'

'He must be unconscious or he would have answered us. I'll go and fetch more help.'

'An excellent notion. We'll need a trestle to transport him and blankets. Get Reynolds to have Mr Bennet's fire built up and have bed-warmers put through his sheets.'

The musty smell of ancient wine filled his nostrils. He told the footman to look into the bays on the right-hand side and he'd do the same on the left. He continued to call but got no response. Then he saw a shape sprawled on the floor.

'Mr Bennet, can you hear me? Take heart, sir, we'll soon have you safe and warm again.' He dropped to his knees in the dirt and placed his candlestick beside him. The footman crouched down, holding his candle steady so it illuminated the crumpled figure.

Darcy was relieved to find his father-in-law still had a pulse and that his skin was warm. He checked for broken limbs or anything that could have caused this catastrophic collapse. There was no sign of any injury. His initial optimism faded. If Bennet hadn't hit his head then he might well have had an apoplexy, which would be far worse.

He took off his jacket and tucked it around the unconscious man and then propped himself against the wall and placed the patient's head in his lap. His beloved Lizzy would be devastated if she lost her parent, as would all her sisters.

'My boy, don't look so downhearted. I'm not about to kick the bucket just yet.'

Darcy blinked back unwanted tears and looked down at the smiling face of his father-in-law. 'What happened, sir? How do you come to be in this predicament?'

'I was nosing about admiring your claret and dropped my candlestick. I became disorientated and walked into the wall. How long have I been down here? I must have ruined dear Jane's dinner party.' He attempted to sit up but Darcy gently restrained him.

'You ruined nothing, sir. We told everyone that you had retired to bed with a bilious attack. Lizzy worked out that you must be in here somewhere. Excellent – I can hear the rescue party approaching.'

Despite his protests Mr Bennet was safely installed on the

trestle after being enveloped in warm blankets. With Lizzy holding his hand and offering comfort, he was carried briskly through the cellars and, with some difficulty, to his own apartment.

'Has the physician been sent for, Lizzy? Your father was unconscious for some time. His head injury must be attended to.'

The patient, now installed comfortably in his own bed, looked remarkably robust. 'I've no need to see a doctor, Darcy. I've a sizeable lump on the back of my head but nothing more. What I need is something to eat and drink, not fussing over.' He waved both hands in a gesture of dismissal. 'Return to Jane and Bingley – you must miss no more of this jolly evening on my account.'

'If you're quite sure, Papa, then I will leave you in peace.'

Once she was sure she could not be overheard, Lizzy voiced her concerns. 'He has no bump on his head. I checked myself. He had a seizure of some kind. I think we should send for the doctor whatever he says to the contrary.'

'My father suffered from something similar and there was nothing a physician could do that we're not already doing.'

'Did your father die from his attack?' Her voice was commendably even, but her posture showed her concern.

* * *

Lizzy watched his face, praying she wouldn't hear the news she feared. He gathered her close and once she was warm in his embrace he answered her question.

'My father suffered several of these minor attacks over a period of many years before finally succumbing to a major seizure. I'm sure it will be the same for your papa.'

'Thank God. Do you think we should tell my mother? I well

remember how she almost succumbed to her hysteria when she thought he might be killed in a duel with Wickham. I believe her concern is more the fact that the house and estate will go to the odious Mr Collins than for any affection for my father. She's more delicate than she appears and I fear her reaction might exacerbate the situation.'

'Are you suggesting that Mrs Bennet's behaviour could cause another apoplexy?'

'I am. He must be kept calm and comfortable; having my mother weeping and wailing over him would do nothing to aid his recovery.'

'In which case, my love, I'll be guided by you. I'll have Doctor Bevan call in tomorrow as a precaution but we'll tell no one what actually happened. Both Kitty and Jane are increasing – it might be best if they didn't know either.'

'You're right, Fitzwilliam. I've no need to go next door again but, now the worry is over, I find my appetite has returned. If Cook is preparing a tray for my father she can do the same for me.'

'Return to our rooms, sweetheart; I'll join you there soon. I'll speak to Reynolds for you.'

The tray arrived before he did and she was already halfway through her supper when he joined her.

'I checked on Mr Bennet and he's enjoying his meal as much as you are. I've spoken to Peterson and Reynolds and we can pray that none of the servants will gossip about the events of this evening.'

'I've been thinking about that, my love. I don't see how we can keep secret the fact that our entire staff both inside and out were involved in the search for my father.'

His smile, as always, righted her world. 'Of course I didn't intend to maintain the fiction of his bilious attack. We will tell everyone that he got shut into the wine cellar, but is none the worse for his experience. I sent word next door that all is well, so we can retire confident tonight's drama is over.'

'Would you object if I invited my parents and Mary to remain here for a few months – at least until Kitty and Jane are delivered?'

'They will be very welcome. Our home is large enough to accommodate half a dozen families as well you know. As long as we don't have to keep *all* the guests for months I shall be content.'

'I meant to ask you, Fitzwilliam, what did your cousin say about the likelihood that neither Sir Robert nor Mr Hall will come here?'

'We haven't discussed the possibility. To tell you the truth I am heartily sick of the whole business. I'm sure this matter could have been resolved without involving bringing the suspects to my home.' He rubbed his eyes and, with a flick, untied his stock. 'I can only surmise that Mr Perceval is so unpopular in London at the present that Hugo deemed it safer to keep his machinations away from the scrutiny of the prime minister's detractors.'

Whilst he'd been talking she finished the last delectable morsels of her supper and was now ready to retire. 'I can't remember having such a prodigious appetite before. If I continue in this way everyone will imagine that I'm in an interesting condition too.'

His eyes widened and he snatched her from her chair. 'Of course you are with child – it must be more than two months since you had your last monthly flow. Why didn't I realise it before now?'

'It has been some time, but you know I'm not someone who can work out these things with any exactitude. Last time I was unwell from the outset and scarcely ate at all in the first few months. I haven't felt nauseous at all so, much as I wish that I was, I don't believe I can be pregnant.'

'There is one way we can be sure...'

'If you think I'm going to endure the indignity of an examination by Doctor Bevan you can forget all about it.' She stepped away from him and walked briskly into their shared bedchamber. 'I'm going to bed. I don't intend to discuss it any further.'

In two strides he was ahead of her, blocking her way; his eyes glinted and she recognised the signs. He had more than sleep on his mind.

# 20

Darcy was certain he was correct in his assumptions. Lizzy was increasing. He was sure if he looked at her without her garments on he would be able to detect any changes to her shape. She had recovered her slim figure within weeks of producing the twins, so any roundness in the belly or fullness of the breast would be immediately noticeable.

Although they indulged in vigorous lovemaking more often than most couples she was a modest woman and he rarely saw her as God intended. It had taken him weeks to persuade her to remove her nightgown when they were intimate.

'My darling, I'm quite sure that not every pregnancy is the same. The fact that you feel well and are eating more could mean that this time you are not expecting twins.'

He saw the glimmer of hope in her eyes. 'I did think I might be a month ago, but decided I was mistaken.' She ran her hands over her body. 'I can't feel any difference.'

Lizzy took little persuading to remove her clothes and stand naked in front of him. 'You are with child – I am absolutely certain. Your breasts are bigger and there's a slight curve to your belly.'

Her look of joy almost unmanned him. Then she flung herself into his arms and he forgot about everything apart from showing her how much he loved her.

When Dr Bevan examined his father-in-law later, he confirmed what they suspected. 'Mr Bennet suffered a mild seizure. He has fully recovered and can continue his life as normal after another day of rest. It might be many years before he is so afflicted again or he might be unfortunate and be struck down much sooner.'

'Is there anything he can do to prevent such a thing happening?'

'No, Mr Darcy, nature will take its course. He must continue his life as normal – although if he was a heavy drinker, or ate to excess, I would suggest he was more moderate. But as this is not the case there's nothing he needs to do in order to prolong his life.' The doctor picked up his bag and prepared to leave.

'There is another matter I require to discuss with you before you depart.' Darcy described Lizzy's symptoms.

'Congratulations, sir, you will be a parent again in the autumn. There's no need for me to examine Mrs Darcy, unless you wish me to – she is obviously perfectly healthy.'

'Thank you, Doctor Bevan, it's good to have one's opinions confirmed by you. Perhaps you could call in and see my wife when you visit Mrs Bingley again?'

The matter happily decided between them the doctor left and Darcy went to give Lizzy the good news. However, when he arrived in the Great Hall he was met by Peterson.

'A letter has come by express for you, sir. A reply is required.'

Darcy removed the missive and stepped aside so he could

read it in the morning light that streamed through the long windows. He scanned the contents and then turned to the butler.

He needed to speak to Hugo and Lizzy about this matter, preferably together to save him having to repeat himself. 'Find Colonel Fitzwilliam and have him join me in the study immediately. Do you know the whereabouts of my wife?'

'Yes, sir, she is in the small drawing room with Miss Bennet and the other young ladies. Do you need me to send a message to her?'

'Do that. Make sure the messenger has rested. He'll have his reply within the hour.'

The study was one place he could be sure he wouldn't be interrupted by any of his guests. Indeed, only Lizzy was welcome there without an invitation.

He paced the room, trying to marshal his thoughts so he could explain the matter succinctly when they both arrived. Ten minutes passed before there were hurrying footsteps – Lizzy was on her way. Then there was the heavy tread of his cousin.

They arrived together and he ushered them in before closing the door firmly behind them. 'I've just received this letter from Sir Robert.' He tossed it across to Hugo but continued his explanation for Lizzy's benefit. 'He enquires most politely if he and Hall will still be welcome here after the unpleasant business in Town. I can't discern from his writing if he assumes we know what actually happened or if we believe the fabrication about blackmail that we put about.'

'If you're asking me if I'm happy to have them here, then my answer is in the affirmative. I believe that their presence is essential if Cousin Hugo's plot is to succeed.' She frowned before continuing. 'As to your other question, I've no idea. If that's all you wish to say to me, dearest, I must return to my guests.'

'Yes. No. God dammit! I didn't intend to make this a public

announcement. The doctor confirmed our suspicions that there is to be another happy event at Pemberley in the autumn.'

'Might I be the first to offer my congratulations on your happy news?' Hugo said with a smile.

'Thank you, sir. I'm so happy I could burst.' Her eyes brimmed with amusement. 'Perhaps not the most felicitous choice of phrase in the circumstances. Pray excuse me, gentlemen, I must go at once and tell my sisters my good news.'

She rushed off, her steps light and looking even more beautiful than usual. He raised an eyebrow in the direction of his cousin who had just completed reading the missive.

'Well, Hugo, shall I tell this traitor he and his crony may come?'

'If you will. As to the matter of whether he knows that we are aware of his treachery I assume that he doesn't. He would have expected us to hand him over to the authorities if we knew he was passing on state secrets. Therefore, unlikely as it might seem, I must surmise he thinks us in ignorance of the true state of affairs.'

'I only met him a couple of times and wasn't impressed by his intelligence. His son, I must say, is a different prospect. I will have a letter sent to young Hall and his family and make sure they know that they are welcome here despite what happened.'

* * *

Lizzy was occupied the next few days welcoming new guests as they arrived. Sir Robert and Mr Hall turned up and Fitzwilliam said they were behaving impeccably. Thomas Hall, his mother and sister were the last to come, but despite their delayed appearance they soon blended in with the other guests.

Mary had blossomed and was now as popular with the young

ladies as she was with the young gentlemen. This had not gone to her head, however, and Lizzy believed her sister had finally grown up. The only worrying aspect was that Mary appeared to be partial to Richard Sinclair.

Her father remained in his room, ostensibly resting from his experience, but she rather suspected he preferred peace and quiet upstairs rather than the hectic toing and froing of downstairs. The twins were safely installed with their nanny and nursemaids in the east wing with their cousin Charlotte.

Her mother had much to say on this matter. 'Elizabeth, surely your sister has more than enough to do without burdening her with your children? She is in an interesting condition and any added upset might be bad for her and the infant.'

Lizzy and Darcy had decided not to announce their good news as she was feeling perfectly well and didn't intend to be treated as if she was an invalid. Her mother's remarks prompted her to reveal that she too was with child.

'Good heavens! Am I to become a grandmother three times over yet again? My dear girl, you should not be dashing about the place as you are. You must allow your mama to take over the running of the household whilst you have this house party here.'

'That's most considerate of you, but this time I've never felt better. We wondered if you and Papa would like to remain here until after all three of us have been delivered. Mary appears to be enjoying herself and I'm sure will be happy to remain until the autumn.'

'Stay at Pemberley? Are you quite sure Mr Darcy is in agreement?'

'This was his suggestion and I thought it an excellent one. Things will be much calmer when our guests depart in two weeks' time and we will be able to enjoy the summer together.'

'I must speak to you about Mary. Lady Sinclair tells me that her son wishes to make an offer for your sister. Imagine that! One of my daughters will eventually be a member of the aristocracy.'

Lizzy had difficulty hiding her dismay. 'They scarcely know each other and I'm sure neither of them will do anything precipitous. He is a pleasant young man but I cannot like his father.' She hesitated and then decided to continue. 'I must tell you that he was involved with Mr Hall in some unpleasantness in London whilst we were there. Would you still be happy for Mary to become entangled with the family if his father was forced to leave the country?' Even this was revealing far too much, but she had no option.

Her mother clutched her bosom in dramatic style. 'Sir Robert a villain? I'm sure that you're mistaken, for he is a most charming man. Lady Sinclair is my dearest friend and I won't hear a word against her husband.' She stalked off and Lizzy swallowed the bile in her throat. This was an absolute disaster and of her own making. Her mother would go immediately to Lady Sinclair and soon word would be all around the house.

Both Fitzwilliam and the colonel would be furious with her – and rightly so. She had been given information in the strictest confidence and she had betrayed their trust. The gentlemen had organised an impromptu game of cricket for all the guests who wished to play – even the young ladies were included if they so wished.

She ran to the rear of the house and out onto the terrace. The warm mid-April sunshine was perfect for playing outdoor games. She put her hand up to shade her eyes and squinted across the parterre in the hope she might be able to see who was taking part in the game. Even from her vantage point she was unable to see more than their heads.

There was no option but to move closer so she could see

properly. As she was about to descend the steps someone called her back.

'There you are – I've been searching for you.'

'Fitzwilliam, I've done something absolutely dreadful. I was looking for you or your cousin in order to warn you.' She quickly explained what had taken place and instead of being angry he laughed.

'That explains why Mrs Bennet is causing such a stir in the garden room next door. Bingley just came over to warn me that trouble is brewing.'

'I don't understand. Have I not ruined everything?'

He dropped an affectionate kiss on top of her head. 'You didn't reveal anything important – merely repeated what might well be common knowledge by now. Certainly Lady Sinclair is well aware that her husband is treading on very thin ice indeed. She will confirm what you said and this will prevent the romance between Mary and her son from progressing.'

'Actually I think it might have the reverse effect on my sister. I think she secretly envied Lydia's escapades although outwardly she always disapproved. She might well find the notion of becoming entangled with the son of a villain romantic.'

'I like the young man. Whatever happens to his father, Mrs Bennet is quite right to say that Mary would become Lady Sinclair eventually if she marries into the family. Your sister has sufficient money to keep them both, so why not let the relationship continue?'

'I've no intention of interfering. I just hope that she doesn't choose to go ahead for the wrong reasons. There is something else that worries me – what if Mr Sinclair is pursuing her to gain respectability for himself and his sister?'

'You refine too much on the matter, Lizzy. There's nothing we can do about it either way. Mr Bennet can refuse his permission if he so wishes, so we must leave it to him. By the way, do you think he intends to remain closeted in his apartment indefinitely?'

'I hear on reliable authority that he makes clandestine forays to the library in the middle of the night. As long as he has books to read I believe he will remain in hiding. He has never enjoyed socialising.'

'I wasn't looking for you to discuss Mary's romance but to tell you we are to expect the first of the gentlemen from London to arrive after dark this evening. Whatever is going to happen will take place in the next two days.'

* * *

'Will the villains be apprehended by their peers? Where will they be put until they can be transported to London to face trial?'

'Hugo has not thought fit to tell me those details. Suffice it to say that I shall stay as far away from the procedure as I possibly can. I have no intention of standing in the line of fire if I can avoid it.'

'Good gracious, Fitzwilliam, I never expected you to be personally involved in the matter. You are not a soldier as the others are.'

A flicker of annoyance ran through him at her words. He might not be a natural killer of men but he was quite capable of pointing a gun and firing it if necessary. 'How perspicacious of you, my dear. If you had not pointed it out so clearly I might have thought myself a soldier in disguise.'

She chuckled at his sally and then dashed off to attend to some domestic duty or other. If she was not so obviously blooming he might have been concerned about how much she had to do. His lips curved as she vanished around the corner.

When the autumn came he would be inundated with infants – not only father to three, or possibly four, children of his own but also uncle to three more.

In his opinion it was a great shame that unless one restrained from lovemaking, one's wife was obliged to produce a new offspring possibly every year. Good God! This meant that Lizzy, who was only three-and-twenty, could have a further dozen children if they continued to share a bed.

There must be some way of preventing conception without abstaining from bedroom sport. He would begin to make discreet enquiries and hopefully come up with a satisfactory answer to this conundrum. Not every married couple had a constant stream of new babies in their nursery. So either the husband satisfied his needs outside of marriage, which he was not prepared to do, or there was another solution and he intended to find it.

He had politely declined to participate in the game of cricket that was taking place outside and had been somewhat mystified by the fact that his cousin had agreed to take part. He made his way outside, along the parterre, until he could see the players.

There were sufficient numbers to make up almost a full team for each side. At least half the young ladies had had the courage to join in such a robust sport. The game was progressing with a deal of merriment and nobody seemed to be taking it very seriously.

At first he couldn't see his cousin – his side must be batting as he certainly wasn't in the fielding team. He scanned the group sitting on chairs but couldn't see him – he must be standing to one side. Yes, Hugo was deep in conversation with Miss Hall and they were both ignoring the efforts of their teammates. Presumably both participants were aware of Mr Hall's precarious situation and neither seemed put off by it.

He shrugged and left them to it. Bingley wasn't among those

exerting themselves on the field, so he would search out his friend and see how things were in the east wing. He had no intention of going in, not whilst the three redoubtable ladies were holding court there. With luck he might find him at the stables.

These housed both his and Bingley's horses and no doubt would now have many more filling out the barns. The weather was more clement and the spring grass growing, which meant that half the mounts could be turned out during the day.

He'd not reached the yard when he was hailed by the very person he was looking for. 'Darcy, shall we go and visit Jonathan or Adam? If we remain on the premises we will be inveigled into some activity or other. Both Jane and Lizzy seemed determined everyone must participate in something today. Mr Bennet has the right idea hiding away in his apartment.'

'I was going to suggest that very thing. The Old Rectory is nearer, so Adam and Kitty will have the pleasure of our company for a while.'

They cantered and galloped across country and arrived at the village far quicker than they should have. He reined back to a walk, thus allowing his mount to cool down. 'I believe it's a musical evening tonight and we will have to endure an hour or more of caterwauling and indifferent piano playing.'

Bingley laughed. 'As long as I don't have to do either I'm quite content to listen. You seem rather blue-devilled today, my friend. Are you concerned about Lizzy overdoing it?'

'No, I might as well tell you as you are privy to everything else. Hugo's colleagues arrive under the cover of darkness tonight. That's why it's essential to have everyone in the music room and not prowling about outside.'

'Well, the colonel seems remarkably sanguine about the whole business – if he was worried surely he wouldn't be gallivanting about the place playing cricket and flirting with the daughter of one of the traitors?'

'This business seems doomed to failure. I cannot think why these men agreed to travel to Derbyshire.'

Bingley looked puzzled – but he was not famous for his sharp wit.

'They could have met in perfect secrecy a dozen places much closer to Town. It doesn't make sense to have come so far,' Darcy explained.

'These military coves are a strange lot and it's best not to get involved, in my opinion.' Bingley nodded sagely. 'But seeing as you are, I should leave them to it. We can pretend to enjoy the entertainment this evening and the matter will be resolved without your assistance.'

Darcy laughed. His friend never failed to cheer him up. 'I sincerely hope that your summation of the situation is correct. Come, we shall put the matter aside and enjoy our visit. I can see King at the window waving to us.'

# 21

The twins were content in their new surroundings and Lizzy was confident they would come to no harm living with Jane and Charles for the next few days. Her mother approached as she tried to slide past the drawing room without being seen.

'There you are, Elizabeth. I must tell you that I've debated the matter you mentioned with her ladyship and am satisfied dear Richard will make Mary an ideal husband despite his father's peccadilloes.'

'Have you discussed the matter with Papa? After all, it's he who must give his permission if they want to become betrothed.'

Her mother's mouth pursed. 'He will be as happy as I am when I explain the situation. Dear Richard cannot be held responsible for his father's actions as I'm sure you will agree.'

Lizzy didn't wish to continue the conversation in case she revealed the true state of affairs. Whatever her mother's feelings on the subject were, if Sir Robert was arraigned her father would never agree to a union between Mary and Richard.

'They have only known each other a few days and I'm sure

that Mary is far too sensible to commit herself so soon. Please excuse me, I have so much to do and must return home immediately.' She dashed off, not allowing her mother to reply.

No sooner had she set foot indoors than she was accosted by Reynolds with a list of queries regarding the arrival of the secret visitors. Obviously, it had been necessary to take both the housekeeper and the butler into their confidence, and no doubt half a dozen members of staff would also be aware there were extra guests lurking in a part of the house that was never used.

'I'll leave this in your capable hands, Reynolds. Is there anything else?'

'No, ma'am, I'll not hold you up any more. A cold collation will be laid out in the dining room at one o'clock for those who desire to eat.'

The cricket players would be ravenous after all that exercise, so this was a sensible suggestion. 'Make sure that the gong is banged loudly outside so that everyone can hear it.'

* * *

The remainder of the day sped past and allowed her no time to dwell on what might, or might not, happen. Fitzwilliam had returned in high spirits and refused to discuss the affair. They strolled through the house to join their guests in the drawing room where they were all gathered before going in to dine. To her surprise the colonel was there and engaging in an animated discussion about the price of corn with Miss Hall.

'Look at that, Fitzwilliam. If your cousin isn't worried then neither should we be. I'm determined to enjoy myself tonight.'

He grinned and lowered his head to speak quietly into her ear. 'I think it might only be possible to enjoy oneself, sweetheart, if one was stone deaf.'

'Do you really think it will be as bad as that? I've no idea of the musical talents of the other guests but Mary, Kitty, Georgiana and I are all competent pianists. Both you and Charles can hold a tune as can Jane. After we have performed there will scarcely be time for anyone else, so don't look so perturbed.'

'I've absolutely no intention of participating, as well you know. It would be unpardonable if only the family got the opportunity to shine; you must allow anyone who wishes to take centre stage to do so before you or your sisters.'

She sighed. 'In which case, my dear, it will be a lottery as to whether we enjoy ourselves or not.'

'Do you not have a list of those wishing to perform tonight so that you could draw up a programme?'

'Good heavens! Of course I do – I've become quite featherbrained of late. Come with me and we can arrange things together. I left a list in the study on your desk and fully intended to do exactly what you've just suggested but quite forgot.'

She found the piece of paper where she'd left it and read out the names of those who'd signed and what they intended to do to entertain the audience. Fitzwilliam, who had the neater hand, compiled the programme.

'There – we have three duets plus accompanists, a recitation and a variety of willing pianists. More than enough for an evening, don't you think?'

'Indeed I do. I'm glad that we have left Georgiana and Kitty on the list as they play so beautifully together. I must say that I'm relieved our other guests have stepped up as I'm not sure Mary will actually wish to participate.'

They hurried back to the drawing room to find Peterson hovering anxiously at the doors to the dining room, waiting to announce dinner.

In some grand houses the owners insisted that guests entered in order of rank, but here, as in most other establishments, the guests made their own way in. Only two seats were reserved at the head of the table and these were for herself and her husband. Fitzwilliam had decreed she sit with him and not at the far end of the table as would be normal in other houses.

Tonight her appetite had returned and, despite having devoured a substantial meal at one o'clock, she was able to do justice to the appetising array of removes that appeared on the table. At Pemberley they preferred not to keep country hours and rarely sat down to table before six o'clock.

When eventually she stood to lead the ladies out, it wasn't to the drawing room, but to the music room where the elegant gilt chairs from the ballroom had been set out in rows. Fitzwilliam had written this evening's order of appearances in his clear, flowing style so that everyone concerned knew what was to take place.

The gentlemen didn't linger over port this evening and soon the room was filling up and the musical entertainment began. Not everyone who participated was as talented as Georgiana but all acquitted themselves well. As the final applause faded away she noticed that Sir Robert and Mr Hall were no longer in the room.

* * *

Darcy saw Lizzy scanning the rows of chairs and understood at once why she raised a quizzical eyebrow. Not only was his cousin missing, but also the two gentlemen they were hoping to trick into revealing the real traitor.

'God knows how those two already know that there's a meeting going on elsewhere in the house,' he whispered.

'Peterson told me the last of them only arrived just before the entertainment began.'

She clutched his arm. 'You promised me that you wouldn't become personally involved in this issue. Leave it to those who are trained to deal with such things.'

Someone called her name and she was obliged to move across in order to speak to them. She was quite right – he had given his word he wouldn't put himself in danger. He would take the servants' passageways and by doing so would remain out of sight but would still be able to discover what was taking place. Lizzy didn't understand that as the owner of Pemberley it was ingrained in him to be involved with anything that took place under his roof.

Whilst his guests were milling about discussing the musical entertainment they had just listened to he took the opportunity to slip away. It took minutes to drift into the gun room and arm himself with a loaded pistol. He doubted this would be necessary – but in his experience it did no harm to be prepared.

Unfortunately his evening rig didn't have the deep inside pockets that his everyday jacket did. There was no option but to tuck it into the waistband of his trousers and hope that the distinctive shape was disguised by the fall of his coat.

He paused for a moment to visualise the maze of passageways and stairs that dissected this huge establishment. There was no necessity for taking a candlestick as wall sconces were lit everywhere, thus allowing his staff to move about freely even when carrying unpleasantly filled receptacles.

The route he must take was now clear in his head. He checked nobody was watching him before pushing open one of the cleverly disguised doors in the wall and stepping through. What the hell he was going to say if he came face to face with a member of his staff he'd no idea – but hoped this circumstance would not occur.

The footmen and parlourmaids would be busy serving tea and supper in the drawing room, or restoring the music room and taking chairs back to the ballroom. As he made his way along the narrow corridor he caught the occasional sound of laughter coming through the wall. Then he could hear nothing apart from his own breathing.

He must now be in the west wing and should be able to pick up clues to his whereabouts from any voices he heard.

Something crashed against the wall and he fell backwards. He froze, fearing the noise he'd made might have revealed his presence. Then he heard voices he recognised.

'God dammit, Sinclair, I don't like creeping about the place. I almost went head first in the darkness. If we're discovered, how are we to explain our presence here?'

'My man said there's something havey-cavey going on in this part of the house. He recognised one of the horses as belonging to Brigadier Stanley – what the devil is that man doing so far from London? It has to be a cabal – you know as well as I do that trouble is afoot in the prime minister's camp. Knowledge of this should earn us a pretty penny.'

Sinclair moved away from the wall and Darcy had to strain to hear his words. 'You're right. Don't you think it's damn strange they should choose the very place that we happen to be to discuss their conspiracy?'

'Coincidence – a fortunate coincidence. We need to come up with something worth having for our next drop after the rubbish we passed over last time. This could be the very thing we need. It will be the last time – we both agreed about that,' Hall replied.

The two men moved away. Darcy pushed himself upright and

took several steadying breaths. They were right to be suspicious, as this wasn't going to end well for either of them.

If these two thought it strange a meeting should have been called in Derbyshire rather than one of the Home Counties, surely the real traitors – the members of this inner circle who were revealing state secrets – must also be concerned?

This entire enterprise had been flawed from the start. He should never have agreed to help – it would have saved him a deal of expense, and the aggravation of having a house full of unwanted guests. Too late for regrets; he was committed to this venture and must see it through.

He made sure, on resuming his cautious progress, that he was ready for any sudden noises and wouldn't react so violently a second time.

If he remembered rightly there was an exit just ahead, so he must be extra vigilant not to place his hand on it and inadvertently alert anyone to his presence. Although he could no longer hear Hall or Sinclair, there was the definite sound of men talking coming from a few yards ahead of him. He edged his way past the door that would allow a member of staff access to this chamber and moved closer so he could place his ear on the panelling.

What he heard almost made him exclaim out loud. He was quite sure his cousin would be equally shocked by the conversation taking place.

* * *

Lizzy moved from group to group playing the perfect hostess. If this house party had been arranged for any other reason than the apprehension of the traitors then she would be able to enjoy it. Entertaining so many guests was most gratifying especially when they were all so complimentary. Her husband had been gone for an unconscionable time, so she would send a footman in search of him before his absence was noticed.

More than an hour had gone by before both he and his cousin rejoined the company. Sir Robert and Mr Hall had also wandered back in a short while ago. All four gentlemen appeared to have a great deal to say.

'Fitzwilliam, Cousin Hugo, might I enquire where you two have been for so long? As the ostensible reason for this gathering is to find you a suitable bride, cousin, then it behoves you to be here.'

He nodded but didn't respond and marched smartly away to immediately engage Miss Hall in conversation. She tapped her foot and stared pointedly at her husband.

'We have all been duped – the military gentlemen have not come here to discuss secrets but to entertain their mistresses without their wives being aware of it.'

Her mouth dropped open. 'Are you telling me that Pemberley is being used as a house of ill repute?'

He nodded solemnly, but his eyes were glinting with amusement. 'I fear that is the case. Hugo should have realised when he saw who was coming that there was more to this than he understood. There are notable absences and those missing are the gentlemen with happy, stable marriages.'

'I still don't quite understand how this can have happened. I always believed your cousin to be an intelligent man, but was obviously mistaken.'

'No, you're right in your assumption. In his desire to apprehend the traitor in the inner circle he allowed himself to be bamboozled by these reprehensible rakes.'

She smiled but then something else occurred to her. 'Am I to take it that you have been eavesdropping on the debauchery, my love?'

'I'm afraid so and I can assure you I've been scarred for life by what I heard.' He chuckled and glanced in the direction of the other two gentlemen. 'I should think that Sinclair and Hall must be disappointed they are not to glean some nuggets of information.'

'Why didn't Peterson inform you of the true state of affairs?'

'I believe he thought that I had sanctioned their debauchery and this was why I requested the guests were put in a private part of the house.'

'Good heavens! This gets worse and worse. You can be very sure word will filter around the house before the end of the house party and we'll never be considered respectable again.'

'Smile, my love, your scowl is attracting unwanted attention from your sisters. They will be over here in a moment to do battle on your behalf.'

She took his hand and led him purposefully from the drawing room where they could talk without risk of being overheard or observed. 'You must evict the unwanted tenants immediately. The military gentlemen may remain, but their light-skirts will not spend another night under this roof. They will be gone before anyone gets up tomorrow.'

He knew her well enough to accept that he had no choice. 'Hugo and I will speak to them as soon as everyone else has retired. To try and do so now might well provoke exactly the sort of scenes we're hoping to avoid. I'll alert the stables that the carriages will be needed at dawn.'

'Presumably your cousin doesn't intend to apprehend Sir Robert or Mr Hall whilst they are under our roof? I would much prefer it if he didn't.'

'I gather that your sister Mary is interested in Richard Sinclair – are the feelings reciprocated?'

Just talking about this made Lizzy feel unwell. 'I fear she is determined on the match. Mama is equally enthusiastic as you might imagine. Even your wealth and prestige is as nothing beside the thought of having a daughter marry into the aristocracy.'

Her husband didn't seem particularly bothered by this news. 'As Hugo also appears to be enamoured with Miss Hall, both sides of the family have become entangled with unsuitable partners. Therefore it's a distinct possibility we will be disgraced one way or the other.'

His mouth twitched and she couldn't prevent herself from smiling. It was indeed quite ridiculous that the Darcy family had not one, but three disastrous events about to break over their heads.

'We survived the ghosts and the scandal, but I fear having a spy at Pemberley might prove our undoing.' A gurgle of laughter escaped. 'That is always supposing our house being used as a bordello does not become a topic of drawing room conversation.'

He slid his arm around her waist and drew her close. 'Well, sweetheart, we cannot complain that our life in the country is dull. Let's not forget the unexpected arrival of Miss Bingley and her betrothed a few weeks ago.'

All desire to laugh vanished. 'I wish you hadn't reminded me. That pernicious woman has caused nothing but trouble in this family and I sincerely hope she never returns.'

'Of whom are you speaking so vehemently, Lizzy?' Charles had drifted up unnoticed beside them. 'I assume it was my sister. I give you my word she will not be seen at Pemberley ever again. I've had my lawyers contact her as I could not bring myself to write.'

Jane was beckoning to her most urgently. 'Please excuse me, I must see what is agitating my sister.'

As she hurried away, she heard Charles laughing and guessed

that her husband had told his friend the true state of affairs. She hoped she would never have to discuss the topic with any other members of her family.

As she made her way across the room, it occurred to her that the traitors might not actually be amongst those who had come with their mistresses, so the whole enterprise had been doomed to failure from the outset.

# 22

'On reflection, Bingley, I'm wondering if Sinclair and Hall will leak the information to my guests.'

'I doubt it, Darcy; they would have to explain what they were doing creeping about the place. More to the point – have you spoken to the colonel about his intentions towards the girl?'

'Not as yet but I intend to as soon as he leaves her side for a moment. It's beyond the bounds of credulity to assume he's going to offer for her in the circumstances. His career would be over if he married the daughter of a traitor.'

'All this excitement has made me a trifle peckish, so I'm going to find myself something to eat. Are you joining me?'

Darcy shook his head. 'I believe I might insinuate myself between the happy couple, as Mrs Hall has called her daughter away for some reason.'

He walked swiftly to his cousin and gripped his elbow firmly before the man could escape. 'Hugo, we need to talk. My study – now – if you please.'

His cousin tensed beneath his hand but then sighed with what could only be construed as resignation. 'Very well, my friend, I shall come with you although I know of what you wish to speak.'

They strode side by side to the designated chamber and Darcy didn't speak again until they were safely closeted inside. 'Lizzy is furious with you for bringing those bits of muslin to Pemberley. They are to be evicted at dawn tomorrow.'

Hugo shifted from foot to foot like a schoolboy caught out in a prank. 'I'll be the laughing stock at Horse Guards after this debacle. If I'd examined the list of those that had accepted the invitation more closely, I would have realised something wasn't right. All these gentlemen are renowned for their cavalier attitude to their marriage vows. God knows if there is a traitor amongst them but being here is not going to reveal it, that's for sure.' He shrugged. 'I can't apologise sufficiently for this debacle. If I'd known for one instant that they intended to bring their doxies with them I'd have put a stop to it.'

'I don't understand how they believed there would be sufficient accommodation when these women were not invited.'

'That too is my fault. I explained to them that they would be accommodated in a separate wing as I intended to keep their presence secret from your other guests. This gave them *carte blanche*. The whole world knows one could get lost in the hundreds of rooms at Pemberley.'

'The situation is beyond ridiculous and we'll say no more about this issue. Which brings me to my second point: what do you intend to do about Sinclair and Hall? Are they not to be arrested? After all it was they who passed on the secrets to the French, whoever might have given the information to them in the first place.'

Hugo shrugged and wandered disconsolately to the sideboard and poured himself a full glass of brandy before answering. 'That's an even bigger mess as you might imagine. I know this house party was no more than a charade but I find myself enamoured of Miss Hall. My intentions are honourable and I'm sure she reciprocates my feelings but...'

'But you can hardly remain in the military and marry the daughter of a traitor.'

'You have the right of it, Darcy. I don't know what the hell to do – do I offer for her before or after I arrest her father? And at what point do I resign my commission?'

'I'm not sure if you're aware of it, but my sister-in-law, Mary, has set her sights on Richard Sinclair. You can imagine what the reaction of Mrs Bennet and her husband might be when Sir Robert is taken into custody.'

'I can see no happy outcome for any of us. Miss Hall will blame me for her family's disgrace and that might well be the end of my hopes. Not only will I be without a career, but I shall also be without the woman whom I wish to marry.' He dropped his head into his hands – a picture of despair.

Darcy thought for a moment. 'Shall we deal with each subject in turn? Send the gentlemen and their mistresses away first and wait for the dust to settle. There will be time enough to tackle the other two problems.'

'The majority of those cavorting in your west wing are my superiors. It will give me a great deal of pleasure to be in position to give them their marching orders. One of those we originally suspected is amongst the rest of them but I can think of no way to reveal his involvement.'

'Surely there must be some you can rule out categorically? Come – we have a while before everyone retires – let us make a list of who is here and who absent and see if we can make some sense of it.'

After the first hour went by, Darcy believed they had narrowed it down to three possible candidates. None of them were known to him, and only one of them was with the other reprehensible gentlemen in the west wing. 'This brigadier fellow seems the least likely of the three – is there any way we can rule him out too?'

'If word of his misdeeds here reached his wife, there would be hell to pay. I'm sure with a little gentle persuasion, I can convince him to answer a few questions.'

'Are you suggesting blackmail? That doesn't sit well with me.' Darcy pushed back his chair and went to fetch himself a third glass of brandy. 'It's damnably quiet out there – I think my guests have already retired.'

Hugo held out his glass. 'Another for me, if you please. I've no intention of doing anything as unpleasant as blackmail. It should be relatively simple to get him to give me sufficient information to either convict or clear him. He's terrified of his wife.'

Darcy replenished his friend's drink and downed his own. 'I'm going out to the stables but will then go and speak to your cronies. Are you coming with me or do you intend to skulk in here?' His smile took the bite from his words.

'I'd much prefer to remain here but shall not do so. I'd like to solve this case before I resign.'

When they emerged from the study the wall sconces were still flickering, but there was no evidence of either staff or guests. Peterson would be lurking somewhere waiting to douse the remaining lights as soon as he was certain his master was abed.

* * *

Lizzy was satisfied the evening had been a success and none of her guests were as yet aware of the unwanted occupants of the west wing. How her staff had kept the matter secret from the other servants she had no idea, but she was pleased with their loyalty and discretion.

Everyone had either departed or retired, apart from herself and her father. She was disturbed by his expression. He had something to say and she doubted she was going to like what it was. With a sigh of resignation she beckoned him to follow her upstairs to her private sitting room. Once safely inside she gestured towards an armchair and waited until he had flicked aside his coat-tails and settled himself.

'Papa, tell me at once what is troubling you.'

'Your sister is determined to have young Richard Sinclair and Mrs Bennet will not hear a word against the match. However, I don't like Sir Robert; there's something untoward about him.'

She kept her face averted, hoping her disquiet would not be revealed. Although her father was somewhat lackadaisical in his duties as a parent, he was not a stupid man and would immediately recognise her expression for what it was.

'Lizzy, look at me, my dear. There's something you need to tell me before things progress any further.'

Reluctantly she looked up. 'I have been sworn to secrecy, it's a matter of national security and however much I want to tell you the whole, I cannot do so.' No sooner had she spoken than she realised her catastrophic error. She should never have mentioned the words 'national security'.

His eyes widened and then his lips thinned. 'There's no need to say anything else, my dear. He, and that unpleasant friend of his, Hall, must be up to their necks in treasonable activities.' He raised a hand as she was about to protest. 'I'll not have any daughter of mine associated with such a family. She needs my permission and she will not get it. The Bennet family might not be wealthy or important, but they are honourable and loyal to King and Country.'

There was nothing she could say that could remedy the situation. She could hardly lie to her own father. 'What are you going to do? Mama will have a conniption fit when you tell her Mary cannot marry Richard Sinclair. I should never have said anything to you. You must give me your word you will not reveal the reasons behind your refusal.'

He nodded and pushed himself upright. 'Believe me, Lizzy, it gives me no joy to deny Mary her heart's desire. I never thought she would fall in love and I doubt she will do so again. She will remain a spinster and take care of your mother and me in our dotage.'

He left the room without bidding her goodnight and she was too miserable to go after him. Her maid was waiting to help her disrobe and was full of chatter about the other servants. She didn't appear to notice how quiet Lizzy was.

When she was down to her petticoats she stopped the flow of words. 'Thank you, I can do the rest myself. Goodnight. I shall ring when I require you tomorrow morning.'

Somewhat surprised by this abrupt command, but too well-trained to comment, the girl curtsied and slipped away. As soon as she was sure she was alone, Lizzy rummaged through the shelves in the dressing room and found herself a warm, long-sleeved, cambric morning gown, which dropped over her head and did not require any lacing at the back.

She pushed her stockinged feet into indoor slippers, found a suitable wrap, and was ready to find Fitzwilliam and warn him that Pemberley was about to erupt in the most hideous fuss. Dealing with the spectres that had been resident for centuries paled into insignificance in comparison to her mother in one of her spectacular rages.

Where would her husband be? He and his cousin had retreated to the study an age ago – would he still be there? She prayed that he might be because she was certain her father would not wait until the morning to issue his ultimatum.

With her skirts held clear of her feet, she dashed down the wooden staircase that would lead more directly to the study. As she skidded around the corner, she saw Fitzwilliam and Cousin Hugo emerge and turn to stride off in the opposite direction.

Forgetting she was supposed to be a mature and sensible matron, she raised her voice and yelled at him. 'Wait. I must speak to you. Something appalling is about to happen.'

He stopped so abruptly that his cousin cannoned into his back and they both staggered about, as if in their cups, before Fitzwilliam managed to regain his balance. He did not look particularly pleased to see her.

'Good God, Lizzy, what were you thinking? You cannot go about the place yelling like a fishwife.'

She arrived at his side and clutched his arm. She could not help but be aware that Hugo was leaning nonchalantly against the wall, his eyes brimming with amusement. He might find the situation funny, but he would change his tune when she told him what had transpired upstairs.

* * *

His wife seemed unperturbed by his reprimand. 'I must speak to both of you immediately. I've no intention of doing so out here.' She pointed to the study and he exchanged a resigned glance with Hugo before following her inside. When she had revealed the extent of the disaster he was dumbfounded.

Hugo rallied first. 'Mrs Bennet will let the entire establishment into our secret. Sinclair and Hall will take off and I shall be lucky not to be court-martialled.'

Darcy had been thinking the same but an alternative

occurred to him. 'Could you not get to them first? If they agreed to become double agents in return for their immunity...'

'Devil take it! That might work. Lizzy, can you try and forestall Mr Bennet? Explain that both men are working with the government, not against it, and to reveal their identity could place all that has been worked for in grave danger. I need to speak to both gentlemen before the house erupts.'

'Will agreeing to your proposition mean that the families will not be disgraced? That Sir Robert and Mr Hall will no longer be in danger of losing their estates and reputations?'

'I will not be able to get them off entirely. However, if they agreed to live quietly abroad, then I believe I can keep the affair quiet and both Lady Sinclair and Mrs Hall will be able to continue to live their lives untrammelled by unsavoury rumours.'

'I think that will be a solution that appeals to everyone, apart from the gentlemen themselves. Mary will be able to marry Richard Sinclair and you can offer for Miss Hall.'

She didn't wait for confirmation of her statement – they all knew what she said was true. 'I shall expect you in our apartment in due course, Fitzwilliam. I sincerely hope my disastrous indiscretion can be rectified to everyone's advantage.'

Hugo looked happier than he had for years. 'We shall go and speak to them together – I've no idea where their chambers are situated in this vast place.'

'I hope this doesn't take too long, as we've yet to tackle the matter of the west wing.'

He led the way through the silent house, at any moment expecting the air to be met by wails and screams from his mother-in-law but, so far, all was well. He stopped in front of the room Sir Robert occupied.

He knocked and his summons was answered immediately.

The door swung open a few inches – then it was pulled right back. 'Come in, come in, I've been expecting you.'

This was a curious greeting – had he somehow learnt what was going to happen? 'We need to talk to you and to Hall. Send your valet to fetch him here.'

The man nodded and disappeared into his bedchamber to pass on this instruction. Whilst he was busy, Darcy spoke quietly to his cousin. 'Something is wrong. Why should he be expecting us?'

There was no opportunity for a response as Sir Robert returned. He was unnaturally subdued – his usual bombastic character no longer in evidence.

'Would you care to sit down, gentlemen? Forgive me if I do so – I'm not feeling at all well.' He collapsed onto the nearest chair, leant his head against the back and closed his eyes.

There was little point in starting this discussion until both gentlemen were present. Less than ten minutes later the door was pushed open violently and Mr Hall burst in.

'What the devil do you mean by it, Sinclair? I ain't one for being dragged from my bed by anyone.'

Darcy hid a smile when he saw Hall wasn't wearing a shirt under his jacket, but his nightgown. 'Take a seat, Hall, and hold your tongue. It was I who sent for you.'

For a moment it seemed that the man might bluster, continue to protest at his rude summons, but then he exchanged a glance with his friend and subsided onto a chair.

It didn't take long for Hugo's proposition to be set before them. The pair of them were like deflated balloons by the time he'd finished explaining in great detail what awaited them if they didn't agree.

Sir Robert eventually cleared his throat and answered. 'If you want to know the truth, sirs, I'm damned glad we can stop. We have no notion who is passing on secrets as we picked them up at a variety of hiding places. However, as our very lives depend on it, we will discover who's behind it and lead him into your trap.'

Hall looked ten years older than he had when he'd come in. 'If I have this straight, once the traitor has been captured we are to exile ourselves abroad?'

'I can arrange for you to be attached to the East India Company and you can then legitimately go away on business for several years. If you are astute, you might well return wealthy men. However, you will remain overseas until you are given permission to come home. You must hand over the running of your estates to your sons before you leave.'

The deal was done and he and his cousin left the two of them to discuss their fate. In Darcy's opinion they had got off lightly and should be thanking God they had been spared the noose.

'I suppose we must now get on with the other business, although I would much prefer to retire.' He rubbed his eyes and yawned loudly.

His cousin clapped him on the back with such vigour he was sent staggering forwards. Darcy turned, about to snarl at Hugo but was forestalled.

'Leave this to me, my friend – I'm made of sterner stuff than you. I can go several days without sleep and still fight a battle. I give you my word the old reprobates and their strumpets will be gone before you rise tomorrow.'

'In which case I shall forgive you for the unnecessary violence to my person.' He grinned and raised his hand in salute. 'We will convene at eight o'clock before we break our fast. My study?'

'I suppose I must speak to Mr Hall and ask his permission to address Jennifer, but I am loath to do so. I think in the circumstances I shall speak to young Richard instead.'

'I think the sooner this affair is brought to a conclusion the better. I intend to give false information to each of the men I suspect and then we will know his identity when either Sinclair or Hall are given the papers.'

'That should work, my friend. It's a great pity you didn't think to do this before you dragged me into your machinations.'

Hugo shrugged and they parted company in good spirits. Darcy strode through the house, eager to reach his own apartment and discover if Lizzy had indeed averted a family crisis, or if that was yet to come.

# 23

Lizzy flew into the house and arrived a trifle breathless at the door to her father's sitting room. Thank the good Lord! She could hear someone moving about inside, so she wasn't too late to avert a disaster. She tapped politely and whoever was inside hurried across to open the door.

'Good evening, Mrs Darcy. Mr Bennet isn't here. I believe that he's gone to see Mrs Bennet.'

She thanked her father's valet and dashed off to the suite of rooms that her mother occupied. These were a distance from this apartment and she prayed she would be in time to prevent Papa from poking the hornet's nest.

There was no need to knock as the door was open – it was strangely quiet. She stepped in to find the room deserted. 'Mama, are you there? I require to talk to you immediately.'

Her mother's elderly abigail shuffled out from the bedchamber and curtsied. 'Madam is with Miss Bennet – the master was just here asking after her.'

Fortunately Mary's room was only two doors down. As she raised her hand to knock her mother screamed. Lizzy was too late. She burst into the chamber just as her mother opened her mouth to howl a second time.

Her father was clutching the back of a chair but looked fiercely determined. Mary was ineffectually patting Mama's hands but looked equally shocked.

Lizzy closed the door and reached her mother in two strides. 'Enough. Do you intend to wake the entire house with your caterwauling?'

Her appalling rudeness was sufficient to prevent the next outburst. Her mother straightened as if stuck by a hatpin. 'How dare you speak to me like that? Mr Bennet, are you going to let your daughter treat me so shabbily?'

Her sister, instead of joining in the condemnation, collapsed into an abject heap and tears streamed down her cheeks. Lizzy drew a steadying breath and faced her family.

'I'm not sure what Papa has just told you, but I can assure you he has spoken out of turn and has quite misunderstood the matter.'

Now she had mortally offended her father as well. He glowered at her but made no comment. It was Mary who recovered from her misery and scrambled to her feet.

'Oh dearest Lizzy, please tell me my life is not in ruins. That Sir Robert is not to be taken away in shackles as a traitor.'

'Sit down, all of you. What I'm going to tell you is in the strictest confidence and must not be spoken of anywhere. Do you understand me? I could be sent to the tower for revealing this information.' Her mother was an inveterate gossip but when the happiness of her daughter was at stake, Lizzy believed she would hold her tongue.

This was a master stroke and all three focused their full attention on her. 'Both the gentlemen in question are double agents and this must not be revealed. It's imperative they complete their mission.'

Her mother mopped her eyes but still looked bewildered. 'I don't understand. Are they traitors or are they not?'

Mary quickly explained what being a double agent meant and her mama eventually grasped the salient points. 'I knew it all along; Sir Robert and Lady Sinclair are now my dearest friends so could not possibly be involved in anything nefarious. Mr Bennet, you must speak to Richard tomorrow and give your permission. I think I shall ask Mr Collins to conduct the service. I'm sure he will be honoured to do so. I don't expect he will have officiated at such a prestigious service before…'

Her father called a halt to this babbling. 'Mrs Bennet, have you lost your senses? Are you suggesting that our daughter marry the son of a spy? When word gets out – and you can be very sure it will – the family will be ostracised. Nobody will wish to be associated with a man involved in such dubious dealings, however noble his motives.'

This wasn't going well. It seemed that her father was not going to give his permission after all. Then before her mother could resume her screeching, Mary stepped in.

'Papa, I don't care what Sir Robert has done. As long as he isn't going to be arrested, then I see no reason why Richard and I cannot be together. You can hardly blame my future husband for the behaviour of his father.'

'I wasn't aware that he had made you an offer. He should have spoken to me before doing so.'

Mary's cheeks coloured. 'I told him not to do so until I'd broached the issue with you first. We have only been acquainted for a day or two, but we both know the moment we met that we were destined to be together.'

For a moment it hung in the balance and then her father

nodded. 'Lydia married a villain and was bitterly unhappy. Lizzy, Jane and Kitty have all married exemplary young men and I don't have the heart to deny you despite my reservations. Reluctantly I'll give you my blessing, Mary.'

Lizzy began to relax but then he continued. 'But you will be married by special licence, in private, and there will be no announcement made in *The Times*. I hope you will have the decency to keep your distance from Longbourn and not taint your family by association. The Bennet name must not be dragged into any unsavoury scandal.' He frowned. 'Whatever your assurances, Lizzy, I'm certain Hall and Sinclair are not to be trusted.'

Her sister smiled. 'Thank you, Papa, as long as my family is present I need no one else. Richard has told me he has an excellent estate in Kent and I'll be perfectly content to remain in seclusion with him there.'

'Then I shall speak to your young man tomorrow and have him set things in motion. Perhaps Darcy will allow you to marry in the chapel here.' He nodded at his wife, smiled at Lizzy and walked out, presumably satisfied events had turned out as he wished.

'Mary, I'm so happy for you. Richard is an excellent young man and I look forward to welcoming him into the family. You might not be welcome at Longbourn, but you may visit here as often as you wish.'

Her mother was the only one less satisfied with the outcome and she continued to protest that there was to be no wedding breakfast, long list of guests or public celebrations. Lizzy embraced her sister and left her to escort their parent back to her own apartment.

Fitzwilliam appeared in the passageway outside their bedchamber, just as she arrived.

'Everything has been smoothed over, my love, and it would appear there's to be another Bennet wedding in our chapel.'

* * *

He took her hand and led her into their rooms. 'My cousin intends to offer for the Hall girl – so no doubt he will expect to be married here as well.'

'I take it you've left the eviction to him – a wise move. I sincerely hope that this year will prove to be the last one so packed with drama and intrigue. I long for quiet days filled with our children and family.'

'About these weddings, Lizzy, I think they should take place as soon as can be arranged. It will be impossible to keep the Sinclair and Hall names out of the hands of the gossips when they eventually unmask the traitor.'

'My father is determined to have Mary marry Richard by special licence – it might be wise for your cousin and Miss Hall to do the same.'

'If they send to Doctors' Commons by express, they should have the licences before the ball. Why not have the weddings in the morning and the ball as a celebration in the evening? I know Mr Bennet wishes to keep the event intimate, but he can hardly object to it being announced that evening.'

'My mother, no doubt, will take to her bed in high dudgeon and bemoan the fact that there are to be no visits to warehouses or purchases of bride clothes. That cannot be helped – we shall see the last two unmarried members of our families tie the knot and then we are done with it.'

'Until all the children are grown and need to be married.'

'I refuse to contemplate such a thing. I intend to enjoy a peaceful decade or two before that happens.'

As both their personal servants had been dismissed, he would have to assist her disrobe – this was something he enjoyed.

* * *

He had barely drifted into a contented sleep when there was a furious hammering on the door. He jerked upright and was out of bed and pulling on his boots and breeches before he answered.

'Who is it, Fitzwilliam? Why is someone banging on the door in the middle of the night?'

'I'm not a clairvoyant, my love, but I'd wager it something to do with the unwanted visitors downstairs.'

'Do you require me to get dressed and come with you?'

'Absolutely not. Remain where you are and allow me to deal with it.' By this time he was more or less decently clothed and strode to the door. Rather than speak to whoever it was from inside the bedchamber he stepped out and closed the door behind him.

Peterson stood there, his hair on end and his expression far from sanguine. He was correctly dressed, so obviously had not yet been to his bed.

'You must come at once, sir, someone has been shot. I've sent for the doctor.'

Darcy took the secondary stairs at a run. When he was still a considerable distance from the west wing he could hear the rumpus. There were women shrieking, men shouting and it was only an issue of time before all the guests were awake and wondering what was taking place below them.

'Where is Colonel Fitzwilliam? Dammit, man, who has been shot?'

The butler was barely keeping up with him. 'One of the

gentlemen, I think, but there is such a furore going on it's hard to tell. The... err... ladies are fighting amongst themselves. It's like a bear garden – forgive me for saying so, sir.'

'Are carriages ready to depart? Is the baggage loaded?'

'Yes, sir.'

'Fetch all the footmen, make sure they are armed with cudgels. This ends now.'

They had arrived at the double doors that led into this section of Pemberley. It was hard to distinguish one voice from another and he wasn't even sure if his cousin was actually in there. Darcy stiffened his spine and flung the doors open.

He'd snatched up his loaded and primed pistol as he'd raced from his apartment. He pointed it at the ceiling and pulled the trigger. The deafening noise had the desired effect. The gaudily clad women ceased their screeching and their companions turned as one to stare at him.

Only then did he see the person who had been shot was his cousin. He was slumped against the wall, a spreading red stain on his left shoulder. He raised a hand to indicate he was not gravely wounded.

'You will all leave my house this instant. I don't care who shot the colonel.' Whilst he was speaking he drew the second of his duelling pistols, thanking God that he'd had the sense to bring both with him. 'I'm quite prepared to shoot anyone who doesn't follow my instructions to the letter.'

There was a scuffle behind him and he was surrounded by two dozen men eager to show their loyalty by forcibly evicting anyone who didn't move of their own volition.

There was another door halfway down this large room, which led to a corridor, which in turn opened onto the path that led to the stables. He gestured with his gun and stepped forward – this was enough to set things in motion and within a short while the final carriage was clattering down the drive.

He returned to see that Hugo, looking a bit pale, was on his feet. Peterson had handed him a folded square of clean linen to press against the wound.

* * *

Lizzy ignored Fitzwilliam's order to remain where she was and tumbled out of bed. She grovelled for her discarded garments on the floor where she'd thrown them earlier. This was no good – she would have to light a candle or she would never be able to dress herself successfully.

Once there was illumination she recovered her undergarments and petticoats and stepped into them. Then it was simple to drop her gown over her head and push her bare feet into her slippers. There was no time to put up her hair, so she quickly braided it and left this plait dangling down her back.

Her mother would be scandalised to see her in such disarray. As Lizzy didn't anticipate meeting her parent before noon tomorrow she believed herself safe to venture forth. Peterson, a normally phlegmatic person, must have been deeply disturbed to arrive at the door in such a state of agitation.

Whatever her husband had said to her on the subject, she knew what her duty was. If someone had been shot then as the lady of the house she must take care of the injured person.

It had taken her far too long to get ready and she increased her pace determined to arrive at the west wing as soon as possible. She had expected to hear raised voices and shrieks but all was quiet. The double doors ahead of her stood open and it was obvious the unwanted guests had already been evicted.

On stepping inside she saw Fitzwilliam approaching with his

arm around his cousin's waist. Hugo didn't look at all the thing and she saw it was him who had been wounded.

'Bring him to your study, my dear; we can attend to him there. Has Doctor Bevan been sent for?'

'He should be here within the hour – unless he's already attending a confinement or someone on his deathbed. You should not have come down, Lizzy; this is no place for a lady.'

She ignored his comments and issued clear instructions to Peterson about her requirements. It took longer than it should have done to reach the study and she was concerned that the patient was now barely upright.

The sofa, at least two yards in length, had been prepared as she'd asked. There were also basins of hot water, clean cloths and a variety of other things set out neatly on the table standing to one side.

The colonel's manservant was waiting to help her husband undress the patient. The sofa, now it had the necessary linen, would make a more than adequate bed until he was well enough to return to his own apartment.

'I'll leave you to get him settled and then return to do what I can.'

The clock on the mantelshelf struck two as she left. It was unlikely any of them would get further rest tonight, as by the time the physician had attended to the patient it would be dawn.

Two footmen were waiting outside. 'Can either of you make coffee? I should like jugs fetched to the study as soon as may be.'

The taller of the two nodded vigorously. 'I reckon I can, ma'am. The range is burning well, as Mr Peterson wanted hot water.'

'Thank you. If there are any pastries or biscuits available bring them too. We will need at least four cups.'

He bowed and hurried away to do her bidding. The other

servant stared studiously at a point above her head in order to avoid seeing her hair undressed. She wanted to know how Cousin Hugo had come to be injured but could hardly ask a footman. Her lips curved. It was quite ridiculous that she'd been calmly ordering refreshments when Hugo had just been shot.

Fitzwilliam called from the study. 'You can come back now, sweetheart; we are ready for you.'

She deftly cleaned the wound and was concerned to see the bullet remained in his shoulder. It had to come out or the wound would turn putrid. This was something she was not sufficiently skilled to do. 'There, sir, the bleeding has stopped. You will have to wait for the physician to arrive and do the rest.'

Hugo's valet removed the bloodstained water and dirty cloths, and left them alone.

'Thank you for your ministrations, Lizzy. I expect you're both eager to know how this injury occurred.'

Peterson knocked on the door and ushered in the two footmen carrying what she'd requested. They placed it on the table that had been used to hold the basins and bandages and then they too disappeared.

Fitzwilliam followed them out and she could hear him talking quietly. She hoped he was telling them to retire – but she supposed that wasn't possible until the doctor had completed his task and departed.

Her husband carried over two straight-backed chairs and placed them beside the sofa whilst she attended to the coffee.

'Now, Hugo, explain to us two things. The first being why you were still in the west wing at two o'clock in the morning, and the second why you were shot.'

Lizzy interrupted. 'I also need to know who did it and why they haven't been apprehended.'

'I could hardly storm in there making demands as they were

all my superiors. I talked to the brigadier – you remember he has the fearsome wife – and he agreed immediately to facilitate the departure of them all.' He sipped his coffee thoughtfully and then with a wry smile continued his story.

'All was going well and even the ladies seemed resigned to their fate when one of them accosted me. She was less blowsy than the others. I believe she might have been a real lady once, and she demanded to know why they had been invited if they were to be evicted so rudely. I explained that only the officers had been included in the invitation. She took offence and struck me across the face...'

'Good heavens! Why should she do that? You were merely answering her question.'

His cheeks coloured and he exchanged a helpless glance with her husband, as if expecting him to explain. Fitzwilliam left him to flounder before supplying her with the explanation.

'I expect that Hugo didn't put it as politely as that. He's never been one to mince his words.'

'Exactly so, Darcy. Unfortunately all might have been well if I hadn't retaliated. My slap landed the doxy on her backside and her protector took offence.'

Lizzy stared at him. 'In which case, sir, my sympathies are with the female in question. No gentleman slaps a member of the weaker sex.' She placed her cup rather more firmly than was necessary on the tray and stood up. 'If I had known the true circumstances...'

Fitzwilliam shook his head and his eyes flashed a warning. 'I believe quite enough has been said on the subject, my dear. I shall remain here with my cousin. I suggest that you go up.'

* * *

Darcy scowled at his companion. 'You got your just deserts; I've no sympathy for you. Ah! I can hear footsteps approaching. I shall speak to the doctor and then retire. You must remain in my study overnight. No doubt your man can take care of you.'

Doctor Bevan was indeed outside. Darcy briefly explained the circumstances and then took the backstairs to his bedchamber. He was shocked that the man he thought he knew so well had behaved so reprehensibly.

Lizzy was sitting up in bed waiting for him. He stripped off his clothes in the dressing room and joined her. 'This is a damnable mess,' he said. 'Do you think we can let the marriage to Miss Hall proceed knowing what we do about my cousin? Shouldn't we tell her about her future husband?'

He had thought she would agree with him and demand that he interfere. Yet again his wife surprised him.

'Initially I thought the same, my love. However, on reflection I think you might have done exactly the same. We didn't enquire, but it's quite possible your cousin warned the woman what would happen if she struck him and she ignored this warning. I'm certain that he would never raise a hand to his wife or a child, whatever the provocation.' She stretched and smiled. 'Anyway, it's none of our business, is it?'

'In which case, darling girl, can we finally go to sleep? We will need our wits about us in the morning if we are to come out of this unscathed.'

She stretched across and kissed his cheek. 'Our guests will be so excited at the prospect of attending not one, but two weddings that everything else will be forgotten. All we have to say is that your cousin injured his shoulder falling down the stairs when in his cups, and that he must remain incommunicado for a few days.'

He blew out the candle on his bedside table. 'I suppose you intend that I act as proxy for him with his future in-laws?'

'You will do it splendidly, Fitzwilliam.'

He slid down beneath the covers, taking her with him. The fact that she was now wearing a voluminous nightgown did not pass unnoticed. He abhorred these things and always slept as nature intended.

'I will speak to Mr Hall but I draw the line at proposing to his daughter in my cousin's stead.'

She snuggled into his arms, where she was meant to be, before replying. 'I love you, dearest, and have every faith that you will surmount that difficulty as well.'

Almost immediately her breathing calmed and she was asleep. He was the luckiest man in Christendom to be married to this woman and however much he might dislike it, he would do what she asked of him.

# ABOUT THE AUTHOR

**Fenella J. Miller** is the bestselling writer of over eighteen historical sagas. She also has a passion for Regency romantic adventures and has published over fifty to great acclaim. Her father was a Yorkshireman and her mother the daughter of a Rajah. She lives in a small village in Essex with her British Shorthair cat.

Sign up to Fenella J. Miller's mailing list for news, competitions and updates on future books.

Visit Fenella's website: www.fenellajmiller.co.uk

Follow Fenella on social media here:

facebook.com/fenella.miller

x.com/fenellawriter

## ALSO BY FENELLA J MILLER

**Goodwill House Series**

The War Girls of Goodwill House

New Recruits at Goodwill House

Duty Calls at Goodwill House

The Land Girls of Goodwill House

A Wartime Reunion at Goodwill House

Wedding Bells at Goodwill House

A Christmas Baby at Goodwill House

**The Army Girls Series**

Army Girls Reporting For Duty

Army Girls: Heartbreak and Hope

Army Girls: Behind the Guns

Army Girls: Operation Winter Wedding

**The Pilot's Girl Series**

The Pilot's Girl

A Wedding for the Pilot's Girl

A Dilemma for the Pilot's Girl

A Second Chance for the Pilot's Girl

**The Nightingale Family Series**

A Pocketful of Pennies

A Capful of Courage

A Basket Full of Babies

A Home Full of Hope

**At Pemberley Series**

Return to Pemberley

Trouble at Pemberley

Scandal at Pemberley

Danger at Pemberley

**Harbour House Series**

Wartime Arrivals at Harbour House

**Standalone Novels**

The Land Girl's Secret

The Pilot's Story